INFLICTED

SOMETIMES THE ONLY DIFFERENCE BETWEEN DESPAIR AND RESURRECTION IS KINDNESS

Britain's Next
BESTSELLER

First published in 2014 by:

Britain's Next Bestseller
An imprint of Live It Publishing
27 Old Gloucester Road
London, United Kingdom.
WC1N 3AX

www.britainsnextbestseller.co.uk

ISBN 978-1-906954-81-9 (pbk)

*This book is dedicated to all those who were imprisoned
in Theresienstadt*

*. . . and also to
Oliver, Charlie, Robbie and Reuben,*

for whom everything is done.

Acknowledgements:

With special thanks to Natalie Wills and Murielle Maupoint for believing in me when I could not believe in myself, to Richard Rogers and Charlotte Bowbrick for reading and reviewing the manuscript and to Carrie Nicholls, Valerie Sutherland, Oliver Levine and Debbie Lance for their constant support, love and enthusiasm. Also thank you to Cheryse Rahaman for giving *Inflicted* to the younger generation; to a teacher there is no greater compliment.

INFLICTED SUPPORTERS LIST

Carrie Nicholls, Ben Nicholls, Sarah Sweeting, Chris Pegrum (Mr Awesome), Mrs Jane Chalcraft, Amanda Hislop, Sara Doyle, Natalie Wills, Adam Wills, Thomas Wills, Beth Wills, Matt NJ, Charlie NJ, Robbie NJ, Reuben NJ, Olly NJ, Vicky Imray, Amelie & Christian Maupoint, Ian Jones, Val Sutherland, Amanda, Sara Doyle, Debbie Lance, Kim Samson, Turbo, Georgina Flitney, Toni Treloar, Laura McKee, Rosemary Needs, Jade Terry, Sheila Lelliott, Cerys Elvery, Mrs Vyle, Chloe Hammond, Natascha Ashford, Jodi Bowbrick, Elaine Brown, Diana Norris-Jones, Kerry Wilton, Nick Elliott, Lyn Edgar, Robin Edgar, Oliver Levine, Oliver David, Liane Richardson, Florence Rust, Claire Bolsover, Jenny & Peter Milford, Juliet Murray, Susanne Williams, Brenda Bishop, Mandy Moore, Mary Greening, Becky Tilley, Jo Wright, Jan Donovan, Julia Roberts, Alison Crane, Siobhan Birds, Jaime Younger, Sarah Boyle, Claire Lynch, Debbie Collier, Louise Micu, Charlotte (Lotte) Bowbrick, Mary French, Jade Cooper, Andrew Levine, Gary Keen, Mark Grove, Brittney Cronin, Esther Jury, Karen Judge, Jane Rowlands, Verity Martin, Paddy Watts, Cherry Taylor, Lucy Bond, Tracy Pengelly, Sharon Rance, Emma Enticott, Pamela Monaghan, Richard Rogers, Ryan Nelson Robertson, Cheryl Stockwell, Jo Grange, Steve Hall, Sue Wildish, Carol Aylward, Janice Hosford, Amanda Gates, Margarita Smith, Lisa Cox, Tina Pearce, Kate Ruby, Samantha Barber, Hilary Gilbert, Su Curtis, Fiona Robison, Lesley Fraser, Jason Stamp, Emma Wallace, Annika Eade, Pip Pranskus, Christine Goodman, Jen Taper, Sonbol Shahid-Salles, Annie Rance, Nina Garrard, Jane Graves, Sarah Newman, Elaine Eales, Nicky Wall, Aimee Gray, Guiletta Venturini, Bridge Bug, Steyning Grammar School, Worthing High School, Juliet West, Genesta Luxmoore, Kim Morgan ... and to all the other wonderful supporters that preferred to remain anonymous.

"We make a living by what we get, but we make a life by what we give."

WINSTON CHURCHILL

"A single act of kindness throws out roots in all directions, and the roots spring up and make new trees."

AMELIA EARHART

CHAPTER ONE

MONDAY, 15 FEBRUARY 2010

WHEN Theo opened his eyes, his first thought was that he should be dead. The thought swung like a pendulum then vanished without scorching his memory. An iron sky rushed towards him. He lay helpless beneath it, waiting for oblivion. For a while he was aware of nothing, except a deep thirst and an excruciating pain along his forearm. A welcoming darkness oozed over him, bringing a wave of nausea. He forced his eyes apart, battling the queasiness. Blinking into the silvery light, he thought he could see leaves swaying above him. He lifted his head to make sense of his surroundings, but the shimmering light began to spin on an unsteady axis. He moaned as the darkness threatened.

He was aware of a weight against his leg. Wrenching his neck forward, he blinked until a black dog came into focus. He was lying beside him in a pile of leaves, his ebony eyes watchful as he held his head aloft. His great paws stretched out towards Theo's body.

Theo tried to move his arm but it hurt too much and felt too heavy. He strained to look at it. Tied around his wrist were scraps of pale blue material through which his blood seeped in great pools. With a gasp of horror, Theo realised what he had done. He realised what had happened since he had passed out from the pain. Tears of rage filled his eyes.

He couldn't even do this one last thing properly, could he?

Blindly he groped for the knife. It was lying half-buried beneath yellow leaves just beyond his reach. The blade glinted with knowing eyes. He scuffled across the ground to grasp it in his good hand. The effort made him retch as the darkness flooded his consciousness. He fought against it, choking on the bile in his throat. The dog did not move.

Aware of a ripping sound a little way behind him, Theo started as he realised he was not alone. The light flooded back.

Kneeling in the leaves was a slight woman whose head was covered in white curls. She was frowning as she frantically bit, then tore at a piece of material that Theo realised was a shirt. It matched the makeshift bandages around his arm. When the woman had contented herself that she had torn away enough of the cloth, she moved with aching slowness to her feet.

Theo desperately wanted to shut his eyes, but he continued to stare as the woman bent over him and continued wrapping his wound.

"Ah, good. You are awake."

She spoke without looking at him in a voice that had a slight accent. She was very old, Theo realised, although her dark eyes were bright above the slack swell of her cheeks. From her ear to the corner of her mouth ran a shocking white scar that traversed the sags of skin, converging with wrinkles and slashes of crimson and purple that branched beneath the loose folds of her chin. Theo couldn't stop staring at it, but the woman did not seem to notice.

The scar jolted his memory. Theo realised he knew this woman. This scarred human who was saving him from his sixteen-year-old self; the one who could not face what he had done to Eden.

He knew her from the beach; she baked cakes for the mobile coffee van on the big green where the tough boys played football. He knew her from his memories, standing at the junior school gates, waiting for the children in his class that she fostered; difficult children who had often antagonised him with their interpretation of the pain in their past.

Theo did not know her name, but he knew that from her reputation as a kind, yet solitary individual, his attempt at suicide remained in constant hands: he did not know if he still wanted to die after the horror of it, but for her renowned reserve, he was thankful.

"I'm Anete," she said, "but you can call me Anna. Everyone else does."

With a sigh, she climbed to her feet, using the tree as a crutch to shoulder her weight. Brushing the leaves from the front of her trousers, she whistled to the dog that leapt up and stood expectantly at her side. She tussled with a thick navy jacket that had been hanging from a branch.

"Now," she said, between deep breaths, looking at Theo for the first time. "Do you think you can walk?"

Theo stared at the dog. He nodded.

"Good," she murmured, zipping the coat slowly up to her chin. "Because these days I am far too old to drag you... here, lean on me and the tree, boy. We'll help you stand."

Theo stumbled to his feet as the world gushed around him for several moments. Anna held onto his hand with a firmness that belied her advanced years. After a while, he took a hesitant step beside her. Together they hobbled through the empty woodland behind the black Labrador who gambolled ahead. The bare trees berated him in the murmur of the wind. They seemed to part, permitting passage through the muddy crumble of rotting leaves. The unsettling disdain of winter.

Anna did not speak to him during the short walk from the willow tree to her house. Theo was grateful. How could he possibly explain to her what he had done or why he had done it? Sneaking looks at the ugly scar on her face, Theo wondered how she had become so mutilated. He had heard people whispering about it when he was smaller, the life of this woman as of everyone else in this sleepy, coastal part of Sussex, being a public affair.

He hated the gossips. He hated that privacy was attacked by spiteful claws masked in cotton gloves. It was even worse since Eden. He wanted to kill them, those women who lingered in pairs too long outside of the house, with their pushchairs and yapping dogs. They feasted on his mother's suffering.

He vowed not to ask Anna about the scar even though part of him wanted to know; to find out if she was like him. He remembered her greeting him every day when he passed her in the playground after school; a striking woman with distant eyes and long dark and silver hair woven into a plait. He thought she must have been ancient even then, but somehow she had not seemed old, unlike his crusty headmaster. Every day, Anna had smiled at him and somehow that crinkled smile at the school gates had faded the depravity of the tormenters, before the moment when his brother Seb appeared beside him on the pavement, skidding to a noisy halt on his bike as the bullies vanished like smoke.

Theo wasn't sure whether to be pleased that Anna had saved his life or furious that he had to face the consequences of his actions by continuing with his pathetic existence. He searched for a sense of relief or the familiar foreboding to restore his equilibrium but found only a hollow numbness. He trailed beside Anna because his exhausted brain could not suggest an alternative.

"Blackie, sit!" she commanded when they stopped outside a bungalow with wide windows looking out over a small front garden that featured one rose bush surrounded by a bed of gravel.

Theo smiled. Anna caught his eye.

"I know! It isn't a very original name for a black dog is it? But there you are." She shrugged, unlocking the front door. "He doesn't seem to mind. Come through. I'll make you something to drink."

Anna ushered Theo through the door. The warmth of the house engulfed him, as Blackie slid quietly past him in the airy hallway. Anna turned to lock the door. She pushed three bolts across, before patting the door and hobbling past Theo. She turned before reaching the door at the end of the hall through which Blackie had disappeared. Theo shifted on his feet, clasping his arm.

"Well come on then."

Anna beckoned him over her shoulder with papery fingers. Theo kicked off his shoes, placing them on the brown mat under the radiator. He followed Anna.

Theo found himself in a spacious kitchen with freestanding units and an enormous sink. An ancient sofa covered with dog hair and faded pillows sat beneath an expansive window giving a view to the back of the property. The garden, a perfect rectangle, stretched away from the house with a lawn lined with empty, immaculate flowerbeds. The soil seemed to be waiting for the prospect of life, below the spectre of high, wooden fencing. There was a faded photograph of a sullen child above a dresser housing a dusty array of literature. Magazines depicting glorious cakes lolled over books, their titles scrawled in a foreign language. Theo shuffled from foot to foot. He hugged his arm to his body, trying to concentrate on his surroundings, but the pain had become unbearable.

Anna waved towards the sofa. "Sit boy. Please."

Theo sat, closing his eyes as the warmth of the room enveloped him. How could he bear the pain? It was tearing at him. Anna shrugged out of her coat, pulling a new shirt from the wicker basket by the back door to cover her vest. There was a blue bow below at the base of her throat. It matched the ripples of her scar. Theo tried not to stare.

"I remember you when you were small. At the school."

Theo nodded, struggling to concentrate on her strange voice over the volume of pain.

"Yes," he grimaced. "I remember you."

"You must be at least sixteen now, no? Here…"

Anna was leaning over him with a glass of water in one hand and a couple of painkillers in the other. Theo nodded, trying to thank her with his eyes he tossed back the pills whilst Blackie circled in front of him before lying upon his feet. Anna smiled, then left him, busying herself in the kitchen. Theo sank back in the mound of pillows, his suffering vivid in each deep exhalation of breath.

Anna glanced at him over her shoulder as she washed dishes in the sink. There was a comfortable silence between them. As Theo watched her shifting around her home she felt familiar to him; the curve of her cheek, the hunch of her back, her hair nestled in the nape of a neck that would not look out of place on a much younger woman. Her clothes were youthful too, Theo decided, her legs clad in denim below the white shirt patterned with blue flowers. He thought she might have been beautiful once, before age withered her skin; before the scar.

Theo tried to focus on what she was doing, but with the warmth of the room and the incessant throbbing, his eyes became heavy.

When Theo woke up there was an old song playing on the radio. Anna was standing over the stove, stirring something in a saucepan. The smell made his mouth water. The pain in Theo's arm was less chronic than before. He noticed that it was now properly bandaged. Anna must have done it while he slept.

Anna took two bowls from a cupboard above her head and poured the liquid into them. Placing them on the table, she started when she saw Theo staring at her.

"Good," she said. "You are awake. I've made soup."

Theo continued to stare at her without moving. She bustled around the kitchen.

"Come on, it will go cold."

"Thank you." Theo hauled himself upright, shuffling towards the wooden table. He summoned the courage to look directly into Anna's eyes. "You have been very kind to me even though you don't know me at all."

Anna smiled. "You are welcome, boy." She picked up a spoon and handed it to Theo. "We are not strangers and I could not just leave you alone and bleeding."

"My name is Theo."

Anna shrugged, putting a crusty loaf of bread on a wooden board.

"I see you walking on the beach often, when I deliver my cakes to Antonio the coffee man. I see your brother..."

"Seb."

"Yes, Seb. He loves my cakes. He buys slices for a girl."

"Girls like Seb."

Anna nodded. She tore great chunks of bread and urged Theo to eat them. They ate in comfortable silence. He was grateful that she did not ask him difficult questions about what he had done and why he had done it. If she had, he wouldn't have known how to answer her. As he spooned the delicious soup into his mouth, his eyes were continually drawn to the scar on her face. It moved when she ate, becoming more pronounced.

"It's not so bad now, but at the time it was very bad indeed. Like your arm."

"What?"

"You are staring at my scar, wondering how I got it."

"No." Theo looked down at his plate, his face flushing.

"You are," she insisted, clearing the plates and rising stiffly to place them in the sink. She filled two mugs from a pot of coffee that was standing on the drainer. "It is natural for you to be curious. I'm used to it. Would you like me to tell you how I got it?"

"No." Theo gulped. "No, you don't have to."

"Of course I don't have to... but it has been a long time... a very long time since I had a good lunch time companion. Maybe if I talk you will not think about you…" She glanced down at his encased arm. A slow grin began to spread over her craggy face making her dark eyes glitter. "And… as we've already decided, we are not strangers."

Theo smiled shyly. He opened his mouth to thank her for the food, but Anna was already talking. He was ashamed that she had caught him staring. He was behaving like everybody else. He hated that, because mostly, he considered everyone else to be an idiot.

"I am old," she began. "Older than your grandparents I should imagine. But I remember like it was yesterday…" Anna's dark eyes rolled towards the ceiling, seeing something more, something beyond.

"Theresienstadt," she whispered.

Theo took a sip of his coffee. It burned his tongue. His eyes watered. It was strong but not unpleasant.

"Theresienstadt?"

"Yes," she insisted. Her eyes no longer sparkled. "Have you heard of it?"

Theo shook his head. She looked directly into his eyes.

"Theresienstadt, in what is now the Czech Republic. Perhaps you have known it as Terezin?"

Theo's face remained blank.

"It was a ghetto, a camp, where they imprisoned people like me."

"People like you?"

"Yes, Jews."

Something inside Theo jolted when she said that. His arm began to pound again. "You… you are German?"

Anna tutted, rolling her eyes in the soft sags of their

9

lids; she shook her head.

"German? No boy, I am Czech. Before the war, I lived in Prague." Her chin jutted forward and her back straightened momentarily. "My father was a doctor."

"They put doctors in the camp?"

"The Nazis put everyone Jewish in the camp: doctors, factory workers, shop-keepers, babies and children, old people – all Jews were put in the ghetto, an old town built fortuitously with walls so that nobody could escape."

Theo's face creased as he searched his mind for all his knowledge pertaining to the Second World War, but his books were about the battles, about the tanks and the ships, the armies and the Commandos. He knew nothing about the Jews except for the fact Hitler and the Nazis had hated them and put them in gas chambers, but he had no idea how many or why.

"... because Hitler hated them?"

"Yes." Anna spoke solemnly. "That is how it started."

Theo searched her eyes for vestiges of hatred, anger, but all he saw was a mysterious veil. He had never seen anyone look that way before. When she stared it was as though she was somewhere he could never go. The lack of emotion reminded him of his mother as she was now. It made Theo worry even more about her.

"You aren't angry?" Theo said.

"I am too old to be angry Theo."

"I think I would be angry."

Anna smiled. "You are young; the young are so often angry. I was young when I found myself enslaved in Theresienstadt, only fifteen. As I was growing up, I had high ideals. I wanted to be a doctor like my father. I had great ambition for I grew up in the bountiful, beautiful city of Prague with its fairy-tale buildings and glorious culture."

Theo watched her eyes as she spoke; Anna seemed suddenly young to him. Her eyes had shifted again to a place that was not present.

"People came from all over Europe to feast on the music and theatre; to marvel at the magnificent city I called home.

"I lived with my parents; my father, Emil, a highly respected Jewish doctor and my mother, Isabella. We enjoyed a comfortable lifestyle in an elegant house with a sweeping entrance." Anna gestured with her arms like a ballerina. "We had servants and learned friends and we were invited to salubrious celebrations. Important people came to dinner… my parents went to elaborate parties… I went to a wonderful school with girls who came from all over Europe.

"Yet… there was sadness within our family also. When I was ten my mother gave birth to a boy who passed away when he was only a few weeks old. After Josef died, we never spoke of him again and my mother hardly smiled again."

Theo flinched; his heart began to quicken.

"It was a very sad time for us…" Anna bent down to rub Blackie's ears, shaking her head.

Reality flooded back to Theo in that moment. He saw his mother clutching Eden as she was led from her home. His legs didn't feel like they were attached to the rest of his body anymore. He clutched at his thighs beneath the table.

He tried to speak. The words fell from his lips in a jumbled mess.

"Why did he die?"

"Pardon, Theo. I did not hear you," Anna inclined her head towards him. He could smell the powdery warmth of her skin. "My ears are not so good."

"I said – why did he die?" Theo croaked.

Anna shrugged. "Nobody knew why. One minute Josef was asleep in his crib, the next he was dead..."

"Someone did it?"

Anna frowned, glancing at him. She shook her head slowly. Worry clouded her eyes, like the pretty English teacher at school who seemed to know more about him than he had ever let on.

"No," Anna murmured. "It just happened. Sometimes these things just happen... don't you think?"

Theo jumped up. His arm seethed at the movement. "But babies don't just die, do they?" he yelped.

His eyes rolled like giant marbles in his face.

Anna drew back. "Theo, be calm... I have upset you..."

Theo trembled. He bit down hard on his bottom lip. A tooth pierced the skin. The metallic taste of blood filled his mouth. He swallowed, cradling his throbbing arm against his body. He could feel blood pulsing in his neck.

"Theo, please," Anna spoke quietly. "Please Theo. We'll talk of something else."

Theo closed his eyes. He took several deep breaths. When he opened them, Anna was handing him a glass of water and more painkillers. She squeezed his shoulder then eased herself into the sofa.

She patted the cushion beside her. "Sit here with me Theo. You need to rest."

Theo did as she asked. He felt comfortable in her presence although somehow it felt wrong; like loving Jon as much as he did when he was only his stepfather.

"Tell me more about your life," Theo said when the pain became manageable.

Anna patted his leg.

"You are a good listener."

Theo smiled at the rare compliment.

"The Nazis took the Sudetenland in Czechoslovakia in 1938; later the country came under their rule which meant the Jews were persecuted. In 1939 they began to segregate us… in restaurants, from certain industries. We were not allowed to go swimming anymore."

Theo frowned.

"They did it slowly. Little by little they took our lives away from us; snatches of pleasure… our radios, so we could not hear the news. A curfew was imposed meaning we could not leave our homes before sunrise or after dusk. A slow persecution of the Jews… and I was one of them.

"When war broke out it became worse. Even our money was controlled. We were forced to sell jewels… gold, silver, Mother's platinum and diamond ring… for little money. Hotels were closed to us. We were forced to sit at the back of the trams. The country became separated… known as the Protectorate of Bohemia and Moravia and the Slovak Republic. The Protectorate government banned Jews from public service which now meant Father's patients were limited to those in the Jewish community."

Theo looked directly into Anna's eyes. He was enthralled by listening to her, yet horrified by the details.

"What did you do?" he asked.

Anna smiled, the lines around her eyes creased like crumpled paper. She reached out one knobbly hand and patted his hand.

"At first, we tried to pretend it was not happening, but when we realised that the Nazis were rounding up Jews who were not obeying their rules, we did the only thing we could do," she said softly. "We ran."

CHAPTER TWO

Anna, 1942

THE village of Lidice is close. It is in Czechoslovakia, north-west of Prague, but we have been moving from place to place so often that I hardly remember where we have been. Now we are on the way to Mother's sister. She, like Mother, was not born a full Jew, but she is offering us shelter, a place to hide, at great personal risk. We have already been to most of our other relatives. As the years pass, we find that we cannot stay long at each place because, with the SS conducting increasingly virulent searches, we are putting the lives of those we love in jeopardy. The hideous situation is a double-edged and bloody sword for, as we try to protect ourselves, we place others in danger. When the Nuremberg Laws became enforced here, they forbade all Jewish doctors from practising. Father, who cannot abide such restrictions, surreptitiously treats any sick person who crosses our path or asks for our assistance. I have become his valued helper; I am a quick and enthusiastic learner. This clandestine behaviour puts us at even greater risk of capture for we are giving the authorities every reason to arrest us.

I long to return home to all the familiar things, I can almost smell the polished wood floor in the hallway and the pungent aroma of coffee brewing in the kitchen, but returning home is impossible. Home, as it was, does not exist under the rule of the Nazis; everything is different. It has been three years since we started running. I was only twelve when I last climbed the steps to our front door. I doubt that I will ever do it again.

Mother is sick. Father won't tell me that she has pneumonia and that she is dying, but I know it is the truth. I try not to be frightened of her death. Part of me thinks that perhaps to die now is better; at least she will go to Gan Eden to be with Josef. If she is with him again she will be happy. Her soul may have lived briefly on earth, but there her spirit can live with God for eternity. If we are to believe the rumours then there is very little left for her here; prison camps I have heard, execution, utter degradation: that is the truth of what we face. Mother cannot bear that, so it is best that she dies in Lidice beside her husband, her daughter, her sister; she should not bear witness to the unreserved humiliation of the Jewish race. She could not abide seeing her family face such utter ruin.

The going is slow due to the thick mud and heavy rain. My boots clog with every step below the hem of my dirty pinafore dress. I carry most of our paltry belongings as Father half carries, half drags Mother as she coughs and weeps piteously. Her pale hair is plastered upon her face, which is barely recognisable beneath the splatters of mud and the spectre of the illness.

I try not to think of her as she was before; in her glamorous dresses, a feather in her hair, glorious perfume wafting from her throat. The thoughts make me angry and I choke on them, biting back tears. I have sworn not to cry. When Hitler came, implementing his brutal, anti-Semitic laws, I vowed that whatever happened, I would not cry; whatever terrible fate befell me, I would never show that they had broken me. I am a Jew; a proud Jew.

Matylda rustles through the gate of her homestead. A goat grazes as we limp towards her. She welcomes us into her home, immediately tending to her delirious sister. Perspiration drips from Mother's face like water from a sheet hanging on a line. I know that she hardly knows Matylda is there. Her eyes flicker and close, sunken in her flaming cheeks.

After Mother is settled in a bed hidden in the attic, Father and Matylda sit beside the fire talking in low voices. She tells us the SS are actively searching for Jews in villages nearby. She says that her house was checked recently. She explains that they ransacked the house, but did not find the concealed attic entrance. She is confident that we will be safe staying with her for some time. My Father thanks her profusely. There are tears in his dark eyes as he clutches her hands in his, then takes his leave to nurse Mother in the attic room. I hear him move the heavy wardrobe from the concealed entrance.

I sit in front of the fire and realise I am shaking. The flames flicker and I imagine bodies burning in their heat. Matylda touches my shoulder. I turn to look into her kind eyes as she hands me a bowl of thin soup. Saliva fills my mouth as I anticipate the first food to cross my lips in several days. I gulp it like a baby sucking milk, hardly tasting it at all. Matylda watches, handing me a hunk of bread. I tear at it with my teeth and I am reminded of the birds of prey we have seen on our travels, ripping at their kill with a disturbing ferocity.

The kitchen door opens and Matylda's husband Jurik enters with her only child. They have been working on the land. Both men are tall and they are forced to duck under the door frame; cold air follows them and the earthy scent of the land. Michal stares at me blankly then begins to make noises at his mother. She signs to him and he steps towards me so that he is standing too close. I try not to flinch. He puts his rough hand under my chin. I close my eyes, trembling. Unexpectedly, this giant bends forward and kisses the top of my head. I open my eyes in surprise. He does not smile, but stomps from the room without removing his muddy boots. Matylda stamps her foot in annoyance. Jurik places his hands on her shoulders and speaks to her in a low, gentle voice. She reaches up to rest her hot cheek upon his unshaven one. The familiarity between them makes me self-conscious. I stare at the flames again, thinking of Mother.

The time in Lidice passes slowly. The family are not great talkers so the house lingers mostly in silence. I am not really allowed to venture outside in case I am seen; unfortunately I look typically Jewish with my wavy dark hair, long nose and black eyes, and in these dark times it is difficult to know who to trust. My appearance, it seems, makes everyone more uncomfortable, as though it reminds them constantly that my presence puts them in danger.

When Father is not secretly called out to treat a patient in the village, he spends most of the time in the attic with Mother. I know she is declining: she hardly knows who I am when I place my cold hand on her fevered brow and whisper affectionate words in her ear. Father remains constantly by her side, holding her hand, rubbing his cheek on her burning forehead. Their unconscious intimacy makes me feel awkward, so I slip away to the kitchen to help Matylda bake or read Father's medical books by the fire. Sometimes I read Matylda's treasured poetry book that sits alone on the mantel. There is one poem that I read over and over again by Karel Hynek Mácha. I love the way the words taste on my tongue; I practise translating it into English as I used to with Father.

> Late evening, on the first of May –
> The twilit May – the time of love.
> Meltingly called the turtle-dove,
> Where rich and sweet pinewoods lay.
> Whispered of love the mosses trail,
> The flowering tree as sweetly lied,
> The rose's fragrant sigh replied
> To love-songs of the nightingale.
> In shadowy woods the burnished lake
> Darkly complained a secret pain,
> By circling shores embraced again;
> And heaven's clear sun leaned down to take
> A road astray in azure deeps,
> Like burning tears the lover weeps.

I believe that the countryside around this village would once have been rich and fragrant; before Hitler, before the occupation, before the Nazis tainted it with their stench. The poem laments as I did for a time long past. Matylda asks me what I am doing. I read the poem aloud to her in both languages and she cries. As she weeps on her knees upon the splattered ashes before the fire and I hold my hand over my mouth in dismay, I hear Father's heavy footsteps on the stairs. When he stands in the doorway, I already know what his words will be before he speaks. A strangled sound escapes my throat. Somewhere, far away, I hear the keening of a wild animal in pain. Matylda weeps into her apron, her body rocking back and forth like an over-painted jack-in-the-box. The words "Barukh atah Adonai Eloheinu melekh ha'olam, dayan ha-emet" spill from my lips and though I cannot hear my voice for the pounding of blood in my head, I know I have spoken Hebrew: 'Blessed are You, Lord, our God, King of the universe, the True Judge.'

I rush upstairs to the attic. Mother is lying on the bed. Her face is white now that the fever has gone. She looks like she is sleeping. I think she is beautiful, even in death. The tears catch at the back of my throat but I swallow them. I will not give Hitler the satisfaction. I hold her hand. It is cold. I am reminded of the Rodin statues I have seen; when I reached out to touch them, they were cold too and even though I knew they would be it was somehow unexpected.

Mother was designated a Mischling by the Nazis at Nuremberg; meaning that she and Matylda were at that point beyond persecution because they had fewer than three Jewish grandparents. Despite her status, I know that Mother was devoutly Jewish and I hope she finds happiness in Gan Eden with Josef. Part of me feels that part of her left us long ago to be with him. I do not resent it: it is just the way it is.

I lay my head down upon her, speaking to her of happier times, thanking her for being a wonderful mother. As I speak, I am filled with an absolute resolution that I will survive this war in her honour. I will beat the odds even if I am a Jew, even if I am petrified of what the future has in store for me. I will face my fear, head on. I will concentrate on life here on earth as my faith counsels.

Father's body presses against my back. I turn into the living warmth of him. He holds me so tightly I feel I may suffocate. His unique, musky scent is almost more than my senses can bear and the tears catch in the desert of my throat. The sound of his weeping resonates in my ear like the music from the theatres that used to float through my bedroom window. We stand together like this until Matylda prises us apart.

Matylda knows that as a Jew my father will want to bury the body soon after the death. She knows he needs time to pray. She begins guiding me out of the room with gentle hands, but our way is blocked by Jurik and Michal. They move over to Mother's body, taking it in turns to kiss her forehead. I can see that Father is overwhelmed by the gesture. He nervously strokes his beard. Jurik takes Father into his arms then, as he releases him, he and Michal begin to pray in the Jewish tradition of men praying together. Father is so touched by this that tears cascade freely down his cheeks. Matylda and I slip away unnoticed. I steal one last glance at my mother before I leave and I am filled with the utter certainty that her essence is gone. Her body will soon unite with the earth, whilst her spirit has returned to God. I find solace in this.

Theo was, in equal measure, appalled and fascinated by Anna's story. She was suddenly silent after telling him about the death of her mother. Theo looked at her and saw that her eyes were closed. He was certain she was praying so he did not speak.

Theo had never really prayed before. He knew that his mother had denounced all religion. He believed Jon had chosen Eden's name and that if his mother had been sane after Eden's death, she would never have agreed to the memorial service in a Protestant church. Nana Dora had tried to protest to Jon, but for once he stood up for himself and insisted. Theo didn't know why his mother wasn't religious, but he sensed it had something to do with his grandmother. She seemed to be at the root of all the unhappiness in their family. Theo found himself thinking that he wished she were dead instead of Eden, but quickly quashed the thought in case Anna could somehow read his mind.

Theo didn't really know how he felt about religion. He thought the Bible made sense in some of the stories they had read at school, and that the Ten Commandments were a good code of living, not that he had been disciplined enough to obey them. He and Seb talked about it sometimes, which he privately thought was a strange thing for teenage boys to do, although he and Seb were anything but stereotypes. They had pretty much decided that religion was a way to control communities of people and persuade them against lawlessness; also that it was the most common excuse for war, which seemed to be in direct contradiction to what the main religions preached. Neither of them believed in heaven although, since Eden had died, Theo was beginning to believe in hell.

"I am sorry," Anna murmured, dabbing at the baggy droops of skin under her eyes with a squashed tissue. "I have not spoken of my mother to anyone for many years."

Theo felt awkward but he knew he should not. This was not a normal situation. It was not a usual day. There were no ordinary days for him anymore. He should not be surprised. After all, he had inadvertently trusted Anna with his secret hadn't he? She had found him, lying there. In the aftermath. Now she was entrusting him with her truth. Wasn't this the way it was supposed to work, even if he had not realised it until now?

Theo was conscious of his arm, heavy against him under the pain.

He leaned towards Anna and put his hand over hers.

It was dark by the time Theo left Anna's house. She had given him enough painkillers to allow him to sleep, but expressed the wish that he return tomorrow so that she could replace the dressing on his forearm. Theo had agreed, offering to take Blackie for a run on the beach before she did it; after all, he was alive and it was half-term. He hoped that Anna would continue with her story, although he couldn't figure out whether he was more captivated by the solace he found in her company or the desire to find out how it ended. All he knew was that being with Anna right now was better than being anywhere else.

When Theo arrived home, he was greeted by ferocious yelling coming from upstairs. Aware of the familiar anxiety rising within him, he climbed towards the commotion. Seb was standing on the stairs with his back to Theo. From out of nowhere, a shoe with a spiked heel flew through the air, just missing Seb's head. It would have caught him directly in the temple if Theo had not thrust him forward. A hailstorm of random objects rained down on them as Theo dodged and ducked his way up the stairs.

Jon was leaning against the banister on the landing with his arms protecting his face. Tears were running down his cheeks as Theo's mother, Sophia threw the contents of her bedroom at him. She was yelling but her words made no sense. Theo watched her, appalled.

She looked like a maniac. Her unwashed hair framed her face like an enormous birds nest. She was naked except for a pair of holey shorts and a nursing bra that was not fastened properly. One damp breast hung over the loose skin covering her rib cage, vulnerable and exposed. The whites of Sophia's eyes were crimson in her ashen face. Seb tried to pull Theo away, back down the stairs, but Theo fought him. Seeing his mother like this was terrifying, but he felt a violent compulsion to bear witness to it. The burden of guilt came crashing down on him again. Mindlessly he moved in front of Jon, standing with his back to him. He shoved him away so that he instead, could suffer his mother's onslaught. Cold coffee, eyeshadow, tubes of moisturiser bombarded him followed by nappies, a breast pump, and a leaking bottle of baby lotion.

Item after item hit him savagely in the face or on his torso. Seb tried to pull him out of the way, but Theo punched him. He fell into the wicker washing basket. Seb screamed at him angrily, but Theo ignored him. Jon sat on the floor with his head in his hands, unable to look at Sophia who was now pelting the contents of her cosmetic drawer at Theo's face. She didn't seem to realise that it was her son standing before her. His prostrate form was an outlet for her rage, a punch bag for her to pummel with her grief and disappointment, though her fists made no contact at all.

Theo knew he must hurt all over but, like the emotional pain from losing Eden, the physical throb was significant in its absence. Horror and personal revulsion held him there; once again, Theo was utterly sick of himself.

The thing that finally brought Sophia to a standstill was the sound of the doorbell. It hailed through the darkness of the house like a bomb siren. The family froze, staring at each other, exhausted and disbelieving. Sophia woke from her stupor and saw Theo for the first time. Dismay dropped over the features of her face. Her wide eyes, saturated with terror, flitted from Seb to Jon to Theo. She brought one trembling hand up to her mouth, then fled into her bedroom and closed the door.

The doorbell rang again. Seb and Theo collided on the stairs as they attempted to answer it. Theo looked through the stained glass window beside the front door to see who was there. The doorstep was empty; there was no one on the garden path or outside the front gate either.

Theo caught a glance of himself in the hall mirror. His hair was soaked with coffee and red blotches now joined the bruise on his forehead. His cheeks were smudged with makeup and white spots of lotion. There was a nasty cut below his left eye; it oozed with blood. Jon appeared on the stairs with a ghostly smile that didn't reach his eyes. He wiped a hand under his streaming nose, pulling a creased, white handkerchief from his jeans' pocket. He blew his nose noisily.

"We need to clean that cut on your face," he murmured. His eyes were red and watery. "Then I'm going to order my two favourite boys an enormous pizza for dinner."

He put an arm around both of them and drew them into a firm embrace. Theo closed his eyes. He smelled of easier times, familiar and earthy.

They all jumped apart as the front door swung open. Nana Dora appeared, looking cold and flustered. With one manicured eyebrow raised, she surveyed the mess on the hall floor.

"Good gracious, what on earth happened here? I only popped out to the shops..."

She bustled into the kitchen, emptying the food from several plastic bags onto the worktop then began to pick up pieces of broken debris. Clearly baffled, she tutted as she collected the contents of her daughter's bedroom from the hall floor, "Sophia did this?"

It was a statement of truth rather than a question.

Anxiety clouded her hooded eyes as Jon sighed and nodded.

"My poor girl," she murmured, shaking her head. "My poor, poor girl."

CHAPTER THREE

TUESDAY, 16 FEBRUARY 2010

THE morning after Sophia's offensive, Theo woke with a headache and a burning sensation in his arm. He had fallen into an uneasy sleep sometime after the light on his watch showed three am and bird song was already anticipating the winter's dawn. The places on his face where the harder things had hit him were stinging and the bruises on his forehead and cheek throbbed. This time he didn't bother to look in the mirror; he already knew he looked like the school bullies who cruised for a fight. He didn't care. The pain on the outside of his body distracted him from the lack of it within him. The dogged void almost ached in its perpetual emptiness.

He left the house before anyone else was awake, with the penknife safely in his pocket. He closed his bedroom door behind him so that they would think he was sleeping. The air was icy and still as he ran down the quiet streets to Anna's house. The gulls were calling to him again from the steely sky. She opened the door before he reached the top of the driveway. Blackie leapt towards Theo, wagging his tail. Anna's eyes travelled over Theo's face, surveying the damage. Much to his relief she said nothing. Fixing a red lead to Blackie's collar, she handed it to Theo. He noticed that her knuckles were swollen and the veins on the back of her hands were erect through the skin. It made him think of the blood dripping from his arm when he had tried to end it all. He shuddered.

He saw Anna glance at his arm. "We'll see to that when you get back. Enjoy your walk."

She patted Blackie on the head then turned to close the door.

Blackie walked obediently beside Theo as they headed to the beach. The tide was low. He released the dog from its lead and they ran down to the water's edge. For as far as they could see, beyond the distant pier on one side and an empty horizon on the other, there was no one to be seen. Large stones turned to small gravelly ones under foot and then finally to dark grey sand that became softer beneath the springy soles of his trainers. Theo felt that if he stood there for long enough the earth might gladly engulf him.

Theo looked out to the horizon, throwing stones for Blackie to fetch and thinking of Eden. He thought that maybe her body should be cremated and her ashes scattered out to sea; at least then she could be remembered in a place of beauty rather than in a morbid graveyard, littered with the bodies of old people from old times. He didn't want that for her. He wanted her to join the fishes and the sea birds, to soar with the porpoises that occasionally graced this coast with their extraordinary presence when the summer sun shimmered on the water; better the cold English Channel than the unforgiving English soil. Part of him wished the waiting was over, that the coroner would release her body, and another part of him wanted to survive in these days of limbo when nothing was certain and no one could reach him.

Once again, Anna was waiting for him as he walked up the drive. She called to Blackie. Theo wondered what had drawn him back to her after yesterday. Was it the lure of her story or his ghastly secret? Was it the black dog, so like the one he had always longed for? Or was it because, with school being closed for half term, he really had nowhere else to go? Theo followed her into the kitchen. A medical kit was open on the table beside two cups of steaming coffee and a plate of biscuits.

"Sit with me."

Theo sat, allowing Anna to tend to his wound with gentle hands that made tears spring to his eyes.

"Anna…What happened after your mother died?"

Anna, 1942

In the wake of Mother's death, we enter a period of mourning. I try to acknowledge this with my dress, but my wardrobe is now so minimal that an outfit of all black is not possible. On the day of her burial, I borrow one of Matylda's long coats. The funeral takes place after dark so that we do not draw attention to our affairs. Jurik and Michal have dug a grave in the area of woodland by the lake. We use the old cart to carry her body that, after helping Father wash and dry her, Matylda has meticulously wrapped in cloth. Over her face, she has laid a silk scarf, which I know to be the only reminder of their English mother who mysteriously left when they were children. All I know about her is that she was called Henrietta.

Surprisingly many others leave their homes to join our procession. They offer Father and I their condolences. Mother was well known in Lidice. I struggle to look at people's faces. I do not want to see their sympathy. I need to keep my emotions closely hidden, knotted like the scraps of wool in Matylda's knitting basket. It is the only way I can survive. I'm sure they think I am hard because my tears don't roll like Father's. The bags of skin droop beneath his eyes like pillows of sadness; he looks exhausted. In a mark of respect for Mother, a tattered piece of black ribbon hangs from the top button of his shabby overcoat. As we walk, he holds my hand tightly the whole time. I feel small and protected as I did as an infant, but I know this to be an illusion. No one can protect me now any more than I can offer protection to anyone else. All of us, Jews and non-Jews are at the mercy of the Nazis. I know the SS are coming. I feel it in the deep recesses of my body, the places I am normally unaware of.

I like the place that Jurik and Michal have chosen for the interment. It is peaceful amongst the trees and the lake shimmers beneath a large, melancholy moon. The burial ground is dipped in silver, which I find most fitting for it reminds me of Mother's favourite evening gown in Prague. I wish the fine, silver satin was draped over her skin now rather than the unseemly, colourless cloth.

My Father manages a few lines of eulogy before her body is lowered into the muddy hole. I try not to think of the lack of coffin and the worms that will crawl across her inert form. I try to remember that her essence is living on beyond her mortal state. A spade is passed among the mourners. Each person takes a turn throwing soil onto the body then places the shovel back into the ground for the next person to take. This is to ensure grief is not passed from one person to the next. As I am last to take the shovel I feel grateful that the assembled party have honoured this tradition, for my own grief is burden enough; if their grief were to eclipse me also I believe I would plummet into the grave with Mother.

During the walk back to the house, I feel that I am not part of my own body. I long for my bed in Matylda's attic room with its makeshift mattress of blankets and pillows. I want to be alone with my thoughts even if sleep eludes me. Matylda seems to sense my exhaustion for upon our arrival she leaves Father and Michal to take drinks with Jurik by the fire whilst she escorts me to bed. I find myself half leaning on her as we climb the narrow stairs. She helps me undress as Mother did when I was a small child and tucks me under the covers. I think she will leave, but she stays at my bedside, singing softly as she strokes my hair. Slowly I am lulled into a peaceful slumber. This is to be the first night in years when the spectre of death does not slither through my sleep. It is also to be the last.

As Theo listened to Anna talk about her mother's death, he found that his feelings towards his own mother were beginning to change. For so long he had felt only bitterness and resentment towards her and the new feelings nestling in corners of his psyche felt strange. The way Anna spoke about the death of her mother with such tenderness, made Theo begin to think about how he would feel if Sophia became sick. He had never really considered the end of her life before, the possibility that she wouldn't be there forever, but now it seemed conceivable; especially if she remained slightly mad as he thought she was right now. What if she never recovered from Eden's death, and Sophia as she once had been, was gone forever? What if she was unable to visit him in prison? The knife seemed to throb in his pocket.

"Anna," Theo said in the silent place between her words.

"Yes Theo."

"Do you think your mother loved Josef more than you?"

"No Theo." Her answer was patient and deliberate. "Of course not. She loved us equally." She shook her head, marvelling at his question. "That is a very odd thing to ask."

Theo raised his eyebrows. "Is it?"

"Yes Theo," insisted Anna. "It is."

She touched his arm then, running her gnarled fingers over his injury and down to his pale hand. Theo choked. Her gesture was filled with a tenderness and understanding that he hadn't known before. The silence between them felt like something he could touch.

"You don't like yourself very much, do you Theo?"

Theo shrugged and swallowed. "Not much to like, is there?"

"I don't agree," said Anna, softly. "I see much to like."

"Well, nobody else does," he whispered, wrapping his body with his bad arm and using his good arm as a sling.

"Do you want to tell me how you got those bruises on your face?"

Theo shook his head, "Not particularly."

"Are you bullied at school?"

Theo nodded.

"Does anyone know?"

He swallowed. "My brother, Seb."

"The teachers?"

"No."

"Why?"

He thought of his English teacher, the meaning behind her words; her concern biting away beneath her skin. Sometimes he wanted to fall into her arms and disappear.

"Because," Theo muttered scratching his head irritably through his curls. "If I told them then I'd just get even more of a beating."

"That's terrible," murmured Anna.

Theo shrugged. "It's not so bad; others get it worse than me."

"That doesn't make it right."

"No, but what can I do?"

"I don't know Theo, but something must be done, I think."

"Perhaps," he agreed reluctantly. "But I think you of all people know that it is not that easy."

"No, I agree, it is not easy, but I think you have to fight it somehow."

"Did you?" Theo looked at her with sad eyes.

She did not break eye contact. Her shoulders shuddered.

"No," she whispered. "Not at first. At first the fear made me weak."

Anna, 1942

A scream of pure terror wakes me the next morning. I leap from my bed as a hand is placed firmly over my mouth. Father's voice is in my ear urging me to get dressed. He moves over to the attic door, trembling as the voices with harsh German accents draw closer. I have barely tied the laces on my boots when the door bursts open, knocking Father backwards. He loses his footing and falls heavily to the floor. The menacing figures of three SS men emerge from the dark stairway into the room. Dressed in intimidating grey uniforms with the SS emblem clearly displayed, and imposing caps hiding the whites of their eyes, they tear through the room, brandishing rifles and revolvers, pulling at furniture and bedding. One of them begins slapping Father hard around the cheeks as he screams at him in derogatory German. They want to know if we are the only ones hiding there. Father tries ineffectively to explain that we are the only ones taking refuge in the attic but the man continues to shout.

Reeling with horror, I back away from the intruders, sliding down against the wall as I struggle to hold my bladder. This is the moment I have dreaded since the day Hitler claimed the Sudetenland. This is the beginning of the end for Father and me.

Feeling like a coward, I shake and cower, watching helplessly as the soldier bullies Father. He yanks at Father's sleeve, berating him for not displaying the compulsory Star of David on his clothing. Another soldier is holding our identity papers in his hand. He shakes them in Father's face, demanding to know why there is not a J marked on them. The soldier then tells him that he is arresting him for breaking the law because he has been practising medicine when it is forbidden. Father closes his eyes as he reels from another slap and I know he is praying. His interrogator drags him to his feet. I realise with dread that he is drawing a knife from the inside of his long coat. The blade glints grotesquely in the beam of sunlight penetrating the tiny attic window. I strangle the scream emerging from my torrid lungs as he brings the blade to rest at Father's throat. One of the others laughs hideously. The blade is drawn under Father's chin; the soldier grips his long beard in his left hand. He rips the knife through the hair; the sound reverberates off the silent walls. I retch.

My bowels turn to water as the SS men turn their attention to me. They do not look at me as they brutally haul me to my feet and drag me down the stairs in front of Father. I wrench my neck round to look at him. I see that his face is red and his beard is ragged, but he is mercifully unhurt. We are pulled into the kitchen. The soldier is gripping my arm so tightly that, at first, the pain prevents me from seeing the horror within. I scream when I see a pair of work boots pointing up to the ceiling. They are Michal's and I know he is lying motionless on the flagstones. I am hauled over his body; the SS men stamp on his inert torso. I look at Michal in horror as I see his open eyes staring senselessly towards the ceiling and blood pouring from his open mouth. There are bullet holes in his stomach and chest. In the corner, Matylda cowers, weeping in disbelief and terror, staring at her son. There is a pool of urine spreading out from beneath her dress.

In a futile act of defiance, I try to struggle. Like a ferocious beast, I bite at my captor's hand. He yelps, but uses his rifle to clout me around the head. I see strange spotting before my eyes then nothing.

My head pounds as I regain consciousness when someone prods at me with a rifle butt. I am sitting in what seems to be a vehicle for transporting animals.

Time has passed and darkness is beginning to crawl over me. I scan the faces around me for Father, but he is nowhere to be seen. A heavily pregnant woman is crushed against me as we are ushered from the vehicle. She stumbles and I grope between our lumbering bodies for her hand. I look at the people I am with and realise they are all girls or women; most of the younger ones are crying into the folds of their mother's clothing. The guards circle us, like great cats on the plains circling their prey; weapons hang over their torsos as a sign of their strength and intimidation.

My fear has dissipated, although I know not why or where it has gone. I am numb to the events unfolding around me; I feel as though I am slowly drowning without the associative pain. The guards holler expletives at us, coercing us forward with their aggression: we are sheep, herded by a rapacious dog. A toddling infant begins to wail uncontrollably; her mother tries in vain to placate her. To our collective horror, the most imposing of the SS men holds aloft his rifle. In one swift click of the trigger, he shoots the child dead. Her body crashes to the floor. A woman shrieks. She runs at the guard and claws at his face with her nails. He pulls a knife from his coat, it is the same knife that cut Father's beard, and plunges it straight into her heart.

Our captors tell us that if we fight or protest then all of us will meet our deaths at the end of his blade. We fall silent, faltering onwards through the thick mud; there are indeterminable buildings on either side of us and we are on the edge of what seems to be a park. The mother of the infant is dragged by two girls who appear to be even younger than I am. I think, absurdly, that they should be at school. The ill-fated infant is left where she fell, blood seeping from the bullet hole at her temple. My stomach heaves with revulsion and loathing. I have no choice but to look away and plod on. The pregnant woman's clammy hand is still clinging steadfastly to mine.

After we have walked for what seems like hours, the guards stop outside a gate to a walled courtyard or military barracks. Over the arch are painted the intimidating words, 'Arbeit Macht Frei' meaning 'work will make you free'. I believe this to be an extortion of the sentiments voiced by a German rhetorician in the nineteeth century. The guards call for the gate to be opened and I know we will not be free here, work or no. This is prison.

CHAPTER FOUR

"THIS was the ghetto, the walled town of Theresienstadt?" Theo asked.

"Yes," confirmed Anna. "This was the place I was to spend the next few years of my life. A ghetto made for Jews and other people the Nazis found offensive... It was apparently an old prison adapted to house important Jewish dignitaries; it was presented as a gift from Hitler but in truth, it was no more than a concentration camp like all the others. There were thousands of Jews living their everyday lives there, but in dismal, overcrowded conditions with guards and barricades all around."

"And you couldn't fight them..."

"No not openly. We had to find subversive means of undermining their authority."

"What they did to that child was barbaric..." Theo's horrified eyes were wide as he stared in disbelief at Anna.

"Yes..." she agreed. "Yes Theo, it was. I would like to tell you this was an isolated incident, but it was not. Things like this happened all the time. It was... it was beyond words."

Anna closed her eyes tightly.

"Murderers," Theo whispered, thinking that perhaps he was just like them. Was what he had done to Eden so different?

Anna rubbed her eyes, rising stiffly from the sofa to let Blackie into the garden. Theo watched him sniffing around the flowerbeds. Anna filled the kettle before calling him back into the warm.

"I've been talking so much Theo. Tell me something about you whilst I make the coffee."

"What do you want to know? I'm not very exciting."

"You have a family?"

"Yes."

"A brother, you said. A sister too?"

Theo felt the anxiety ignite within him. He rubbed his forehead, taking a deep breath. He couldn't mention Eden, could he?

"Just Seb. He's going to university soon."

"That is a big step. I expect you will miss him."

"Yes. My stepdad Jon jokes that he'll be having such a good time that he'll never come back. He'll miss him too."

"What about your mum? Is she nervous about him leaving?"

Theo smirked. "God knows – all Mum ever wanted was a girl."

The words were out of his mouth before he realised what he'd said.

Anna stood very still. Theo brought the back of his hand over his damaged cheek then stared at his feet.

"A girl? Why?"

Anna handed him a cup. She tilted her head to one side, her dark eyes mixed with bewilderment and unveiled curiosity.

Theo shrugged. "Who knows?"

She sank into the seat beside him, shaking her head. Anna's awkward movements made Theo's joints ache in sympathy with hers.

"She told you this?"

Theo laughed and shook his head. "She didn't have to."

"How do you know that is the truth then?" persisted Anna, coughing into a screwed up tissue.

"Because everyone knows. She and Nana Dora are always talking about it."

"Your mother and grandmother talk about this in front of you?" Anna coughed again.

"Yeah," Theo said wearily. "I think Mum had Seb and that was alright, but then she had me and that wasn't really alright because she and Nana Dora had planned for me to be girl."

Anna laughed. "But that's preposterous. Life doesn't work like that."

"No," Theo agreed. "Mum had two boys; she really wanted a girl, then Dad pissed off and she was even more miserable. On top of that her mother, Dora Doom is a right old bag – Seb and I can't stand her – and kept pushing Mum to find another bloke so she could get her little girl. Mum found Jon, who is actually pretty cool, and spent the next few years trying for another baby."

Theo stopped, aware that he was ranting and that he sounded bitter.

"I see," Anna murmured and although Theo thought she couldn't possibly, it somehow made him feel better.

They sat in companionable silence, watching Blackie chase his tail. Eventually Anna spoke.

"So…did she get it?"

"Get what?"

"A girl?

"Yeah," breathed Theo. "She did."

"And?"

"And nothing," Theo stared at his wounded arm. He could feel the panic returning. He said hastily, "Tell me about the ghetto."

Anna, 1942

Nothing could have prepared me for Theresienstadt. The truth was the ghetto was ugly in its entirety. This place that barely registered as civilisation was a grid of murky, run-down streets with blocks of non-descript buildings rising from its grimy depths. These edifices, naked in their neglect seemed to hang their shabby heads in shame, capitulating to their decay. Barricades, ditches and trenches provided a constant reminder that those incarcerated here were part of an even darker war than the one that was being fought outside its walls. Yet the physical horror of the ghetto was completely emasculated by the people themselves; they were the greatest shock of all. There were so many of them: young, old, dark, fair. They were wholly distinguishable except for their eyes which were undifferentiated. The expression in them was one I cannot describe because it was something that one felt when looking at them. My inexperienced eyes perceived them to be broken and though that scared me far more than the surroundings, I made a pledge to help mend at least some of them. As time passed, this would prove to be a more and more difficult undertaking.

I am taken to the barracks where I am to be housed. As we walk, the people who live there pass us unsmiling. I am struck by how thin most of them are. They are so emaciated that their faces look like skulls with a transparent skin hanging over them. Their hair is ragged and often missing in places. Every visible bone is prominent; shoulders and ribs protrude through threadbare shirts. The spine is horribly visible at the nape of the neck. It is clear that many are suffering some kind of illness and that all are starving. I wonder where Father is. I wonder if he has seen these poor, sick people too. I wonder if we are soon to end up like them.

The smaller children are ripped away from their mothers. Screams fill the air and I close my eyes because I cannot bear to see the agony on the children's little faces. The pregnant woman staggers against me; I know she is about to faint. It takes every ounce of my strength to hold her up. The mothers beg their children to be quiet and strong; they are panicking that their child will be shot like the poor infant lying in the road. Eventually under the stern supervision of our guards the children are led away to a place the guards call the Girls' Home, where they are told a Jewish Elder will meet them. Although I am still a child it is clear that they find me too old to be sent there.

I am led to the Military Barracks with the pregnant lady still labouring at my side. We shuffle into a building and one by one we are shoved into rooms. One glance reveals the living conditions to be insanitary and inadequate for the crowds of women who seem to inhabit them. Three storey bunks tower from the floor each containing more than one person. Many of those sleeping there seem to have the sickly pallor of impending death; my heart shrinks and misses a beat as I am reminded of

Mother. The rooms are alive with the rancid stench of stale sweat and the air excreted from bowels of bodies suffering stomach infections. It is impossible not to reel in abhorrence, but in time to come I am to find that I hardly notice the smell at all.

My companion and I are not separated but rudely thrust into an already overcrowded room. This room is larger than the others, but has no beds and even more occupants. The stench is even more overpowering and as I scan the faces of the inhabitants I know that many of them should be hospitalised. On the cold, wooden floor, straw is scattered to provide makeshift mattresses and the women cover their scarcely clad bodies with thread-bare blankets.

Nobody moves to help us as we stand on the threshold of our paltry new existence. I wait for several minutes before my companion's weight is too much for me to bear. When I turn to look at her I see she is barely conscious. I drag her forward to a corner of the room that seems suspiciously vacant; at this point I do not have time to consider why. Lowering the pregnant woman onto the straw, I murmur words of reassurance in her ear that sound hopeless and pathetic even to me. As I take off her shoes, the residents of the room watch me with wary eyes that seem to droop in the shape of a falling tear; eyes sunken with malnutrition and sadness. I try to ignore the many pairs boring into my skull. Fussing over a dirty blanket that I find discarded beneath the straw; I try ineffectively to cover my needy charge. The holes are so large; the material has been eaten by moths. I lay down, turning my face towards the grubby wall. I have seen enough for today. Lying with my eyes tightly closed to blot out the reality of my surroundings, I think of Father and where he may have been taken. There are men in Theresienstadt also, housed in another building in another part of this uninhabitable ghetto. Tomorrow I will try to find him; if he has also been taken here then at least we will have the comfort of being together even if we are living apart; at least we will know that the other is not missing or worse, dead.

Sleep eludes me, despite my physical exhaustion and the nagging pain in my head. I recite my prayers, one for Mother, one for Father and one for every unfortunate person in the ghetto; everyone here needs my prayer that is certain. The pregnant woman shifts against me and I feel the child within her belly move against my back. I am momentarily filled with hope and bonded to the child, but the hope dies with the bouts of chesty coughing and moans rattling through the darkness. When sleep finally washes over me I am caught in my thoughts in the chrysalis between waking and sleeping. Here I realise that I have learned two lessons today, one to always look as though I am doing as I am told, and the other to hold onto myself at all costs.

"What do you mean?" Theo asked when Anna was silent for a moment, lost in her difficult memories.

"Mean?"

"Yes," Theo urged. "What do you mean when you say you had to hold onto yourself?"

"I mean that I had to always hang onto the person I am; hold onto Anna; hold onto my self-esteem, my self-respect."

"You knew who Anna was?"

"Yes, of course. I have always known who I am;

sometimes I have lost sight of myself in the journey of my life, but back then I loved Anna and I knew I had to continue to love her to survive in the ghetto."

"Oh," said Theo. "I see." He nodded, although he didn't really see at all.

"I don't think you do see actually. If you do not like yourself, how do you expect others to like you? If you do not stand up for yourself, how can you expect others to defend you?"

"This is 2010 not 1942… My life can't be compared to yours! You lived through the Holocaust. You survived the Hitler and the Nazis. I have more respect for you than for anyone else I have ever met!" Theo was breathless with admiration.

"I see," Anna nodded pensively. "You respect me, but you do not respect yourself."

Theo was silent for a few moments. "No," he agreed. "I don't, I don't know how to."

"What would you do if I hit you?"

Theo laughed, his dark eyes creasing as he scratched his bottom lip with his nail.

"You are laughing…" Anna narrowed her watery eyes.

"Yes… yes I am, because I can't imagine you… you hitting me."

"Because I am old?" Anna raised her eyebrows.

"Yes," Theo agreed grudgingly.

"OK," she conceded. "What would you do if Seb hit you?"

"He wouldn't," Theo marvelled. "Seb has never hit anyone in his whole life."

"What about the bullies?"

"What about them?"

"What do you do when they hit you?"

"I wait until they've finished. They don't hit me for long if I don't fight back and they only punch me in the places where the teachers can't see. They've done it since you used to foster kids but it's worse now…"

Anna took a deep breath and exhaled through her nose, shaking her head.

"You don't try to defend yourself?"

"What's the point?"

"There is every point," insisted Anna emphatically. "There is every point. It is like you have given up Theo."

Theo glanced sideways at her. Strangely he felt like he had disappointed her and oddly he found that he didn't like it. Theo was an expert in disappointing people: his Mother, Dora Doom, and his Father also, he supposed, even though he could barely remember him. He was accustomed to people finding him lacking in some way and most of the time he didn't really care or understand what it was he lacked compared to everyone else, even people who didn't seem to be very nice. Now he appeared to be disappointing Anna and for some reason that knowledge did not sit so easily in the pit of his stomach.

"Why did you cut yourself?"

Theo was silent.

"Come on," insisted Anna. "I am telling you my whole life story; you are the first person I have spoken to for years! And I can promise you boy… that is no exaggeration! Tell me why you hurt yourself; tell me about the bruises on your face; maybe if you tell me, you might feel better."

Theo shook his head. "I doubt it."

"Try," declared Anna impatiently. "You never know."

"You are so nosy," huffed Theo.

"Yes," giggled Anna like a small child. "I have been told that many times before. And you," she added sternly, wagging her crooked index finger, "...are rude."

"Yes," Theo admitted. "I've been told that before too. I'm sorry though, I don't mean to be rude to you. I just don't like talking about my mum. It puts me in a bad mood."

Anna's old eyes widened. "Your mother did this to you?"

Theo stared down at his dressing, realising that he had said too much and that he was about to betray his mother.

He nodded. "My face; by accident though."

"What!" Anna marvelled. "You cannot do this much damage to a face by accident, unless you are in a car crash!"

"It's not the way it looks," muttered Theo trembling. "Honestly Anna, she didn't mean it. Mum is not herself at the moment. She's..."

Theo's voice trailed off because he did not know what to say next. He put his head in his hands, scratching at his scalp. The pressure from his hands made his bruises hurt.

He felt her crooked fingers rub his knee.

"I'm sorry Theo," Anna whispered. "I have pushed you too hard. You didn't want to tell me this and I won't try to make you tell me more. I am afraid that one of things that makes me, me, is my tenacity – I am like a dribbling dog that will not release its bone."

Theo smiled into his hands.

He sighed. "I don't think I know what makes me, me."

Anna rocked her body into him. "Then between us we will try to find out."

Theo looked up from his hands realising that he may have just found his first real friend.

CHAPTER FIVE

AS Theo dawdled home his morning with Anna ran through his head like an old movie. He could slow down the frames that he wanted to examine more closely. Listening to Anna's life story was affecting him in ways that he did not understand; it was also giving him blessed relief from the uncertainty of home and his guilt over Eden. When Anna spoke it was like reading his books; he could slip away with her to a time gone by. Her appalling situation in Theresienstadt could in no way be compared to Theo's own circumstances, but listening to her story jolted him out of the cycle of self-pity that had controlled his feelings for so long.

Theo thought about what Anna had said about the bullies. Did they pick on him because he was an easy target? Could they tell he had little self-respect and even less self-esteem? Would they be more inclined to leave him alone if he was more confident about whom he was, if he liked himself better? Why did he see so much to like in other people and so little to like in himself?

Anna seemed to find it so easy to talk to him even though she had clearly not confided in anybody for years: surely he should take that as a compliment. He tried to think of other people who talked to him and found that he could think of quite a few: Seb, his mother, Jon, a boy in his form at school called Lewis whose mother had recently died of cancer. A couple of girls he knew, who were bullied like him for not quite fitting in, had also confided in him on occasion. Maybe he knew how to be a good friend, but he just didn't seem to have any. Maybe he pushed people away like Seb had once suggested.

He tried to think if anyone had ever tried to be his friend and he remembered that Lewis had often invited him to kick a ball about on the green near the beach where Anna's coffee man sold her cakes. Theo always refused because, firstly he was terrible at football, and secondly, he thought Lewis just felt sorry for him because he knew he didn't have any friends. Now Theo considered the fact that Lewis had invited him because he was lonely too. Theo paused at the front gate. It rattled on its rusty hinges as he pushed it, then let it swing back to him. Staring at the house, he felt his stomach jangle with nerves for he had still not seen his mother since she had thrown things at him. He forced himself up the path to the front door, lingering over a lone snowdrop that had bloomed in the hard soil. Taking a deep breath, he put his key in the lock, hoping that Nana Dora had not taken up residence for the day to look after Sophia.

The house was silent when he padded quietly through the hall to the kitchen. Seb was sitting at the table, staring at his laptop with his earphones glued to his ears. He didn't look up as Theo slouched on the sofa, removing his shoes. Theo watched Seb tapping at the keyboard, marvelling at the speed at which he typed. He found himself thinking that he would never be able to match it, but then he thought of Anna and her promise to hold on to herself. Immediately, he quelled the negative thought before it formed completely in the disquiet of his mind.

"Where have you been hiding?" asked Seb, removing his earphones and leaning back in the wooden chair to stare at his brother. "God," he added, looking appalled. "Look at the state of your face. Mum would do her nut if she knew what she'd done!"

"S'alright," Theo muttered. "It'll heal."

"It had better," Seb grinned. "You don't want to spend your whole life looking like that! You'll never get a girlfriend!"

Theo blushed and chucked one of Sophia's favourite cushions at his brother's head.

"How is Mum?"

"Same," Seb made a face and a bubbling noise with pursed lips. "Still won't get out of bed. I think Dora Doom has gone to speak to the doctor about her today. I heard her going on at Jon before he went to work. She arrived at the crack of dawn as usual, not bothering to use her key so that I had to get up and let her in because Jon was in the shower. She gave him a hard time about phoning the coroner's office too: as if he doesn't have enough to do already! They'll bloody phone when they know anything won't they!"

"Probably," agreed Theo, rubbing at a newly forming scab on his face.

"Poor old Jon... He seems stressed out to the max... I've offered to go to the shop with him, but he says it's more important that I keep studying."

"I could go," Theo offered, thinking that it would be an excellent opportunity to escape from the house again.

"That's a great idea – I'd go now though," Seb urged. He took a gulp of cold coffee then spat it back in the cup in disgust. "Otherwise Dora Doom will be back to give you a load of hassle!"

As the words dropped from his lips, the doorbell rang, making them both jump.

"Bugger!" exclaimed Seb. "I bet that's her! You go out the back door and I'll answer it. She won't give me any grief because I'm going to bloody Oxford!"

Theo grabbed his trainers and his coat, tripping over Seb's books in his eagerness to reach the back door before his grandmother caught him. As he reached to close the door behind him, he heard Seb's persuasive tones echoing through the hallway.

"Nana Dora, I would really be most grateful if you used your key!"

Grabbing his bike from the back garden, Theo disappeared down the side of the house and out into the road. The icy air burned his injuries as he cycled quickly towards Jon's antique shop. It was hard going. The pain in his arm prevented him from steering with two hands which meant he wobbled most of the way.

He took a detour along the seafront. He could not resist the vitality of the sea air despite the difficulty in cycling. During the moments when the sea's breath filled his lungs he could believe that everything would be alright; that it was just another day helping Jon at the shop rather than the precipice of chaos. He listened to the pull of the tide over the shingle as he wobbled past the beach huts. An old man sat alone huddled beneath a blanket on a deck chair, staring out to sea. Theo saw his shoulders shaking with the rhythm of the waves. Reaching the road, he navigated a coachload of pensioners, dismounting from a coach. They waved at him and chuckled as his front tyre narrowly missed the sea wall. Theo wondered about their lives; if they had fought in the war against the Nazis. He wondered if they had always been so happy. Their glee seemed to hover in the air around him as he peddled towards the avenues. The pier stretched out into the silvery sea, like a beast flung from the low clouds above. Theo thought about the first day he and Seb had met Jon; when he had taken them to the ice cream parlour next to the old Edwardian cinema whilst Sophia was at work. Theo had eaten a banana split and Seb had teased him about the way he took seconds to demolish it. They had wandered along the pier, with the couples strolling hand in hand, their cheeks pink from the wind. Whilst Jon had joked with Seb about his antics at a nightclub that used to be located on the pier, Theo had stared down at the water at the furthest point, wondering if he would have the courage to jump off and swim to the shore.

Now it did not matter.

Theo swerved across the sea front road, into the wide avenue lined with beautiful houses. The sea, behind him, he rode furiously until he reached the alleyway behind the shop. Leaning his bike against a wooden shed, he bent over his knees, waiting for his burning lungs to recover and his arm to stop throbbing.

Theo loved the shop. He loved the musty smell that clung to the old wood and material. He loved the elaborate jewellery that had once adorned a lady's throat or hat, and the ceramics, beautifully painted by someone whose work was yet to become collectable. Paintings hung from the wine-coloured walls, rugs were draped over banisters, and on the shelves that clung disjointedly to the walls beneath ostentatious wall lights sat the small antiques that Theo and Seb had always found so fascinating. Theo's favourite was a World War One cigarette case that had all the cigarettes present except one. There was a poem inside on a scrap of paper that Theo believed the soldier had written himself in the trenches. It was signed Kenneth Button.

The cigarette box had never sold, despite being collectable to the right person. Theo believed it was waiting for him to buy it and he vowed that he would, when he was old enough to receive his first pay cheque.

Jon was sitting at the computer in the stuffy back office doing his accounts when Theo entered through the garage space at the back of the building. He looked drawn and miserable as he typed numbers and shuffled papers. His black hair stood on end.

"This is a nice surprise!" His brown eyes smiled over the top of his glasses. "I haven't seen you for a while."

"Thought you might like some help... or company."

"Thanks mate. Your company is always welcome. Biscuit?" Jon offered Theo a ginger nut.

"Thanks – what can I do?"

"I'd like to say nothing, but to be honest since my part-timer has been off looking after her sick husband, everything is a bit dusty."

"Hand me the duster then!"

"Are you sure you don't mind?"

"Course I don't mind!" He took a yellow duster and a can of polish from Jon's outstretched hand.

"Anywhere in particular you want me to start?"

Jon sighed. "The big stuff! There's no way you'll get around all of it in a few hours."

Theo smiled.

"What happened to your arm?"

Theo stilled, turning away so that his stepfather would not see his face burning.

"Fell off my bike."

"Oh, want me to take a look?"

"No, it's fine. Just aches a bit."

"Theo," began Jon hesitantly. "I know things are bad at the moment but they'll get better... you know."

Theo nodded, looking at his feet.

"Mum didn't mean it you know... when she chucked the stuff at you... she's just suffering at the moment, but she is going to get better, I promise. The doctors are going to help."

"Yeah," muttered Theo, avoiding Jon's eyes. "I know."

"She does love you. We both do."

Theo fiddled with the corner of the duster. "I'll get started on this..."

"Thanks," said Jon. "I appreciate it."

For the next few hours, Theo was content. He had time alone, being responsible for precious items, doing easy work that allowed his mind time to breath. The antiques shop was warm and quiet and without the constant tension of home.

Theo worked quickly and thoroughly. He knew Jon liked to keep his things in good condition so that they remained as appealing as possible to customers. The bell above the shop door rang many more times than Theo expected for a cold Tuesday afternoon in February. Jon appeared from the office and used his extensive knowledge of antiques to beguile his customers. As sales were made and Jon smiled despite the difficult circumstances at home, the soldier's cigarette case remained untouched.

As Theo dusted he opened sideboard cupboard doors and the drawers of desks and bureaus. They all smelled of a time gone by and Theo inhaled deeply when he was sure no one was watching him.

Sometimes the furniture contained something special. Once he had found a secret compartment to an old sewing box and discovered a diamond and sapphire ring gleaming back at him. The family had crowded around him in delight and admiration. When Jon sold it, to a man wanting to propose to his girlfriend, for a good price, he had taken them all on holiday to Portugal. Theo remembered the pool and his mother smiling a lot. Seb said it was because Nana Dora hadn't gone with them.

The next antique in line was a desk from the time of the Restoration. A small Charles II walnut writing desk, which had a sloping fall flap supported by two gate legs. The interior was fitted with an arrangement of six drawers and its block legs terminated in turned feet. Theo opened the drawers, paying particular attention to each of them. The desk was a new addition to the shop and clearly needed a good dust. Theo came to the last drawer; he opened it gently and was surprised to see a folded, discoloured piece of paper. His heart quickened with excitement. Carefully, he unfolded the frayed corners, sinking onto the velvet chaise longue that languished in front of a beautiful Grandmother clock. He jumped as it began to chime the hour.

As he unfolded his treasure, Theo was surprised to find that there were many pieces of paper locked together. They were flimsy and the edges seemed to have been eaten by something. Theo laid them flat on the velvet and looked closely at what was written on them.

The first pieces of paper revealed themselves to be a

letter. The writing was large and scrawled across the page. It was written in a different language. There were strange slashes above some of the letters. Theo had no idea what language it was written in, but he knew it was not French, German, Spanish or Italian or any of the other world languages which were identifiable by the difference in their alphabet. He guessed it was eastern European, but there were so many countries that he could not pin it down to a certain one.

It was addressed to "Teta" at the top of the first page and signed "Miluji tě rad Ivana" at the bottom of the last one. Theo scanned the page to find some meaning in the words and was disappointed to discover that he could find none. He was just about to turn his attention to the final piece of paper when he spotted a word that sent a bolt of recognition to his brain. In the top right hand corner, where the address should have been written, one word was scrawled above the date: Auschwitz.

Theo's mouth was dry and he swallowed, staring at the word. He knew what it meant. He had read about it in the book he had borrowed from Seb. Auschwitz was the most famous of all the Nazi concentration camps. It was a place built for the mass extermination of Jews; the place where more than a million people were cold-bloodedly murdered in gas chambers.

Theo's blood felt cold in his veins. He shivered. Had the letter been sent from someone who had died in Auschwitz? Was he holding a piece of history in his hands? How had it come to be in this old English desk in Jon's shop?

Tremulous, he lifted up the final piece of paper, examining it carefully. It seemed to be a poster of some kind, advertising an event. There was a drawing of a three-sided fence with the faces of smiling children peering over the top of it. The writing was again in a different language. Theo grabbed the letter and studied the words on each piece of paper, trying to find similarities. After looking at them both carefully, he concluded that they were written in the same language.

The poster had none of the darkness of the letter; on the contrary it seemed to exude fun and a sense of joy. A word in bold script seemed to chuckle on the page: Brundibar, it read. Theo wondered what it meant; he examined every word in turn. Each line of script was written alternately in cursive and bold capital letters. Eventually he stopped at a word he recognised: "opera".

He smoothed both of his remarkable findings over his thighs. He felt instinctively that they were related in some way, not only because they had been bound together in their folds but because he believed both of them had belonged to the mystery Ivana. In his mind he imagined a young, dark-haired Jewish girl dragged off to the hell of Auschwitz, with the sound of children singing opera still in her ears. Theo shuddered then took a deep breath.

Checking that Jon was still busy talking to a customer on the phone, Theo slipped the papers into the back pocket of his jeans. Immediately he felt guilty, as though he had stolen something that did not belong to him. In a way he supposed it was theft, but he fully intended to return the treasure to its rightful home or give it to Jon, so he grappled with the guilt in his mind. Theo could not quite allow himself to turn over his findings to Jon just yet. First, he desperately wanted to show them to Anna. He believed that she, more than anyone, would be able to illuminate the meaning of the poster and the letter. Anna had experienced the madness, the barbarism of the Nazis first hand. He believed that she, rather than some shabby historian, should be given the first opportunity to see them.

With certainty in his gut, Theo continued to dust the remaining large antiques in the shop front. Jon eventually finished his work and wandered around the precious obstacles in his kingdom, praising Theo for his hard work. He offered him money which Theo felt unable to accept with the poster and letter throbbing against his right buttock. As Jon pulled down the metal guards and locked the front door, Theo cursed his blushing face, once again. He shook his head, quietly swearing at himself for his deceit; although as he cycled home through the darkness he had to admit to himself that stealing a few letters from the war for a few hours, faded into nothingness when he was going to prison for killing Eden anyway.

Once again Sophia remained in her bed for the duration. The doctor arrived as Theo and Jon rushed up the path together. As Jon spoke to him, the words spilled from his mouth like lumpy custard from a jug. The doctor had to ask him several times to repeat himself. Nana Dora stood behind the kitchen worktop. She seemed upright and proud, but Theo thought she should be cowering for the mess she had made of her daughter's life. More than anyone, even himself, he blamed Dora for the hideous situation the family now found themselves in. If she had not bullied Sophia... if they lived far away from her... if his mother had not felt like a perpetual failure... then maybe things would have been different. Maybe a dead baby would not be lying, suspended in the morgue, and a woman would not have retreated to temporary insanity.

Feeling Seb's eyes upon him, Theo looked straight at his brother. Everything he thought and felt seemed to be reflected in his face. Seb was glowering at Dora with the same loathing that Theo felt too frightened to expose. He envied Seb his ability to hold onto himself.

The doctor padded upstairs to see Sophia. Nana Dora tried to follow him, but Jon held her back with more vigour than he usually displayed. His face was grim as Dora tried to argue with him. He ushered her onto the sofa, pouring her a glass of port from the decanter on the side board. Theo and Seb both eyed her suspiciously as she sat with her legs folded and one arm crossed across her body. She dutifully sipped at the glass of port, keeping a close eye on the kitchen door.

When at last the doctor returned, his face was unreadable. He asked to speak to Jon privately. Jon quickly ushered him out of the back door, grabbing his cigarettes and lighter from the worktop as he left. Dora leapt up from the sofa and tried to bustle past Seb.

"Don't," Seb countered, stabbing his arm into her path. "I know you want to, but don't! Jon will tell us what we need to know."

Nana Dora glared at him, tottering on her heels as she tried to slide past. "Sebastian, she's my daughter!"

"Yes," agreed Seb grimly. "And she's our mother. We are worried to death about her too. If we can wait, then you can too!"

Her eyes filled with repugnance, but she stopped in front of him, falling back upon the sofa and gulping at her drink. For once, Dora was silenced, shocked by her grandson's outburst. Theo quietly applauded his brother, awed by his assertiveness.

When the doctor and Jon traipsed back through the kitchen they were silent. Jon showed him to the front door then returned to the kitchen, pouring himself a glass of wine before he took a deep breath and started to speak.

"They think Sophia has suffered a nervous breakdown." Jon was candid as usual.

"What does that actually mean?" cried Seb. "I mean I know it means she can't cope with everyday life, but what is it, exactly."

"The doctor thinks that Mum is suffering from an anxiety disorder," explained Jon.

"Post-traumatic Stress Disorder?" inquired Seb wisely. "I did a search for it earlier. That's the answer I reckoned on!"

Jon stared at him.

"Yes, actually." He drank deeply from his glass.

"My poor baby," whined Nana Dora, sniffing into her handkerchief. "My poor, poor girl."

Jon scowled at her, blatant hostility hardening his usually soft features.

"He thinks he can help her," continued Jon, pouring himself another glass of wine. "I have a prescription."

"Not anti-depressants..." snorted Dora, glaring at her son-in-law. "You cannot possibly be thinking of those awful things. Sophia is stronger than that!"

Jon sighed, his eyes weary. "Dora, I really don't think this is the time for mental health prejudice... Your daughter needs your help and support to get through this," he added sternly, leaving everyone present in little doubt of his tolerance for any arguments or recriminations. "You will support her or leave!"

Nana Dora opened her mouth, then clamped it shut again as three pairs of eyes bore into her.

Theo felt jubilant and he could sense from the glitter in Seb's eyes that he did too; Nana Dora, for once, could not dominate the proceedings. Her bullying was left with nowhere to go for the first time in Theo's memory. It was a perfect moment despite the appalling circumstances.

"Right," she began nervously, her top lip twitching. "I see there is little for me to do here, so I will leave you all in peace. I gather you won't mind me looking in on my daughter before I leave."

"She is sleeping Dora…"

Nana Dora stood upright, but her eyes did not meet Jon's. She bustled around searching for her handbag, before standing in front of the gilded mirror hanging above the sofa to tuck her straw-like hair in an ungainly felt hat.

"I had intended to cook for you all tonight, but I don't feel you'd appreciate it," she prattled.

"Thank you Dora, we do appreciate the gesture, but I can take care of my boys very well."

"Suit yourself; though I think it's such a shame to give them soggy old pizza again!" She applied a layer of glossy fuchsia lipstick, smacking her lips together, dismissively.

"Actually," blurted Theo, in a moment of sheer bravery. "Jon cooked steak and peas the other night. It was delicious!"

Theo's face was burning. Nana Dora glowered at him before turning on her ridiculous red heels to flounce out of the house.

Jon and Seb burst into laughter.

"Genius Theo!" Jon applauded. "That was brilliant!"

"Yeah," agreed Seb, slapping Theo on the back. "Absolutely brilliant."

A wide grin spread across Theo's crimson face. He luxuriated in their praise, joining in their laughter.

Chapter Six

Wednesday, 17 February 2010

THE next morning, the laughter was replaced by the familiar panic. Theo had dreamed that he had smothered Eden with a pillow rather than cuddling her. When he became fully conscious he had to pinch himself to remind himself that it wasn't true.

Feeling the contents of his stomach threatening to regurgitate, he raced to the toilet just in time. He retched continuously over the bowl until there was nothing but bile streaming from his lips. Guilt and shame joined the vomit, but no matter how deeply he wrenched his stomach, he could not rid his body of the feelings.

Theo lay down on the floor, holding onto his belly, his legs folded against his shaking torso. The cold tiles cooled his flaming cheek. He lay there, completely still, for a while, feeling unable to move or think beyond the compulsion to confess the truth to his mother. More than anything, he longed to unburden himself of his guilt. Part of him knew that until he had done so his emotional void would remain just that. He could not mourn Eden while the guilt suffocated his grief. Yet right now was not the right time to confront Sophia; he knew that. She would be unable to register what he was saying if she could not even accept his presence.

Somebody banged on the toilet door, making him jump. They knocked again, more forcibly this time, but Theo remained routed to the ground. He did not try to rouse himself until he heard the footsteps retreating and the click of a bedroom door. Hurriedly he wiped his mouth with a handful of toilet paper and flushed the chain.

Nobody emerged from the rooms when he stepped out onto the landing so he slipped quietly into his bedroom to dress for the beach. He clothed himself warmly, pulling three jumpers over his head. He fumbled around in the bottom of his wardrobe in search of the ski gloves Jon's mother had given him for Christmas. Wrapping a scarf around his neck, he belatedly remembered the letter and poster that was still sitting in his jeans pocket from yesterday. He transferred them carefully to the back pocket of the pair he was wearing, then shuffled down the stairs in the darkness.

The morning was still again. The thick aroma of fuel filled Theo's head as a lorry passed him on the corner. The pavements were empty and laced with a ring of frost. Theo's warm breath preceded him like a puff of dragon smoke in the icy air. Breaking into a run, he found himself relaxing in the beauty of the morning and the freedom of the empty roads. As his feet pounded the pavements, so too did his thoughts, each one of them invisibly stamped on the slabs of concrete, moaning to those that had been left before them.

Anna opened the door before he rang the bell. He took Blackie's lead and matched his lolloping pace through the trees to the seafront. As they bounded over the grassy mound, he breathed in the immensity of the channel stretching out before him; it was almost blue under the cobalt winter sky. Shadows from the wisps of cloud lingered on the motionless water. Only at the shoreline did it whisper over the sand, gurgling into the small dips and ravines.

Theo threw a stick for Blackie, enjoying the dog's gleeful anticipation, his muscular, trembling body. The stick bounced on the surface of the water before being caught on a wave. Blackie bounded into the shallows, swimming with his nose and ears above the water to retrieve the stick. He returned to Theo, dropping the stick at his feet before shaking the water from his fur. Theo stumbled backwards, as droplets of salty water smudged his lips. He threw the stick into the sea again and realised that his breathing had returned to normal.

"Your face looks a little better," Anna murmured, when he and Blackie returned to the snug kitchen. She undid his dressing with her knobbly fingers. "I think you are beginning to heal."

Theo nodded, looking glum.

"Inside – it does not heal so quickly, no?"

"No," agreed Theo.

"I've cooked bacon. Would you like some?"

Theo nodded.

Anna handed him a plate that was still warm from the oven. Two rashers of bacon sat beside a chunky piece of bread.

"I have something to show you..." Theo murmured when they had finished eating. He took his plate to the sink and rinsed it under the tap.

Anna smiled.

"This," he began, groping around in the back pocket of his jeans. His cheeks flamed as he offered the old pieces of paper to Anna. "I found this in a Charles II desk in my stepfather's antique shop."

Anna's eyes widened. She unfolded the papers with clumsy fingers that shook with age and then fumbled around between the cushions on the sofa. She pulled out a crooked pair of reading glasses.

Theo watched her face as her eyes scanned his treasure. He saw them twinkle with surprise and fascination.

"Theo," she breathed after several long moments had passed. "This is incredible. Truly... you have no idea what it means to me to be holding this..."

Theo smiled, pleasure thawing the edges of the numbness within him. For once he felt that he done the right thing in bringing his findings to Anna first.

"I...I..." he stammered. The words tripped over themselves trying to escape from his mouth. "I didn't know what language it was... I thought you might know..."

"I do, Theo!" she marvelled. "This is remarkable because both of these are written in Czech and I have not seen this poster since 1943!"

Theo was dumb-founded. "You... you recognise this?"

"Yes," declared Anna, shaking her head in disbelief. "I certainly do!"

Anna, 1942

I am awake long before the wakeup call sounds. In the darkness of the early morning, when demons gloat over a bewildered mind, I lie on my straw bed, listening to the sound of rats' feet scratching on the wooden floor. If I wasn't frozen and miserable, I would still be reluctant to return to sleep because I am sure that what roused me was a rat scampering across my body. I can still feel its smooth, long tail slithering over my face. I am repulsed and absurdly terrified because I know, that of the things that may hurt me here, this creature will not be one of them. I begin to rationalise my fear by contemplating the diseases the rat may harbour. When the wakeup call sounds, I am relieved to rise from my thorny bed.

Rousing my pregnant friend, I speak to her gently. When I lay my hand on her forehead, I am certain she has a fever. I ask her name and discover she is called Viera. I urge her to lean on me as we lumber our way to the cold, ugly washrooms. There are only a few toilets for the hundreds of women who have to use them. Viera seems hardly conscious, so I make it my responsibility to find her food and medical assistance. In the rooms that are scarcely kitchens I squabble over cauldrons of thin soup and wheat grits. I grab what I can for Viera even if I have to starve myself. So far I have not met anyone who is friendly, but I have barely looked anyone in the eye. Everyone seems too miserable and preoccupied with surviving to bother over me. I am new to this place, but I do not believe the others who bed with us have been here long either. They seem to have the same wide-eyed fear that I know is echoed in my own face.

In a way my invisibility pleases me. I am not ready to tell my story. Viera says very little also. I believe she is not just pregnant and sick but also suffering from shock. I believe she may have seen frightful things. I wonder where her husband is. She is hugging her belly and rocking gently when I return to her with the food. I am able to persuade her to eat very little. Her eyes are fearful as she surveys the room and I know she also fears the vermin within.

With one long nail she scrapes viciously at the skin on her calf. I look down and see she is covered in bites. Absently, I begin to scratch at my own body; every part of me feels violated by insects, vermin.

Viera continues to refuse the meagre breakfast. Eventually I give up and eat the paltry offering myself. I try not to notice the unsavoury taste as I gulp at the soup and chew ineffectively at the grits.

We are approached by a woman who smiles with half of her face. Her hair is pinned back in a harsh bun; her long skirt and boots are shabby. She introduces herself as Giza and explains that she will be taking us to our place of work. I protest strongly that Viera is too sick to work, but Giza does not seem to hear me. As I assist Viera and we follow Giza, along with several other women from our barracks, I begin to think that it is not only her features that are harsh.

In the open air the ghastliness of the ghetto strikes me anew in the light of the day. As we walk the dreary streets, a po-faced Giza tells us about the prisoners in the Small Fortress. She explains that the cells are housing prisoners from the Soviet Union and also those who were arrested for political activities or contravening anti-Jewish laws. A shiver runs through me as I think of Father; perhaps he has been taken there. I think of all the terribly sick people he has helped. Giza waves her hand absent-mindedly in the direction of the Commandant's house. Her voice is a growl as she relates that the 'Gate of Death' is believed to be next door to where he sleeps. This gate, she is soon to elaborate is the gate through which one passes on the way to be executed if one is to believe the 'bonkes'. I quickly gauge that 'bonkes' is slang for rumours and that Giza's tour is intended as stark warning to all of us to always obey the rules of the ghetto.

As time goes by, the reality of these rules becomes more apparent.

We stop at various insalubrious buildings within the ghetto; at each stop we shed one of our number as she is prodded towards her place of work. I catch a small glimpse of what is going on in each place and it begins to dawn on me that our work here is in support of the Nazi war effort; that we are assisting the very regime that incarcerates us. I watch two women disappear to spray what seems to be military uniforms with white dye; (I gather they are to be sent to the Eastern Front as camouflage in the snowy Russian ravines.) Another is given the task of splitting mica.

Soon Viera and I are separated. I try to protest once more, explaining that she is too sick to work. My objection falls on deaf ears and Viera is led into a vast room full of women who appear to be sorting through underwear. I am puzzled by this and I wonder if it has been confiscated from Jews in the ghetto. Giza, sensing our unease, explains that it is sorted here so that it can be taken to the people of German cities whose homes have been destroyed in Allied bombing attacks. I shiver and absently hitch up my own tatty undergarments.

When we eventually arrive at my place of work, it happens that I have the most macabre of the jobs that we have seen that day. Inside what has become a workshop there are people sawing and hammering at pieces of wood; most of the workers are men and it takes me several moments to pick out the women. They have cropped hair and melt seamlessly into the nucleus of men as they work. At first the purpose of the woodwork is not apparent, but as I look around, drinking in my new surroundings, the horror of its intended creation reveals itself. The prisoners are making coffins.

Nausea clings rigidly to the well of my stomach; I struggle not to retch as I am introduced to a man named Karel. He is a burly blonde Czech with wide shoulders and guarded eyes. When I greet him politely he grunts in reply. Giza takes her leave without looking back. Karel moves with unusual grace for a man of his stature. He seems to control the mechanics of the room with looks alone. It is clear that the workers obey him out of respect rather than fear. Despite the gruesome product we are commanded to build, there is a bonhomie here that I have yet to experience anywhere else in the ghetto. The unexpectedness of it unnerves me for a while as another man is told to teach me how to prepare pieces of timber using a plane.

I find it difficult to concentrate on his instructions even though he speaks in Czech, because my mind suddenly becomes bewildered by my fate. Everything I have experienced since the moment Mother died begins to whir through my mind like a steam engine, hissing and spitting as the momentum increases. I try to hold onto the present, but the past is engulfing me faster than I can focus. Abruptly my vision turns to snow; strong hands thrust me into a chair and push my head forward between my legs. A Polish voice commands me to breathe deeply. I have no choice but to appease the darkness.

It seems an eternity has passed before my vision returns to normal and I can raise my head.

A Polish woman is kneeling at my side; many concerned pairs of eyes watch me keenly across the work space. Whilst her thumb rubs at my trembling hand she tells me her name is Eliza. She tells me that I am suffering from shock like so many before me, that I must not be ashamed, that I will become accustomed to my life in Theresienstadt. Eliza's kindness reminds me so acutely of Mother and Aunt Matylda that I have to angrily scrub the tears from my eyes. I sit with Eliza for a while. Nobody urges us back to work, but after a while they seem to forget my unsettling presence.

Eventually I stand on shaky legs, thanking Eliza for her kindness and stumbling back to the man who is my teacher. He smiles at me with pale, kind eyes, patting my shoulder. Once again he begins my instruction and this time I am a conscientious listener. When finally he hands me a piece of timber and a plane, I almost relish losing myself in the task. I try not to think of the coffins I am making; the German soldiers they are intended for. I tell myself that I am learning to work with wood, honing a new skill; that there are far worse jobs I could be given in Theresienstadt.

Viera greets me with a surprising smile when I arrive back at our bed of straw. I have struggled with the hordes for tasteless food and grappled with the wood. Every part of me is exhausted from the emotion of being here and those I refuse to acknowledge. The buried emotions squirm in the coffin of my soul, yet seep through my eyes. Tonight it is Viera who is the comforter as I am the comforted. Her bump sits on her crossed legs. It looks uncomfortable, but she looks better than she has done. I think the fever has gone for she tells me she has eaten and her demeanour is changed. If I am honest I thought that I would find death slavering over her tonight, but I try to bury the thought as she voices her concern for my well-being and thanks me for caring for her since our meeting on the transport. She says she will be eternally in my debt; that I can rely on her undying friendship always.

As she strokes my hair, I sense others watching us. Viera greets them unexpectedly, urging them to sit with us. Four women kneel and sit on our bed of straw; it seems Viera has been making friends in my absence. Her extrovert demeanour surprises me for until now I have not heard her speak more than a few words. I had even considered that shock had made her mute.

The women introduce themselves. It is clear they are hardly older than me. I pay each of them careful attention as they talk, trying to imprint their names upon their faces.

Rachel is a beautiful Austrian girl with luminous skin and a long blonde plait running down her back. Her physical beauty seems at odds with her shabby clothes. She arrived at the ghetto three days before us. Her family had fled Austria after the Nazis came to power in Germany in 1933. When the anti-Semitic Nuremberg Laws were passed in 1935 and Hitler turned his imperialist attentions towards Austria, Rachel's father, a Jewish banker, put his family on the first train from Vienna to Prague. She has three Jewish grandparents like me. She talks about her brothers, but she has no idea where they are. The children were separated when their parents sent them into hiding, but Rachel says her eldest brother Fischel has promised to escape to Switzerland. He has vowed to send for her when he reaches safety, but Rachel does not know how he will find her now that she is imprisoned in the ghetto.

Agnes, a serious looking girl with straight dark hair and thick rimmed glasses, tells us she was a violinist in Prague before she was forced to leave when the Nazis arrived. Agnes was shipped here by train, arriving at the small country station of Bohusovice and walking the three miles to Theresienstadt, following her father's arrest as a political activist against the regime. She believes he is a prisoner in the Small Fortress.

Beside Agnes, sitting crossed-legged is gregarious Berta, a Hungarian who seems to talk more than anyone else in many different languages. In the short time I have sat with her, I have heard her greet other women in our barracks in both Russian and Rumanian, although I do not make it clear that I can understand. Her round face is surrounded by a mass of dark curls which bounce as she talks; her eyes remind me of the chocolate discs my aunt used to bring me from her holidays in the Alps. She was living in Prague before the Nazis transported her here.

Sara is the eldest of the girls. She is twenty, like Viera, I am told. This surprises me because I had assumed Viera was older because she is with child. These other girls seem to know more about her than I do, despite the fact I have spent more time with her since our arrival in Theresienstadt.

Sara's mousy hair is cropped short; because it is cut in untidy clumps and the fringe is horribly uneven, believe it may have been cut against her will. Her ragge clothes hang from her bony shoulders as though th are suspended from a knobbly wooden chair. I cheekbones, protruding beneath pale green eyes, l a deathly hollowness to her pallid face. She does volunteer any information about how long she has here or her life before the ghetto. I feel an affinity her closed past. She says very little unless urged by who seems to have appointed herself Sara's ment understand why she believes she needs protectin also think Sara is probably stronger than all of us

The girls whisper of their experiences in th their fear of looking like the emaciated inm have suffered here for years, their hatred of the food and toilet facilities, the awful jobs they have been assigned to, the appalling sleeping conditions, the vermin and the lice and the lingering threat of infectious diseases. I expect somebody to become emotional, but the solidarity between us appears to keep sentiment at bay. Nobody speaks of their family or of what they experienced in the months of living under an anti-Jewish regime before being incarcerated here. The conversation is restricted to topics within the ramparts of the ghetto. Through our mutual predicament we begin to weave the delicate strands of friendship in the unspoken but reciprocal hope that it may contribute to the strength we need to keep us alive."

I
d
ey
Her
end
not
been
with
Berta
r. I can
g, but I

e ghetto.
ates that

CHAPTER SEVEN

sses in Theresienstadt I begin to discern
s about myself. My first discovery is that
remarkable resilience and ability to adapt
ındings despite squalid conditions and an
ture. The second is that I have a natural
orking with wood. Like the happy days
ı assist Father on his medical rounds, I look
ng to my place of work and learning from
thers.

v patient Polish teacher, delights in my
working with the wood. He is an excellent
like to spend time just watching him at
s I am aware that looking at him arouses
ıgs in my body. When I feel like this, I
reen eyes as he earnestly instructs me.
st boy who has ever made me feel shy,
ly is too big for the space it occupies
ıt to look at his thick black hair that still
n glossy despite his decreasing weight
ı not know how old he is, but I think he
same age as poor, dead Michal.

elf to be ignorant of the purpose of
the speed at which I learn. When I

forget about impending death and lifeless bodies in the coffins, I can lose myself in the beauty of the wood and concentrate on the pieces I am shaping. This profession is not medicine as I had dreamed but it does offer blessed relief from this place. I pray every night that I am no moved to a different job as other girls have been, because I believe that if I am here, I may survive, despite the lon working hours and the bleeding fingers.

I have surreptitiously asked questions relating t Father, but nobody I have spoken to has heard of a ma called Emil Levinsky, eminent physician, whose Russi father had stormed the Winter Palace in 1917, whilst h mother fled to her wealthy family in Prague with h four children. As yet I have not entered the barrac where the men are housed in search of him because I not wish to draw attention to myself. I believe that if I to survive then I must fade into the background of ghetto, watching and listening, whilst being shrewd a perhaps a little devious.

It is Sunday. Today I have decided to look for Fath do not tell Viera, who seems to have regressed back a brooding silence, where I am headed. The other have been avoiding us this morning owing to Viera's mood, so I do not have to contend with endless quest from Berta.

I walk sedately through the ghetto, longing to bre fresh air. I yearn for the mountains or the mesmer forests of Moravia. Some of the children here say the see the mountains from one of the rooms where are housed. Here that must be an incredible luxur wander I see children on the ramparts that are acce only to them. Laughter lingers on the air, then is g know that I am still a child, but since I am housed adult women I feel that part of my life is over. I ha felt like a child since leaving my home in Prague.

After trying several different buildings, I eventually arrive at the Sudeten Barracks which accommodates men. The inside does not vary very much from the place where I am housed; endless cramped quarters that spill with people contained, like animals in cages, against their will. As I wander from room to room, many pairs of eyes stare back at me, but none of them belong to Father.

In one room I find a solitary fellow lying on a filthy mattress on the bottom line of a three-tiered bunk. The air smells rancid. He is lying facing the wall with his back towards me. From the colour of his hair and familiar way in which his body is lying, I think he could be Father. An ember of excitement ignites in my gut. Gingerly, I approach the bunk, glancing warily at the door as I bend over the man's inert form. I feel guilty about interrupting his sleep, especially if he has been given special dispensation to remain in bed because he is suffering from an illness. Leaning over his torso, I am overpowered by his reeking body. The smell is utterly intolerable. I cover my face, holding onto my nose as I strain to look at the man's face.

I am completely unprepared for what I see. The man lying in the bunk is not Father. The man lying in the bunk is no longer there at all: his eyes are wide and lifeless staring at the wall. In horror, I recoil from him as I realise he is dead. I discern that he has probably been like that for several hours. Scanning his body I realise that the smell originates from the urine seeping through his trousers and the fact that he had certainly defecated in death as his body lost its muscle function.

I cannot believe he has died here and that, despite the mephitic smell, nobody has realised. Stretching out my arm, I rest my trembling hand on his shoulder, saying a prayer for his soul. I think that just a month previously I had never seen a dead body, but that now they seem to be occurring far more regularly than I can bear.

It takes me several moments to compose myself enough to call for help. When at last I find my voice, several men come running into the room. I try to explain what has happened and a heated debate ensues. They argue about calling one of the physicians, completely ignoring my presence. Finally, a stern, hefty man commands them to lift the man's body outside. Speaking in low grunts, they shuffle out of the room without even giving me a second glance.

Slipping out into the corridor, I convince myself to continue my search for Father despite the unnerving circumstances. I try to rid my mind of the man's empty eyes staring into mine over his stagnating torso. Men of all ages bustle past me. Most do nothing more than raise their eyebrows or mumble when I manage a timid greeting in their direction.

Stopping outside the makeshift kitchens I peer through a gap in the door in search of Father. A young man with straw-like hair and a bulbous nose is peeling a potato. Immediately I find him distasteful for a reason that is not entirely clear. Around him there are men, perhaps ten of them, whose aged faces are sagging under the weight of their wrinkles. These men are hunched over and so thin that they can hardly stand. Their weary eyes watch as the man slowly peels the potato and allows the peeling to fall to the grimy floor. In horror I watch as the old men shove and tear at each other as they struggle to reach the scraps of potato. Some are knocked to the floor, unable to raise their rickety bodies. The space is filled with screaming, groaning and hissing as the men fight each other like dogs. I am appalled and unable to move. The blond man laughs scornfully over their heads then turns to leave the room. I press myself against the wall hoping that he will not see me. He strolls out of the door heading in the other direction along the corridor. Mercifully he does not see me because I do not believe he is a Jew.

Waiting until he has turned the corner, I lurch into the kitchen to assist the men. Most are grateful for my assistance as they explain, in a variety of languages, that they are starving. I try to prepare a meagre meal for them as a man called Jan explains that there are men in the quarters above them who are so decrepit that they cannot manage the stairs. They are dying of hunger, he tells me. When I have fed the men in the kitchen I insist that Jan takes me up to see those who are starving. As we enter the overcrowded rooms, I am shocked by the hideous state of humanity within. I cannot believe these men are not cared for as they lie in their own waste, unable to make it to the toilet or washrooms which are located on a different floor. Their bodies are the size of a child's, the frail skeletons shrinking beneath the rolls of furrowed skin.

I know that food is scarce in Theresienstadt. I know it is a battle to find any nutrition in what is available; that bread is a currency that can be exchanged for nearly anything: clothes, cigarettes, a vegetable, private tuition; that the soup is disgusting; that in their dreams everybody eats the delicious food they once tasted, for it now exists only in the respite of sleep. I know all this, but I cannot believe it is necessary for these old men to be dying of malnutrition. I can help them. I will help them. That Sunday, after I have given the starving what food I can muster and a drink of water, I leave Jan with the promise that I will return, thoughts of Father for once obscured by the miserable fate of the fellows lying before me.

It takes a while to make changes, but with the assistance of the Jewish elders and others who expressed concern, change happens. The old men, and women also, are eventually helped to get enough food and water. Young people from the children's home are encouraged to visit the elderly to provide them with some reprieve from their daily misery. Sometimes they sing to them or give them drawings or meagre gifts. I persuade my friends to accompany me when I visit the elderly. Berta, Sara, Agnes and Rachel share my concern for their well-being, so we decide to visit them regularly to help them wash and toilet themselves and clean their dreary quarters.

My quest to find Father terminates in a dead end. He is nowhere in the ghetto for I have searched every barracks. There is a possibility that he may be imprisoned in the Small Fortress for flouting the anti-Jewish laws by continuing to practise medicine before we were captured, but I am beginning to think that he may have been sent to one of the camps in the east that I have been hearing about. I try to stay positive about seeing him again, envisioning our happy reunion, but it is difficult when I have heard Sara telling the other girls that nobody ever comes back from there. Sometimes it makes me cross because I think they all pay too much attention to the 'bonkes'. Others say that the camps in the east are an improvement on Theresienstadt. Most of the time I just don't allow myself to think about it because surviving here is enough of an ordeal. I have made a deal with God about seeing Father again. I am absolutely relying on him to keep his side of the bargain.

Today has been more horrific than the worst nightmare. This morning when we were working, one of the Czech guards who work for the SS arrived to speak to Karel. When he left, Karel's face was grim. Closing his eyes, he pinched the bridge of his nose tightly, drawing several deep breaths before he was able to speak.

He tells us that a group of thirty of us must be ready to leave within half an hour. There are only thirty-two working in the workshop so we know straight away that only two of us can remain behind. Morris and the other men ask Karel for more information, but he says that all he has been told is that the delegation are going to work for the day in the village of Lidice.

My mind is immediately brought to attention when I hear the name of my aunt's village. It is the opportunity I have been waiting for; perhaps today I will find out where Father is and also whether Matylda is safe. Since being dragged away by the SS on that dreadful morning, I have been eclipsed by a gnawing guilt about Matylda and her family. I know that she lost her only child that day because of us. I know I cannot even begin to repay her sacrifice after this war is over, but I know I must try. I have to take this opportunity to see her again.

There are only three women issued to work with the coffins. Eliza and the other woman immediately start crying when they hear Karel's news. He says that the two left behind must be women and that it is up to us to decide who will stay and who will go. Instantly I am at their side as they try to tell me that I must be one of the ones left behind because I am so young. I know they are thinking that we might be sent to our deaths in Lidice, and because of the barbarism I have already experienced at the hand of the SS I know this could be a very real possibility. As Eliza gabbles fretfully in my ear, I know I must insist that I am going with the delegation.

Gently I begin to explain to her about Matylda and Jurik and my agonising wait for news of Father. I tell her that she and the other woman are needed here because they have other family members within the ghetto who are relying on their survival. I insist that if one of us is going with the men then it must be the one with the least to lose. The women pull me into their teary embraces, asking me if I am sure of my decision. I assure them that if this task is expected of the men then it is expected of me too.

Extricating myself from their arms, I hunt around the workshop for Maksym's sharp scissors. Finally I find them lying under a bundle of tools. I think that if I am to join the men successfully in the delegation to Lidice then I must look like one of them. I am already wearing a pair of trousers that Maksym has found for me in the men's barracks. (He insisted that I needed them for working with the wood.) Now I realise that I must cut my hair. Taking a seat on a wooden stool, I raise my hand aloft with the scissors open. Before I can cut my hair, I hear a wave of Polish expletives pour from Eliza's lips as she realises what I am about to do. Darting across the room, she rips the scissors from my hands, issuing me with a sharp reprimand. Shaking her head and murmuring in Polish, she takes the scissors in one hand and a comb from the pocket of her tattered overalls. The workers applaud as she proceeds to cut my dark mass of hair. Misery clogs my throat as clumps fall to the floor, mixing with the wood shavings. The strands of hair feel like the loved ones I have lost and the years of my childhood, relegated to an old wooden floor. I am now a different Anna to the one who left Prague and entered Theresienstadt; half adult, half child with the adult half forced to emerge and stand to attention.

The nape of my neck feels exposed and vulnerable. Eliza finally puts the scissors on the work bench and stands back to admire her work. The others grunt in admiration, but all I want to know is whether I can successfully pass for a young man. Morris agrees that I can, if a very pretty one. Karel nods in agreement, just as the door opens and the Czech guard reappears to take us to the SS waiting beyond the barricades of the ghetto.

I have been naive about everything that has happened to me. The heinous acts of the SS and the doctrines of Hitler and the Nazis seem so senseless, so utterly evil that it is difficult to comprehend that such depravity is even possible within the realms of humankind. I know the history books will tell me otherwise, and that although I have experienced the atrocities committed by the Nazis first hand, I still cannot quite believe it.

On the day we arrive in Lidice, everything changes; I find that from that moment on, I am forced to believe in actions festering in the very bowels of wickedness. Upon my arrival in Lidice, my innocence is gone forever.

The shock of what I see when we are ushered out of the transport nearly renders my body worthless. As I look around I struggle to control the threatening panic or the speed my heart thuds in my chest.

Lidice is gone. The homes, the buildings, the gardens, everything has been flattened as though a bomb exploded in the very centre rendering everything to rubble. Anything that is left is blackened and smoking. I am utterly confused and I can hardly believe that my eyes are telling me the truth. I feel the warmth of someone's breath on my cheek. I do not turn to find out who it is because I cannot allow their faces to validate the truth of what I see. Also the area is swarming with Gestapo agents and members of the SS. I am so terrified of them that I daren't move a bone in my body unless under instruction. I am grateful to be standing amidst the crowd of carpenters who are familiar to me. Many of them tower above me. A voice murmurs in my ear:

"Stay calm, Anna. Whatever you do, stay calm. I have heard rumours that Hitler has ordered reprisals upon the Czechs for the murder of Heydrich. I think this is about to be very bad indeed. You must stay calm and strong, moja droga."

I know it is Maksym who murmurs in my ear because he speaks Polish. Usually he will not tell me of the 'bonkes' he has heard or the risks I know he has taken to bring news from the outside world into the ghetto. Everyone knew who Heydrich was but, living in the walls of the ghetto where news of the outside world was scarce, I had no idea that the security police chief SS-Obergruppenfuhrer had been assassinated.

My eyes are locked upon the ruins of Lidice. Around us are the remains of uprooted fruit trees and ruins flattened by bulldozers. Derelict walls lie in pools of rubble where charges were set to explode. Everything has been reduced to nothing and there is no sign of anyone who once lived here.

CHAPTER EIGHT

Anna, 1942

WE are ordered past the trucks. Our delegation moves slowly. Behind us is a mound of mattresses obscurely doused in red paint; this confuses me until I see what lies in front of them.

Lying on the earth are rows and rows of dead bodies. Hardly able to breathe, I stare at these corpses with a horror that can never be explained. I feel the men breathing hard beside me, struggling not to cry out in resistance to such pernicious criminality. Every part of my body screams at me to look away from the lifeless bodies, but I force myself to look at every face I can see because I need to somehow validate their existence.

With sudden realisation, I know the abhorrent purpose of our presence here. SS guards yell at us in German expletives, laughing as they light cigarettes and take slugs from a leather hip flask. We are instructed to dig a big hole in the ground. Shovels are passed around and each of us reluctantly takes one. We are being forced to dig a mass grave for these people of Lidice who have been unjustifiably murdered by the Nazis. As I start to dig, a cold numbness washes over me. I am working outside of myself; I am no longer Anna.

There are seventeen rows of bodies, lying in the

meadow of what I know used to be a farm just hours before. The bodies are male and from what I can deduce they have died from an assortment of bullet wounds. I believe they may have been forced to line up in front of the mattresses – because they are splattered in blood, not paint as I had first thought – then shot by firing squad. If I was in a position to try to identify the bodies, identification would have been impossible in most cases. I assume that nearly every man in the village is lying there, because there are so many of them here before me, but I have no way of knowing if Jurik is one of them. Faces are obliterated, visages replaced with splinters of bone and brain that ruptured when the skull was shattered. Torsos are splattered with a hailstorm of bullet holes; intestines unravel from the inside of bodies, like slaughtered pigs suspended by their trotters.

This is a massacre; the total annihilation of a village. A village that has not committed any crime; that has lived quietly with its lake, stream and meadows, providing a home for good men and women as they work, love and procreate children. This tragedy is shamelessly engineered by the hand of evil.

I dig now with absolute fury coursing through my body; I dig with madness in my mind; I dig with thoughts of revenge, escape and anger at the injustice of this attack.

There has been no sign of any women or children. I cannot weep for Matylda, but I long to so desperately. Once again I listen hard to members of the Gestapo lounging at the other side of the ditch we are digging. One of them is taking pot shots into the air with a revolver. This, I know, is done with the intention of petrifying us into working faster and it has the desired effect. My Jewish comrades jump as the bullets explode in the cobalt sky above them.

Two of them are talking loudly about the children who have been taken from Lidice. Either they do not think that any of us understand German or more likely, they do not care, because in their distorted view, our Jewish blood revokes our humanity. They speak of children being sent to Lovosice, and the women to Prague and camps in the east. One of them brags that they will probably be executed for their part in Heydrich's demise. The other laughs in agreement, calling the women immoral and filthy. Seething, I wonder how on earth women from here could possibly plot Heydrich's assassination. My whole body aches with longing for Matylda and Jurik.

I have been digging for a long time, but I do not care that my back aches and my heart aches more. I just want to validate the existence of these men whose lives have terminated at the end of a Nazi weapon, convicted for a crime that they have not committed. I want to think of them as the individuals they deserve to be, so I ignore the purpose and pain of the work and pray for each man.

I think of them as they were, with soft skin that was warm to the touch and smelled gloriously individual. I think of Mother; how her distinctive perfume mingled with the scent of her skin on a warm summer's day. I listen for their laughter echoing through the windows of their homes as they played with their children or drank beer with their friends. I consider the undisclosed sadness that may have influenced the life of each man and the simple things that may have transcended all things to bring happiness. I think of the inimitable mannerisms and characteristics of these men that made them unique individuals. I think of the love they had to give; I think of their humanity.

My thoughts are interrupted by a ruckus at the other end of the monstrous pit we have dug. A man I do not know, who scarcely speaks when we are all in the workshop, has thrown down his spade and is yelling insults at the Gestapo who stand mocking him at the top of the pit. The man is apoplectic in his fury. He tells them exactly what he thinks of Hitler and the Nazis. He tells them exactly how he feels about what has occurred in Lidice. His shouting scares me because I am in no doubt about how the Germans will react. I fear for him and the rest of us. It is not long before my prophesy becomes a reality. A member of the SS with cruel eyes holds his pistol aloft and shoots my comrade in the head. He tumbles, like a puppet with its strings cut, into the mass grave. I know I will have to be eternally grateful to God if I get out of Lidice alive. I know now that, like Mother, Josef and Michal, Matylda, Jurik and Father may be lost to me forever.

My sixteenth birthday has come and gone without fuss. After the day in Lidice I find it difficult to find happiness in anything. Even smiling makes me feel guilty. I do not tell anyone when the day arrives because I believe that even delighting in birthday wishes is disrespectful to those who died an unjust death in such ghastly circumstances. I think the girls think that I am ill, because I say so little but I am not ill, I am mourning.

Berta has been meeting an older boy. They promenade in the evenings together. His name is Stefa. I have seen him a few times. He helps the man from Moravia put on puppet plays for the children in the cellar. I have heard them laughing, and I revelled in the perfection of such a sound. Stefa's eyes are the blue of the summer sky above the mountains and his chiselled features give him the appearance of a Renaissance statue. It is almost difficult to look at him as he is the antithesis to the ghetto. Agnes giggles that he has the stance of a Greek god.

She whispered to me once that in a dream she saw him naked except for a loin cloth. I try not to imagine it the next time I pass him beside the barricades. I know many of the women here stare at Stefa. I wonder if he is aware of the impact he has on females. I do not like to imagine him as arrogant; like the son of one of my father's friends who baited me when I was smaller. I believe that a man who is blessed with such physical attributes has a duty to be humble, for then he may remain an ideal for the girls living in the ghetto, who are in need of a happy distraction.

I cannot allow my thoughts to wander to a man such a Stefa. It would unravel the shackles of Lidice, the steel beneath my skin allowing me to keep my promise to Mother. Whilst I can relate to Berta's elation in my covert admiration of Maksym, I know my feelings do not threaten my will. My fury.

I wonder if this man Stefa is too much for giggly Berta, who dreams of mothering five sons whilst her rich husband makes obscene amounts of money; though perhaps that is only bravado; escapism from this squalor. Stefa is like the sun, and inside I know Berta must luxuriate in his warmth while she can.

I sit half listening, slightly apart from my friends as they gorge in rapture on Berta's tale of love. I find myself hoping that this man Stefa will not hurt Berta, but quickly realise the irony of such a concern abiding within the strict regime of Theresienstadt. Stefa is no threat.

She dissects their first real kiss, as the girls grin and gasp at her boldness. I catch her whisper of his tantalising tongue on her neck, the desire burning in her belly. She says her skin hums, sings like the choir that can be heard resonating from the basement rooms. My throat is full. I try to swallow, watching Berta's animated face; yet envy will not be so easily dismissed. It clogs my veins. I know, however that I am not envious of Berta's happiness, but rather more wistful at the realisation that perhaps my body may never sing. I feel a blush creeping over my cheeks.

The girls salivate as Berta murmurs of her secret engagement. Agnes and Rachel share a clandestine smile that tells me they long to be in Berta's position one day soon. There is high excitement in hushed whispers, a loving embrace; a heartfelt kiss. They gasp at the wooden ring Stefa has fashioned with a knife and chisel. I admire his handiwork. He has an indisputable talent. Berta says they will get married when Hitler is defeated and the Jews are free. She enthuses about seeing an end to our time in the ghetto, for Stefa believes Hitler will be running scared now that the Americans have joined the Allies. I shift uncomfortably on the knobbly floorboards, fighting the urge to reprimand her for the volume of her high spirits, but despite my fear of Berta being overheard by one of the guards, I cannot dampen her joy. There is not enough of it here to dismiss it so callously.

I do not share her optimism about Hitler, for I do not believe a man with such a capacity for wickedness would count America as any great opponent. He may have underestimated the British RAF in 1940, failing to dominate the skies, but this, to a man of such arrogance, would be merely seen as a temporary glitch. All the rumours speak of his dominance. I cannot believe they are wrong even if America has entered this ghastly war.

Sara urges Berta to whisper. Their huddle tightens.

Unconsciously I know I move closer to them, my legs resting softly against Viera's back. She leans into them. I notice her arms are crossed over her enormous belly as though she is settling them upon a table. She tells the girls that she knows of love. She demands they wish for more when they leave this hell. She says romantic love is not always something of which we can be certain. She demands we dream of other things. The girls respond eagerly to her command, for Viera is our silently allotted leader. It is not only her age that has contributed to this privilege, but her aura of wisdom and experience. We all long to know more about Viera than we already do.

The whispers move from Stefa's attributes to other desires. Sara wishes to write a book. It will be published, she says. Berta tells her she will be a great author. We all know, yet do not voice, the knowledge of Sara's diary hidden beneath a floorboard where the rats prefer to defecate. When she leaves the ghetto… if she leaves the ghetto, I hope the diary goes with her. I hope it is published and that one day, years from now, people can share in our experiences here; our pain and our pleasure, our hopes and dreams. I cannot bear the thought of Sara's work being lost to the world. I know if anything happens to her I will keep the diary safe.

It is Agnes' turn to speak; quiet, dependable Agnes with a talent for music and friendship. We are close so I know what she will say. I smile when I hear her longing to play the violin at the Albert Hall in London. She describes the instrument with such passion that my desire to be a medic seems almost meagre in comparison. I hope she goes to London; perhaps we will all accompany her. I squash the thought before it completes itself. I feel the shackles relinquish their grip, breathing in so that the screws may tighten once again.

When it is Viera's turn she does not mention her child, tumbling in her womb. She voices her wish to find a friend who last resided in Germany. The girls silently speculate that the friend is Jewish. They are wondering if this person is contained in a place like this. Viera does not volunteer information about her comrade, yet the sadness shifts in her eyes as though relinquishing a ghost.

The turn becomes Rachel's. She is less serious than the others. Her beautiful eyes shimmer when she tells us of her longing for the tasty Tafelspitz prepared by her father's chef in their mountain chalet. The way she describes the beef dish elicits growls of hunger from the girls. A bead of saliva hovers on Sara's bottom lip. I know she does not know it is there. I think she has been without palatable food for longer than the rest of us. Rachel laments the exquisite clothes than she left behind in Austria, describing haute couture gowns from Paris, made of the finest silk by delicate needlewomen. She tells Berta that she will request that her father commissions a wedding gown after the war. Berta squeals with delight as Sara moves the chain of dreams swiftly on to me. The girls scoff as I turn my body in their circle. I know they do not mean to be unkind, but I feel the sting of humiliation. Viera wraps an arm around my legs. I smile at a patch of straw on the ground. Rachel nudges me. I laugh then with reluctance, begin telling them my dream in words they have already heard. When I have finished they tell me I will be a great doctor; a physician of the highest regard throughout Europe and perhaps the world.

For a moment I forget about Lidice and the ghetto. For a moment I am happy; encircled in the belly my friends.

We sleep huddled together; our bodies drawing strength from the humanity of another. Exquisite music drifts in the air. I close my eyes, pretending I am in my bed in Prague with music floating through the open window. The melodious voices of the choir emanate from the cellar. The SS do not seem to mind such endeavours within the ghetto for they view such pastimes as frivolous. Sometimes the choir sing Czech and German folk songs or Hebrew melodies, but tonight they are practising a classical piece; music that will float from the grave of my decaying body long after I have left. I have heard Verdi's Requiem so often I can sing it in Latin in my head on nights when sleep eludes me. The music is haunting. The voices of the choir are like that of angels fallen from God's grace, limping at the gates of hell. I want them to sing forever.

The birth of Viera's baby is certainly overdue. I have never seen a pregnant woman so large or cumbersome unless she is carrying multiples. Once a woman knocked on our door at home in the dead of night; she was carrying twins and Father allowed me to witness the birth because he knew I was passionate about becoming a doctor. I supported the woman throughout the birth, saying things to her that made no sense. I think I was more frightened than she was. I held her hand as she wept in agony, crouched over the mantelpiece in Father's study. When she gave birth to live, healthy twins it was the greatest miracle I have ever witnessed. When I think of it now, it makes me shiver with sheer wonder.

Viera doesn't seem worried that the onset of labour is slow. She does not talk about the baby or the infant's father. It is almost as if she is in denial about its existence. When I, or one of the others – usually Berta, makes a reference to her heaving belly, she changes the subject, leaving us in little doubt that the subject is forbidden. I wonder what will happen to the child in this place. I wonder if it will be allowed to remain with Viera or if it will be confiscated and kept in the children's home. Another woman has given birth in our barracks and the baby has so far remained at her side, but I know that elsewhere this has not been the case. The rules in here seem to change daily except for those which remain the same, such as the night-time curfew and the fact that unauthorised departure from the ghetto will be seen as an attempt to escape, resulting in the use of weapons.

It is in the dead of night when I awaken with the unsettling sensation that something is very wrong. I cannot feel the warmth of Viera beside me; when I roll over I realise that she is not lying on the thin, grubby mattress that Maksym found for her in his barracks. I sit up and wait for my eyes to adjust to the darkness. There is no sign of Viera. I creep through the throng of snoring bodies that shift uncomfortably on the straw in their sleep.

Wandering in the direction of the toilets, I can hear whimpering. I know it is Viera. I pad over the cold stone floor, banging on the wooden door. A full, luminous moon casts a silver river through the bars on the window, creating ghostly shadows in its ethereal presence. The door opens and Viera is crouched over the bowl. She retches as her enormous body heaves with the strain. Her legs are wide and sweat pours from her forehead and dribbles down her side from the arc of her armpits. I hold her while she retches, then sits on the toilet, expelling the watery waste from her bowels, crying in agony while her belly contracts as it tries to expel the child. I think I should be frightened, but I know from my experience with the twin mother that I do not have time to indulge in such luxury. Viera's time is near. In here, there is little point calling for a doctor. He will either be too late or already busy. I run to find clean rags that I can wrap the baby in and something to mop up the blood; I search for an implement to cut the umbilical cord with; I think I can ensure it is sterile by running it through the flame of a candle.

Returning to Viera, I wait until she is calmer, before I persuade her to let me take a look between her thighs. She groans as her body contracts over and over again. There is barely any time for her to recover. When I look down I can see the baby's head moving down the birth canal to the opening and then back up again. Without any real certainty about whether what I am doing is correct, I urge Viera to pant when the pain abates and push when she feels her belly tightening. Viera does as I ask, but wails as the pain overwhelms her. She will not sit, but crouches like an animal on all fours. I cannot bear to look at the immense pain raging over her face so I force myself to concentrate on the baby's head.

The going is tough; the head does not seem to come freely. I do not know if Viera can cope with much more and I fear for her life and the life of her child. She is practically delirious, murmuring that she is dying, as I urge her through my tears to push one last time. Viera lets out a scream that is utterly primal. When the head emerges followed by the slippery body of the baby, it falls into my waiting arms as Viera collapses on the floor.

I place the baby on her sobbing body as I help her deliver the afterbirth and cut the cord. Viera is weak, but she holds her baby in delight.

"Oh, Anna... I have a girl... a beautiful girl."

I smile at her agreeing that the baby is very beautiful indeed. Handing Viera the clean rags to wrap the baby in, I urge her to put her to her breast as I had heard Father do. I know this to be of paramount importance, especially in Theresienstadt where food is scarce. The baby must have her mother's milk.

Thankfully the infant does not need much persuading. I watch her as she suckles and Viera smiles down at her. As I clear up the mess, I know I am witnessing beauty in its rawest form. I know that being with Viera tonight makes me very fortunate because I have experienced one of life's true miracles.

"Anna, I want you to name her, if it wasn't for you we would both be dead."

I try to protest, but Viera insists that her daughter will take a name chosen for her by me. Finally, I relent, suggesting that she could call the baby Isabella after my late mother. Viera is enchanted by the name and I glow with pleasure. She rocks her child gently, crooning Isabella over and over. We both laugh with the sheer happiness of gazing upon her daughter, for now at least, it does not matter that we are in the infernal pit of the ghetto. For now, we have everything we need.

When I have finished cleaning I tell Viera that we can go back to our dorm. She is reluctant and urges me to sit with her.

"I need to ask you something very important. I think you know that you are the only person I can trust in the ghetto."

I nod.

"I need you to promise that if anything happens to me in here that you will care for Isabella as your own daughter. I give her to you Anna, if I should die or get put on a transport. Do you understand?"

Once again I nod. I want to speak, but tears are clogging my throat and I cannot give them free reign. Viera speaks urgently in my ear. I do not try to interrupt her.

"If you and Isabella get out of here alive I want you to promise me that you will find her father. I do not talk about him in here, because he is German, an Aryan. I met him in Hamburg when he was working on the U-boats. He is much older than me but we fell in love. When it became impossible for Jews in Germany, I left Hamburg. It was too dangerous for both of us. I had been in hiding with some of his friends and they managed to get me forged papers. I escaped to Prague, but eventually the authorities caught up with me and I ended up on that transport with you. By then I was too weak and too sad to care what was happening to me. You brought me back to life, Anna. I will love you always for that. Isabella and I are in your debt. I'm sorry that I have to ask this last favour of you, but I believe that you may be able to understand about Wolfgang and not hold his nationality against him. Wolfie did not care that I was Jewish, he does not believe in the laws of the National Socialists. He is a German, but not a Nazi."

Awestruck, I listen to Viera's story. It is terrible yet romantic all at the same time. I know I will do as she wishes should anything happen to her in Theresienstadt. I know that I have wordlessly been appointed Isabella's guardian; a second mother when a father is absent. I hug Viera tightly, promising that I will carry out her wishes to the very best of my capabilities. She sobs in my ear, saying,

"You are so young Anna, you do not yet know about love."

She strokes Isabella's downy cheek.

"Love, my darling Anna, is madness; utter madness."

There is an epidemic of scarlet fever rampaging through the ghetto. I offer my services in the infirmary, helping to care for the sick. There are so many of them that the infirmaries are overflowing. There have been an unprecedented number of deaths, because so many of the sick are malnourished or old and do not recover from the diarrhoea that is often prevalent among the patients suffering from this illness. There is also precious little medicine to go around. I try not to think of the coffins I have made or worse, the pit that I dug for the victims of the massacre at Lidice. Their fragmented, deformed faces haunt my sleep. I know the Nazis will not exert themselves to ensure we have the medicine and medical equipment we need to preserve Jewish lives. I am angry, but I do not voice my anger for there are people in the ghetto who are still naive to the extreme measures favoured by this regime that imprisons us.

Covering the faces and bodies of many patients, there is bumpy rash that is a vibrant red, as though one has spent too much time in the sun. Their glands are swollen in the groin and neck area and a fever of over one-hundred-and-one degrees causes delirium. I pour water down raw throats, mop fevered brows and empty chamber pots for more than fourteen hours a day, but it is not long before I succumb to sickness myself. It is a debilitating illness.

I do not remember much about the time that I am sick. I am at the mercy of the illness which must run its course. When I am finally well again I am frustratingly weak. This frightens me more than the illness, because emotional and physical weakness makes people vulnerable in Theresienstadt.

When I eventually return to my straw bed in the barracks, I find our space is not as suffocating as usual. Many of the familiar faces have gone and I am told they have either perished from the sickness or been placed on transports to the east. The girls are brimming with news and excitement upon my return, for they cannot believe I have been lucky enough to survive when so many others have not. I cannot believe they have all been fortunate to escape the disease altogether. Isabella sleeps peacefully in Berta's arms. I ache to hold her, but I am not sure Viera will want that when I have been so ill and in quarantine. Isabella looks bigger and quite healthy. During the nights when the fever coursed through my body, I dreamt terrible hallucinatory dreams that Isabella was thrown into the mass grave with the men in Lidice. I am relieved to see her bonny face resting against the dark hair on Berta's forearm.

Viera sees me watching her daughter and urges me to take her. I do not need to be asked twice. I hold her sleeping form to my body, luxuriating in her warmth and the smell of her soft head. I am overwhelmed with happiness; relieved that she is safe and well and with Viera. In the months that follow I spend as much time with the baby and Viera as possible. Her care becomes our joint responsibility and she seems to thrive despite the wretched conditions. Isabella is my one source of happiness and I will do everything to protect her.

In Theresienstadt it is difficult to decide whether

summer is worse than winter, or the other way around. The oppressive heat of the summer exacerbates the vile smells, the spread of disease and the swarms of insects. Lice, fleas and bedbugs reign in tyranny over the residents of the ghetto. They crawl through clothes and blankets, biting exposed flesh, making everyone itchy, irritable and impatient for an end to the war. "Bonkes", pertaining to the progress of the Allies, raise our hopes for a while but it is always short lived.

Winter is harsh for it is impossible to get warm under the thin blankets and our tattered clothes. Food does not provide our bodies with energy or warmth for its nutritional value is so limited. The rooms we inhabit are like blocks of hollowed-out ice. My hands and feet are always numb or aching with cold. Everywhere is continually dank, dark and miserable.

A new year is upon us bringing freezing temperatures and morbid conditions; I am worried about a new sign that has appeared above the taps and wells. There is limited running water in here and we are now to believe that what is available may be contaminated with faeces containing typhoid fever. I know this disease will spread rampantly in the ghetto for the intolerable, unhygienic conditions that we are forced to endure will encourage it to thrive. There are signs everywhere telling us to "Beware: Typhoid!" and to wash our hands, but I know that hand-washing alone will not prevent the progress of this foul disease. It will pollute everything it touches within the squalor and flourish at body temperature. In its own way, the ghetto is slowly killing us. I do not think, with its miserable medical confines, it can cope with a pandemic of a disease as virulent as this.

Although I am concerned for my own health, I am more concerned for Viera. If she is infected then it will place Isabella in danger, not only of losing her mother but also of contracting the disease herself.

I watch my friends closely. At work, many of our number have become infected with the disease. Dear Eliza has lost her daughter already and now she is also suffering from the high fever and chronic stomach cramps. As the number of carpenters dwindles, my workload increases as the number of coffins we are compelled to produce rises. I wonder if they are being used to carry our dead, though I think it is more likely that the victims of this illness will be burnt in the new crematorium that Maksym has heard rumours about. Death, it seems, is everywhere. I cannot escape its baneful clutches, even in sleep.

One morning I cannot find Viera. I place Isabella in Berta's drowsy arms and go in search of her. I find her in one of the facilities which is covered in urine and faeces. The smell is so putrid that I retch and cover my nose and mouth with a tatty handkerchief. Viera is in a terrible state: her face is flushed with fever and she is releasing a noxious pea-green fluid from her bowels. Her stomach pain and delirium is so severe that she barely recognises me. I know from the symptoms that she is infected with typhoid. When I am able to move her I place her in a heap on the icy floor, while I try to clean the soiled area. This disease can thrive adequately in the unsanitary conditions beyond our control; it does not need further incitement. As I wipe, I try not to gag nor think of the infection assailing my own system. I wash my hands several times before I am happy to move Viera.

The girls take the news of Viera's infection badly. Berta

cries and Agnes rants. Rachel is quiet. Sara's pale face is almost cadaverous. We are all worried about the fate of Isabella, for if anything should happen to Viera the Elders will almost certainly rule that she must be sent to the children's home. I cannot bear to contemplate a day without Viera and Isabella at my side. The pain of it is just far too overwhelming on top of what I have already suffered. I cannot consider the infant losing her mother, then leaving the women that love her, to be housed in the girls' home next to the church in the Market Square. It is intolerable.

I do not really understand all of the decisions that are made within these ghetto walls. I know that the Council of Elders make most of the arrangements with their meagre resources and the impossibility of running facilities that are only adequate for a tenth of the number of inhabitants, but I am finding it difficult to believe that they are anything more than the puppets of those residing in the SS commandant's office. I think the Elders, like everyone else in Theresienstadt, are scared of breaking the rules, of provoking the anger of those who rule us. When the names are revealed of those placed on transports to the east, people feel confused. Some are thrilled that they are leaving the ghetto for a camp that is, according to the implausible Nazi propaganda, a better facility and others reel in terror that they are being sent to a place from which they may never return. Knowledge is power and without knowledge we are woefully inept at predicting our futures. Without knowledge, without truth, terror reigns supreme. Fear eats away at each of us whether or not we feel able to voice it, and its only adversary is the solidarity and friendships that the misery of the ghetto has foisted upon us.

Seven days after Viera is taken sick with typhoid fever

I am called away from the workshop to be told that she is dead. I cannot stand to look at the face of the woman who speaks to me, because I want to rip out her eyes and beg her to stop telling lies. Viera's death is just too much for me to contemplate.

When I tell the girls that we have lost our dearest friend, we stand together holding each other whilst we grieve. Around me there is uncontrollable weeping. I will not weep. I will not allow Hitler the satisfaction of my tears. I will not succumb to the pain within me, because I cannot let go of those who have gone.

I am not allowed to keep Isabella despite the fact that Viera has declared me to be her guardian in writing. I refuse to relinquish her to the children's home and it is quiet, stoic Sara who finally prises the sobbing infant from my arms. Tears fall off her chin into Isabella's hair as she bravely marches out of our room and through the barracks.

Agnes is not present to say goodbye because she has also become infected with the disease that is ensnaring so many lives. I cannot think about the possibility that I may not see Agnes again either so I bury myself in the straw, letting the raw pain assail me. I know that I am lucky to be alive. I know that I am fortunate not to be suffering the terrible symptoms of typhoid fever. But today I do not feel lucky. Today I have lost my best friend and a child who feels like my own. Today my physical form is paralysed by my emotional pain and I am powerless to stop it.

Chapter Nine

Anna, 1943

I visit Isabella every day; sometimes I am able to see her before I go to work and after I have finished. On the days that I am not working I am allowed to spend all my time with her. This arrangement cannot compensate for the fact she no longer shares the space beside me on our bed of straw, but it is better than not seeing her at all. I must confess that the conditions are slightly better in the girls' home and the food is more palatable. Isabella greets me with a bright smile when I arrive each day. She is already crawling around and pulling herself up on the three-tiered bunks in the overcrowded accommodation which is headed by Jewish counsellors.

There are so many girls in the room where she sleeps that they all lay top to tail in the cramped bunks which are meant for only one person. Despite the noise and chaos caused by so many children housed in a small space, and the inevitable emotional pain suffered internally by each child, there is an uneasy happiness and solidarity between the girls, many of whom are school age. The natural jollity of the children makes the girls' home a more pleasant place than the adult barracks, but there are similarities to their daily existence. The wake-up call still sounds, announcing daily chores and clean-up duties.

There are stringent rules about the beds which have to be aired each morning. Many of the girls attend lessons, but the nature of their schooling has to be handled delicately because of the Nazis' view on education.

When Hitler marched his troops across Europe, in pursuit of "Lebensraum", he promised to place limits on the education in the countries he ruled. The Nazi ideology, that deems the existence of an Aryan Master Race to be in every way superior to the inferior races of the world, demands that those not included in the Master Race should live within confines laid out by the hierarchy. The restrictions upon education are especially important, because the Nazis view every educated person as a future enemy.

The schooling in Theresienstadt is termed 'activities' as the SS believe that art, singing, dancing and other physical pursuits are mere frivolity; the actual lessons, therefore, are disguised in some way, as an education in history, foreign languages and literature are strictly forbidden. Many of the Jews called upon to be the children's secret teachers are experts in a certain field such as science or music.

Like nearly everything in the ghetto, fear is permanently intertwined with the pleasure of learning. The young people know that if they are caught studying by the guards or the SS, there will be serious reprisals for the children and the adults who are teaching them.

Recently there has been a barracks lockdown which lasted two months and meant that nobody could go out into the streets. During this time I was unable to visit Isabella which was pure torment for me and the other girls. The lockdown was due to a visiting dignitary, the SS Sturmbannfuhrer. Such a visit did not bode well for anybody and further ignited the heart-stopping fear that jangled inside everyone when the SS marched through the ghetto. We all know that he is making plans for us with the SS commandant, but we have no idea what these plans are or how they will be orchestrated. The lack of knowledge is torturous and people make wild guesses pertaining to the purpose of the visit. I keep my fear locked in. Lidice is still fresh in my nightmares which I share with no one. At work it is never mentioned. We continue as if the massacre never occurred. I think it is the only way we can all cope with witnessing such barbarism.

More transports to the east follow the visiting dignitary. I listen for my name but it is not called. I listen for Isabella's name, but that too is mercifully missing from the list. The same cannot be said however of my friends. Today, Maksym has been called. I am crushed by his departure. He spent an hour talking to me before he left to pack his things; he cried silently on my shoulder, we were eclipsed by pain and uncertainty.

There are so many people packing; because it is warm many of them are outside in the square languishing in the chaos of their possessions, choking on their fear and insecurity. Different transports are leaving at different times. There is a queue waiting at three o'clock outside the Hamburg Barracks, I cannot bear to look at them as they wait to enter the sluice and then to board the transport east. They seem to be vacating in their hundreds, some are relieved to be leaving the ghetto and others are terrified; all are uncertain for their destination is unknown.

In an impetuous moment when my anguish over Maksym leaving is at its height, I rise early to catch one last glimpse of him. When I arrive at the barracks I can see people just coming out of the back gate. In an unguarded moment, driven by infatuation, I clamber over the fence. From the gate I see the cattle truck pull up, boarded with wooden planks so that nobody could really see in or out; keening sobs fill the still air. I watch the truck containing Maksym depart and towards its rear, blow a flurry of fervent kisses.

I sleep very badly in the months that follow Maksym's departure: my torrid nightmares match the scorching heatwave that festers over the ghetto. It is ninety-five degrees in the shade. Those who remain in Theresienstadt are edgy and short-tempered. Nobody knows when the next transport will leave or whether their name will be on the list. Opinion seems to be divided over the subject of transport. The stinking ghetto is such an iniquitous blend of filth, disease and crawling insects, exacerbated by the prevailing heat, that some believe the transports must be headed to somewhere that is an improvement on Theresienstadt. Others, believe, as I do, that the transports are headed to a place from which there is no return. The fear of this gnaws away at them hour by hour.

In the heat the overcrowding is even more unbearable. The stench of our bodies in the defiled mire of our quarters, coupled with the lice that crawl incessantly over our itchy skin, aggravates our uneven tempers, jangling nerves to breaking point. Everywhere there are people scratching their skin to the point where it bleeds and allows infectious toxins to penetrate the blood. The bedbugs are so virulent that some have taken to sleeping under the stars. Some nights I join them, staring into the inky sky as I dream of a future for Isabella and I that does not include this hateful place or the wicked people who incarcerate us here. I ask questions about God and the meaning of our existence. Staring at the host of glittering stars that fan above me like angels protecting the earth, I wonder how we have come from nothing. I question how, if God is everywhere, he created us from nothing at all. I wonder if nothing is really something, if energy is created in a void. I curse humankind's propensity for war and those who believe they are superior enough to make judgements upon the lives of others. I curse their bullying, narrow-minded stupidity. I ask myself whether man will always go in search of Lebensraum in places he has no right to invade. My mind whirls with question after question and my sleep is troubled.

The pugnacious heat eventually breaks in a thunderstorm that crashes through the August skies. We all stop to watch the mighty display ravage through the atmosphere, marvelling at the forks of lightening that illuminate the heavens seconds before the thunder roars through the hills beyond the barricades. I am humbled by the power of God, but angry with him for allowing this terrible hardship to befall us. Why does he not look after the Jews? Why does he not bring an end to our suffering?

A group of children have arrived from another camp in Poland, a ghetto called Bialystok. Berta tells me there are more than a thousand of them and that they have been given accommodation in the West Barracks. There is another barracks lockdown and we wonder if this is the reason. I am extremely irritable because it means I am further separated from Isabella.

Rachel, Sara and I see the little children stumbling down the street. The infants grasp at the hands of the older children as they are commanded to march to the Receiving Office. This is evidently a chore for all of them for they are dressed in nothing but rags and shoes that are too large for them or cumbersome wooden clogs. The smallest children wear nothing on their grubby little feet. It is impossible not to stare at them even though we have to crane our necks to do so and we know it is forbidden. The orphans will inevitably be in quarantine until the hierarchy are sure that they do not bring any infectious diseases with them into the ghetto. I ache to reach out and give each child a cuddle as they trail past with fear and misery etched upon their faces. Their bedraggled existence angers me for these tiny frightened human beings should be warmly encapsulated in the protective arms of their parents. Instead, they wear the faces of old men and the demeanour of the starving upon their skeletal form.

Fury makes me tremble as I watch them leave the Receiving Office with bald heads. I know this means that the poor souls have lice, but to me they seem to be shaven like frightened lambs dragged away from the comfort of their mother's teats.

Later when we are discussing the new arrivals in conspiratorial whispers, Berta claims that she has heard a perplexing rumour about the orphans. She says that when they were sent to the showers in the bathhouse to be washed clean, they screamed like piglets taken to slaughter. We mull over this curious fact as we ponder the circumstances of the children's arrival: the event is masked by a great deal of secrecy. Eventually we decide that the children must be suffering from shock because a shower in the ghetto is one of the greatest extravagances afforded to all of us. As we salivate over the luxurious dream of a soapy shower, the cruel eyes of the SS soldier at Lidice clouds my vision for a fleeting moment, sending an involuntary shiver of fear down my spine.

I return from work one day to find Berta in a terrible state. She cannot speak to me because she is almost hysterical. I try hopelessly to calm her down so that she can tell me what ails her, but she continues to sob until Agnes appears in the doorway to our room. Agnes is very pale. She has never really recovered from contracting typhoid and she is struggling to do the physical work demanded of a gardener. Agnes' job is to tend to the vegetable patch which seems to feed the guards and the SS rather than the inmates. She works with an older man called David. He is the head gardener. They have become great friends. When I last saw him he voiced concerns for Agnes' health. I wonder if he is right to be worried, if he is seeing something we are choosing to ignore. The doctor within me reviews her symptoms, her pallid complexion, her obvious disorientation, her racing pulse.

Agnes leans against the door frame, breathing heavily. Her demeanour is rather stooped. I move to help her, explaining that I cannot calm Berta. Agnes stares from me to Berta, the whites of her eyes enormous in her blanched face. Her decrepit glasses fall from her nose to the floor. She does not even bend to retrieve them. I scrabble around in the filth to retrieve them. For a moment I am confused, until I become aware of what is going on around me, what has been going on in the other barracks I have passed: people are, once again, silently packing.

"You?"

I stare at Agnes waiting for her reply, but I know what it will be before the words cross her lips.

"Yes."

She nods, tears flooding her eyes, rolling down her thin cheeks. Her dark hair hangs like a noose around her neck.

I shake my head, sinking to the wooden floor, placing my head between my knees. I take great gulps of air into my lungs, forcing the cannon of pent up pain from my body. I must be strong. It is a struggle not to allow the panic to take control. I concentrate all my effort into channelling my mind. I must help Agnes. I must be courageous in the face of more misfortune. I must be strong for my friends. It is my only choice.

When I finally look up, I see Rachel hugging Agnes. She is smoothing her hair away from her throat, murmuring in her ear with the tenderness of a mother. I swallow hard.

We are all present except for Sara and I know that we are all secretly lamenting the absence of Viera. Her liveliness could be an antithesis of the misery that hangs from the rafters here. I wonder if Sara will make it back in time to say her goodbyes to Agnes.

We all help Agnes pack her things. There is little to do but we help nonetheless. Agnes babbles incessantly about finding her brother when she is taken east. He was an eminent pianist. I marvel that she still has hope. I do not think I would have any if it were my name being called from the list. Although I will not allow myself to dwell on it, I know that since the day in Lidice all my hope has gone.

Agnes must report to the Hamburg Barracks at six o'clock. Saying goodbye is horrendous for each of us, but it seems to hit Berta hardest. She and Agnes are very close. David is beside me. He does not move or speak, but pain emanates from him like a fever. Tears flow into his beard like rain seeping into grass. Sara does not return in time to say farewell. This puzzles me because she is a stickler for routine and it is unusual not to see her here at this time. I know she will be devastated that she missed her chance to see Agnes for the last time. None of us knows when we will be reunited again. Bitterness sticks to the back of our throats.

Before she stumbles away with her battered suitcase in her hand, Agnes reaches into her pocket and surreptitiously hands me a spherical object. She urges me to place it in my pocket and makes me promise to share it with Isabella. Later, when she has gone, I examine her gift. It is a lemon. I have not had one for so long that I cannot remember how it will taste. I do not know how Agnes would have come across such an item: there were none growing on the vegetable patch, but I am extremely touched and enormously grateful that she has given it to me. I will certainly keep my promise to her and share my treasure with Isabella.

A contagious energy crackles in the atmosphere of the girls' home. It reminds me of home and the excitement buzzing through the theatres of Prague before a great performance. When I discover the reason for this unlikely frisson amongst the children, the comparison I feel is almost ironic, for their exuberance is due to the imminent production of the opera Brundibar that is being performed by the children in the attic room of the Magdeburg Barracks.

The girls swarm around me, almost tripping over one another in their eagerness to tell me their news. During my visits to the girls' home, I have made many friends and since Agnes left, I find myself spending more and more time there. The buoyancy of the younger girls helps me ignore my grief. Their squabbles and girlishness ignite tender feelings in the hollow of my stomach.

Brundibar is an opera that was written in 1938 by a Jewish Czech composer called Hans Krasa. It is written to be performed by children, to children. In Czech the word Brundibar means bumblebee, and in the story he is a wicked organ grinder who chases away two children called Aninka and Pepicek from the village square where they are singing to raise money to buy milk for their sick mother. Enlisting the help of a cat, dog and sparrow, the children are able to expel the evil Brundibar and continue singing in the square.

Hans Krasa, having now found himself imprisoned in the ghetto, has adjusted the score to accommodate the musical instruments that are available in Theresienstadt. This includes the guitar, the piano, some percussion instruments, the flute, the clarinet, the accordion, a cello, a double bass and four violins.

My friends plead with me to help with the set and costumes and I readily agree. Such a source of happiness cannot be ignored in times of hardship. My excitement over this great performance will be as unrestrained as every other boy and girl. I will watch my friends with pride and admiration.

Brundibar is performed on September 23rd. It is a magical performance brimming with effervescent hope and enthusiasm for life. On the improvised stage the children perform as though they believe they are the characters in the opera. Their true identities are indistinguishable from the characters they have become. The performance emanates from their very souls. With the borrowed dregs of makeup and boot polish and clothing that has been loaned and adapted, the melodic voices of the cast hypnotise the three hundred members of the audience who do not notice the heat of the tiny room into which they are crammed. Entranced by the musicians and the singing that soothes tired minds, they are humbled to be part of such an exceptional event that honours our cultural heritage.

The wonder of Brundibar lives with me for many months after the performance. When the sordidness of my surroundings overwhelms me or more people are ordered on transports, I listen to Brundibar in my mind, recalling every chord, every melody; the bright, involved faces of the children. The recollection calms me. It is easier than dreaming of happier times gone by because those episodes are filled with the people I have lost, and it is more palatable than dreaming of a future in which I no longer have faith. Brundibar becomes my great solace; the place I drift off to when life becomes unbearable.

CHAPTER TEN

"SO *Brundibar* was an opera," marvelled Theo. "Isn't it amazing that they managed to perform an opera in a place like Theresienstadt?"

Anna nodded. "It was... totally amazing. Luckily for us, the SS found such pastimes meaningless so they were not bothered when music filled the air or children sang."

Theo looked down at the poster, thinking of the girl Ivana who had written the letter.

"Do you think Ivana would have taken part in *Brundibar*?"

Anna nodded. "I know she did Theo. She was a quiet girl with a lovely voice. I did not know her well, but I remember her voice clearly. I remember her being quite tiny with thick black hair and wide dark eyes. She did not live with Isabella so I only really managed to exchange smiles with her."

"Exchange smiles," Theo was thoughtful. "I like that. How long was Ivana in the ghetto?"

The smile died on Anna's face.

"She left on a transport with some of the other girls shortly after the first performance of *Brundibar*." Anna slid her reading glasses over her nose and peered down at the letter again. Her hand shook slightly. "Now I know where she went. Poor Ivana was only fifteen – far too young to die. Would you like me to read the letter to you, Theo?"

"I would," began Theo. "But I sort of feel its private. Maybe she wouldn't want us to read it?"

"Well, I have already read it and though I didn't know Ivana well, I believe she would have wanted this kept as part of this terrible history. I think it is important to share this letter; I think it was perhaps the last one she ever wrote." Anna sniffed and swallowed awkwardly. "Shall I begin?"

Theo shrugged. "If you think it would be ok?"

Anna nudged him gently with her elbow until Theo managed to meet her gaze and produce a feeble smile.

"Dear Aunt, I am writing this letter because I do not know if I will ever be able to write another and I have to tell someone what is happening here. It is forbidden to write letters so I doubt this will ever reach you, but I have to hope that someday somebody will find it and share it with others.

"When we were in Theresienstadt some people believed that the transports to the east were taking Jews to a 'better' camp. I must tell you that this is absolutely the opposite of 'better'.

"I am in hell.

"Upon arriving here we were forced to join a queue. At the top of the ramp there was a member of the SS who was clearly drunk, instructing us to go left or right. I was bustled into the camp with many others and relieved of my belongings. They shaved our hair by force and showered us before giving us an outfit of what seemed to be striped pyjamas. It was the most undignified, frightening moment of my life to that point because I had no idea whether I was to live or die.

"We live in huts in a big compound, sleeping in three-tiered wooden bunks with bugs that suck our blood for company. The inmates here are in an even further state of advanced malnutrition than those of us from Theresienstadt. They can hardly manage to do the work forced upon us by the SS or stand for long periods of time during the tedious roll calls.

"From dawn until dusk I sort through the confiscated possessions removed from the prisoners on arrival at the camp. Today I have cut the fur from fur coats. Touching these beloved objects brings the horror of this place into brutal reality, for as we work the smell of burning flesh from the incinerators hangs in the air. They are burning Jewish bodies as I disembowel their treasures.

"I know I have come here to die. I know I am part of a Nazi death machine which will continue to kill Jews until there are none left on this planet. I know that those in the queue who were ordered to turn the other way at the top of the ramp were actually going to the gas chambers to be exterminated. Children, babies, mothers, the elderly, the sick, the handicapped – everyone who cannot work is immediately gassed. The truth is excruciatingly obvious now. We know that hope is dead. I have lost the will to write more. Everyone I love has gone. Speak of me sometimes with affection. I love you, Ivana."

Theo shook as he listened to Anna read Ivana's letter. The emptiness in him seemed to shake in time with his body and he couldn't stop it. The horror and sadness of the letter sat heavily on his guilt and misery. He thought of those who had died in the Nazi death camps and felt as though he was losing them all himself.

Fury filled the void, like a noxious gas. He thought about the bullies at school and their pointless existence; their blithe disregard for life and pathetic need to dominate. He thought about the ridiculous things people moaned about, not having the latest game or phone, the futility of school. Even Sophia's friends moaned about needing a bigger house or a flashy car like their neighbour. The world, Theo thought, was full of people who were dissatisfied with having everything. Everything was just not enough. He wanted to shout at them all, to wake them up from their apathy and disappointment. Then he wondered if he was the same. He wondered if he was no better than those he despised. He had not treated his life as sacred. He had not treated Eden's life as sacred. He had not tried everything to overcome his problems. He had capitulated to them.

"Theo," Anna's voice broke through his thoughts. "Is it too much?"

Theo didn't answer.

"How many died Anna?"

"In Auschwitz?"

"No," murmured Theo softly. "The final number. How many did those sick savages murder altogether?"

"I think the number is about six million, but maybe that was only the Jews."

"What do you mean?"

"I mean that the Nazis also persecuted and murdered other people too, people who did not fit in with their Aryan dream."

"Like who?"

Theo sat very still and upright.

Anna sighed. "Like Jehovah's Witnesses, Gypsies, political activists, Soviet prisoners of war, the handicapped and even homosexuals."

Theo curled his top lip, his brow furrowed. "Hitler hated gay people?"

Anna nodded. "Yes, they were treated very badly by the regime. In Nazi Germany they were urged to reform their identities and change their ideas."

Theo was incredulous. "You mean they tried to force them not to be gay?"

"Yes."

"But that isn't something you choose, is it? You just are or you aren't."

"Yes."

"That's terrible. Why?"

"Hitler believed they were defective. In the concentration camps doctors did experiments on homosexuals to try to eradicate the 'gay' gene in future generations."

"No!"

"Yes," Anna insisted. "They did – both ridiculous and cruel. They also experimented on twins, thinking that if a German mother could give birth to blonde-haired, blue-eyed twins then the Aryan supremacy would become unstoppable. The experiments hurt the twins terribly."

"What did they do?" Theo couldn't bear to hear the answer but he felt compelled to ask the question.

"Drew countless vials of blood, flushed chemicals into their eyes and performed operations without using anaesthetics. It was, as you can imagine, completely monstrous."

"Sickening. I don't want to believe it."

"It is true."

"Because Hitler wanted a race of blonde, blue-eyed people?"

"Ultimately, yes."

"But life doesn't work like that."

"No."

"You didn't know all this when you were in the ghetto."

"No," Anna agreed. "Absolutely not – it is all too much for you to believe – for us it was the same, even though we were suffering in Theresienstadt and I had lived through Lidice, it would have been impossible to guess that Jews were being murdered in gas chambers and the other terrible things that were happening. The Nazis kept it all a big secret."

"Because they knew the rest of the world would find it abominable."

"Yes, I'm sure that had something to do with it."

"But surely you only keep a secret if you are ashamed."

"I don't think they ever felt an ounce of shame Theo. They believed in the survival of the fittest – a superior race – humanity did not come into it. They just didn't want anyone standing in their way!"

Anna and Theo were quiet for a while, both lost in terror of the past. Theo felt, for the first time since he had cut his arm, guilty about trying to kill himself when the life was taken so ruthlessly from others who knew their lives were sacred. He stood between himself and his own survival.

"There's something I don't understand," Theo began, looking directly into Anna's watery eyes. "How on earth did you escape this? Why weren't you taken to one of the death camps? How did you manage to survive?"

"I'll tell you," murmured Anna. "I'll tell you more if you would like that."

Theo nodded.

Anna, 1943

We are being forced on a march because a census has been ordered. The fear in the air is palpable; I can almost reach out and touch it. We flow from the doors of the barracks in our thousands into the cold, steely morning, fearing that the Nazis have ordered us to march the two miles for the census in a further demonstration of the power they wield over us. I know there is every possibility that they will stand us in lines, then shoot us by firing squad; amongst us are staggering SS brandishing weapons they are too drunk to fire straight.

Rachel, Berta, Sara and I take it in turns to carry Isabella who insists upon tottering at our side some of the time, splashing in the grimy puddles. The sheer number of people is overwhelming. There must be more than thirty thousand of them. Although we are aware that the ghetto is fraught and overcrowded, seeing all these people at the mercy of Hitler is terrifying. The old and frail, clinging to someone for support, shuffle painfully along; desolation woven into the clefts of their wrinkles. Children hold their parents' hands or those of older children. They are guarded and quiet. Babies are hidden in the folds of their mother's clothing; wary eyes peeping out from this farcical blanket of security. The crowd is a great swarm of people moving through the November rain trying in vain to conceal the panic they feel in suffering this Nazi circus. Only the seriously ill or exceedingly infirm remained inside the ghetto walls within the confines of the infirmary.

Recently everyone has been aware of a heightened frisson within the ghetto. The 'bonkes' conclude that it has been precipitated by the escape of several prisoners a month earlier who were later seized by the SS in Prague. Uproar has also been evoked by the arrest of the deputy Jewish elder and several others from the office that keeps account of all those leaving and entering the ghetto. The "bonkes" suggest the SS have unearthed some irregularities which may suggest that names have been faked on the transport list. Apparently those due to be transported have had their names switched with those who have already died in the ghetto.

The atmosphere surrounding the march is menacing in the extreme. The SS are a sinister and constant companion as they ride amongst us on bicycles or stride on foot wielding great whips and displaying weapons over their long dark coats. Every now and then, whips crack through the still air and gunshots can be heard above the ominous barking of dogs. Beyond us, is the baleful figure of the camp commandant, majestically astride a great black horse. Spurs shine at the heels of his gleaming black boots as he urges the great beast forward. His malevolent features are hidden beneath the brim of his infamous SS cap bearing the minacious emblem of a skull upon its rim with an eagle above it.

Whispers melt among us as people wonder aloud if this march is a ruse for reprisals, if today will end in a bloody massacre for acts of disobedience, of which we have been hitherto oblivious. Everyone is edgy and rather emotional as the SS bark at us to stand in groups of one hundred in a valley that we call "the hollow" just outside Bohušovice.

Hours pass like days as we are forced to stand in the low lands with hands and feet that are frozen solid, enduring gliders passing in a gesture of intimidation over our heads as the SS march between us snarling orders. Eventually the old and sick begin to fail, staggering sideways as they struggle to maintain their balance in the harrowing conditions. Maintaining our solidarity, we strive to assist them, concealing their fragility from the suspicious, attentive eyes of the soldiers.

Rachel murmurs that if she is to be shot then she is thankful that she is with us. Berta claims that we definitely are about to be shot and that we should all tell each other something that we wished we had been able to do before we died. We are separate in our thoughts for a couple of minutes, each of us lamenting a youth cut asunder and an evanescent future, before Sara declares in an imperious whisper that she wishes she could taste her Italian uncle's Linguini Puttanesca one last time. We all smile in spite of our fear and Berta declares that nobody else is allowed to choose food because it is cruel to even mention it when we have not experienced a good meal for so long. Rachel says that she wishes she knew what it felt like to fall in love.

I knew that one of us would choose this as her wish because we talk of love often. Except Berta, none of us have even had the opportunity to kiss a boy and we sometimes giggle about what it would be like. Rachel had been contemplating allowing one of the boys with whom she works to kiss her when he walked with her back to the barracks one evening, but he had left on a transport so her dalliance with love had been aborted before it had even begun.

Unsurprisingly Berta's wish is to be reunited with her sister. Of everyone she misses in Hungary it is her sister she hungers for most. We have tried to take her place as poor Berta languishes in Theresienstadt without any knowledge of her sister's whereabouts, but Berta's regard for her is so profound that we can only fail. She vows that she will be present at her marriage to Stefa.

My friends urge me to tell them what I wish for the

most, but before I open my mouth to explain a command is issued from the SS.

"Zpet do ghetta!"

"Back to the ghetto!"

Loud cries echo across the valley.

Relief floats over us, a shroud of gossamer painted crudely with blurred images of a future that stretches beyond today. People grab at each other forcibly as though reassuring themselves they are still alive, bewildered smiles on their thin, blanched faces. My friends hug each other and swing Isabella around in great circles until they are swallowed by a deluge of people swarming forward with a momentum that could outrun a torrent of lava cascading down the gully of a volcano. So great is their desire to return to their pit of perdition which has transformed, on the cusp of death, into a sordid yet tolerable refuge, that individuals seem to be consumed with an egocentric zeal which could topple others in its wake.

Sara thrusts Isabella into my arms. We move with the hordes because we have no choice, carried by the tide of the masses which with the unthinking mind of the individual creates a vicious current of its own. We roll with the veracity of a cannon ball. I force Isabella against my chest and cling on to Sara's hand. Rachel protects Isabella from my other side as she is pushed and pulled by the throngs shoving past her. Berta stumbles before us, finding a safe path forward through the frightening avalanche of reprieve. Nobody speaks during the two-mile roll back to the ghetto and I do not think I even breathe properly until we are safely ensconced upon the straw littering the floor of our barracks.

I do not send Isabella back to the girls' home that night

for she screams whenever I try to put her down. I decide to suffer the consequences of keeping her with me and allow her to sleep snuggled in the warm curve of my belly. I sleep soundly. It is the first night since Viera's death that I do not wake in the early hours with the shadow of death looming in my face.

CHAPTER ELEVEN

Anna, 1943

HANUKKAH arrives soon after the episode in Bohušovice. I know we cannot celebrate this festival in the traditional Jewish way, as those who are suffering the ravages of war in Europe will be unable to celebrate Christmas with the usual zeal, but I feel I must mark the occasion somehow. The parallel between Hitler and Antiochus IV is not lost on me, nor is the need to have enough oil to burn the menorah for we have need of everything in the ghetto and most especially wholesome food.

I have been invited down to the vegetable patch by Agnes' great friend David who is in charge of administering the gardeners who work on the patch. He knows the name of even the most obscure vegetable and his fingers are extraordinarily green. Since Agnes left I have visited David regularly to bring him news of Isabella and the other girls. He and Agnes would spend hours in his shed chatting about their families and the progress of the war. Agnes used to say that he reminded her of her grandfather so strongly that sometimes she had to pinch herself to realise that he wasn't. With his long greying beard and sparkling green eyes he could remove Agnes from the banausic perdition of her daily existence and take her to the places he had travelled before the Nazis came to power. Unusually David does not bear a grudge against them, but quietly declares them to be ignorant in every way. His favourite saying is "God will judge".

I admit that I visit David for the same reasons that Agnes did: he reminds me of someone I love. Father. Somehow when I am talking to him the constant, predatory ache that occupies the hollow of my stomach dulls slightly. I feel closer to Agnes when I am with him.

I look around with apprehension as I leave the barracks. Recently the presence of a certain guard has been making me feel uneasy. A number of times I have caught him following me as I conduct my business around the ghetto. He has appeared outside the coffin workshop and I have also seen him loitering outside the girls' home when I depart from visiting Isabella. Berta teases me that the guard is infatuated by me, but I hate it when she says that because the sharp features of his face frighten me. We have grown used to the nominated Czech guards, the insidious puppets of the SS, moving amongst us, but this man fills me with alarm whenever our paths cross. His eyes are far apart and seem to see all the way around me. I never look at him when he casually steps in my path with an insouciant smile, trying to trip me as I endeavour to pass him without incurring his wrath. The girls think he is playing with me because I am an easy target and prone to blushing, but I find his deliberate presence most discomforting. He also consistently seems to be present when a beating is taking place. Vicious beatings for untimely misdemeanours are commonplace in Theresienstadt and he appears to delight in them.

I am relieved when I see that the street is empty, but I look over my shoulder numerous times as I half walk, half run the distance to David's shed. He is waiting for me with a warm smile when I arrive. The shed smells of earth and fresh air and the richness of green leafy vegetables. The basket of spinach on the muddy wooden shelf makes my mouth water. I can also spy potatoes out of the corner of my eye, spilling from a holey sack in the corner of the shed. I have not eaten a potato in such a long, long time. I am beginning to dream about them like chocolate.

We spend several contented hours together. David tells me about the 'bonkes' he has heard pertaining to the progress of the war. He says that the British RAF has dropped a tirade of bombs on Berlin and that the Italian and German troops surrendered in North Africa some time ago. He praises an English Field Marshal to whom he affectionately refers as Monty. I know nothing about this soldier. The world beyond the ghetto seems vast and terrifying despite my longing to explore it. I believe I must do more than slowly decay in the bowels of Theresienstadt. I think my life must be worth more than that. Anger surges through my belly; but then I think of Viera, Agnes and Maksym. I think of Father.

I ask David whether he believes Hitler will be defeated eventually. David bows his grey head, holding his coarse palms towards the oil lamp. His little finger is slightly buckled as though the layer of flesh beneath the skin is shrinking. I wonder if it is painful. David sighs and tells me that he has to believe that the Allies will be victorious. He says that he if gives up believing in the free world and justice then he may as well hang himself up from the roof of the shed. He doesn't look at me as he speaks and although I long to believe that he is joking about prematurely ending his life, I really don't think he is. Suicide is common in Theresienstadt.

I change the subject by grumbling about food again and more specifically the lack of it for Hanukkah. David chuckles at my childish moaning, but surprises me by climbing off his rickety stool and delving into the sack behind him. Bundling several potatoes into the front of his apron, he shuffles towards me, brandishing a grubby paper bag with his other hand. It takes me a while to realise what he is doing. I shake my head. David plunges the potatoes into the crackly bag as though he is a pirate looting jewels from a ship. When he has finished he holds the bag out to me, placing a finger over his lips. Again I shake my head, trying to refuse the illicit gift he is offering. I know that he offers it with such good intentions, at great personal risk to himself, but I feel too guilty and too frightened to take it. What if I am caught?

David's lips are set in a grim line and he scowls at me from beneath his furry, furrowed brow. He shakes the potatoes in their bag in front of my nose. I can smell the soil that still clings to their skins. This is food intended for the SS, the Commandant. This is contraband; stolen property. I think about how badly I want to taste a fresh potato; I think how badly I want to feel full up from its starchy goodness. I think about Isabella and the girls. I think about how glorious it would be to see their faces as they tuck into the potatoes. Speechless, I finally snatch the bag from David's outstretched hand. I am trembling as I lean over and place a tender kiss on his whiskery cheek. He issues a curt dismissal, indicating that I should place the illicit goods inside my shabby coat between my body and my underarm. I leave the safety of the shed with my heart clanging like a bass drum in my head.

It is dark outside and I jump at shadows around every corner, scolding myself for appearing so culpable. I move quickly past the looming dark buildings, clinging tightly to the booty smuggled inside my coat. Just as I catch sight of the barracks and start believing that I have successfully navigated the breadth of the ghetto without being caught, somebody steps out of the shadows directly into my path. I am so frightened that I jump involuntarily backwards, dropping the bag of potatoes from under my arm. I watch in horror as they roll out from the hem of my coat and trip over the pavement.

Crying out in alarm, I scramble on my knees to grab at the potatoes rolling away from me in different directions. I do not dare to look into the face of my assailant; I do not dare to hope it is a friend.

My arm is forced roughly behind my back. I scream and a gloved hand is thrust over my mouth. My body is compelled upwards. I watch as one stolen potato rests at the end of my shoe. A nasty, nasally laugh vibrates in my ear from lips that are almost sutured to the lobe. I close my eyes as my thudding heart seems to clog my airway. I struggle to breathe with the glove restricting my nose and mouth simultaneously. I kick my legs, using every ounce of strength to free myself, but these efforts are in vain. My assailant only tightens his grip on my face and forces my arm further up my back. Just when I think I will suffocate or pass out from the pain, he throws me viciously to the ground.

Taking great gasps of breath, I raise my face to meet the eyes of my attacker, although I am certain of who it is before I dare to look. It is Slezak, the guard who has been following me.

"He cut you didn't he? That guard? That evil son of a..."

"Theo..." Anna's hand was wavering as she placed it on Theo's furiously jiggling leg.

"I'm right though aren't I?" he stormed leaping to his feet, glaring at Anna with blazing eyes. "He slit your face like you were an animal in the slaughter house, didn't he? Just for taking those potatoes when you were starving and desperate and miserable. He did, didn't he?"

Anna said nothing, her hands clasped together. Her knuckles were white except for one dark liver spot that spread onto her fingers. Theo stood completely still, but his body trembled as the animal chained inside him clawed ferociously at the cavern of his chest.

"It was an accident." His voice was choked and almost inaudible.

Theo stared out of the window. The dying sun shimmering through a veil of silvery cloud cast an eerie glow over the garden.

"My face – it was an accident..." Theo rubbed his brow slowly with the fleshy part of his palm. "Not like yours. Not a punishment. She... she's not herself..."

Theo waited for Anna to say something. He didn't look at her, but took her silence as a sign to continue.

"She's dead you see..." Theo's voice came out as a strangled sob although he wasn't crying.

"Who is dead, Theo?" asked Anna softly.

"The baby."

"Baby?"

"Mum's precious girl."

"I see... that's terrible."

"Yes," agreed Theo. "It is."

"Oh Theo, I'm so sorry."

"Why?" said Theo bitterly. "You didn't kill her."

"Because it is sad – a terrible time for your family."

Theo nodded.

"Mum won't get out of bed... they say she's got post-traumatic stress... Eden's only been dead a few days really... the coroner won't release her body... it's all a mess and Mum isn't like Mum... she isn't like anyone at all."

"She's grieving Theo. Grief can do terrible things to people."

"But I don't think she is," blurted Theo. "I think she's... I don't know... stuck."

Anna nodded. "It is a dreadful, dreadful thing to bury your child."

Theo sighed, shaking his head.

"I got home the other day... it is hell, because we can't even bury her yet or whatever... and Mum was standing in her bedroom doorway throwing stuff at Jon... I didn't like it because Jon is a good bloke and he's been amazing to all of us; since he came along everything has been a lot better."

"What did you do?"

"I pushed her out of the way and let her throw stuff at me instead, nappies, bottles of stuff, cold cups of coffee," Theo shrugged. "Stuff like that. I suppose it was whatever she could lay her hands on. You know, Anna, I was looking into her eyes the whole time and Mum wasn't there... it was like something else was controlling her body."

"I think you are right, Theo," murmured Anna. "I think the pain your mother feels is too great for her to deal with right now, but it has to go somewhere. It was the pain controlling your mother. She is externalising it."

"Will it go away?" Theo asked, his bottom lip quivering and swollen.

"Not until she can acknowledge it; not until she accepts what happened to her."

"What if she can't? I've told you how it was... Eden was precious."

"All children are precious Theo, each and every one of them."

"You know what I mean."

Anna shrugged. "I find it hard; actually... she'll have to accept it sometime. She has no choice. She'll have to move on with her life."

Theo shook his head. "Did you? Did you move on after all those people you lost, after all the terrible things that happened to you... to the Jews? I mean, how do you actually recover from something like that?"

Once again Anna shrugged, opening her watery eyes very wide. She took a deep breath, exhaling vigorously. "I don't know... I can't answer you... time helps, time heals... as they say."

"Does it?" blustered Theo. "Does it really? I'm not sure I believe you, because you are telling me about your life when you were twelve... sixteen, eighteen... like it happened yesterday! Has time really healed those terrible things?"

Anna chuckled. "Oh Theo, you are a wise boy. Time! Time has been a different friend to me. It hasn't healed because I haven't talked properly about this to anyone since it happened... until now. Yes, I have explained snippets of my life here and there... but I have never quite been able to talk about it all."

Theo frowned. "Why now? Why now after so long?"

"Because time," sighed Anna. "Has softened my memories, acceptance has softened my pain and you... you listened."

Theo nodded slowly. "So talking heals..."

"I think so," Anna closed her eyes tightly, pursing her withered lips. "It unleashes the beast... allows it free reign after it has lived in captivity within you for so long. Talking expels that anguished animal, leaving an imprint of what has passed."

"Then talk," said Theo simply, flopping back onto the sofa and folding his arms and ankles. "You haven't finished and I'm still listening."

"Will you talk to me?" Anna asked, her voice barely audible.

"I'll try."

"When Theo?"

"Soon."

Anna, 1943

His mouth twitches as he stares down at me with an imperious expression across his sharp features. I know that he is smiling inside his mind as he regards the nefarious potatoes scattered at my feet. This is the opportunity he has been waiting for to haul me away for a beating.

"Get up and come with me."

I remain immobile. His voice becomes a vicious command.

"I said, get up... you dirty little thief."

He grabs my arm, painfully dragging me behind him. I hobble along because I cannot stand at full height when he is pulling my arm towards the ground. The street is veiled in darkness and I do not have any idea where he is taking me. I try to look around, but he forces my head downwards so that I am forced to watch the rugged ground vanishing beneath my feet. I think I am more scared than I have ever been.

Slezak finally yanks my quaking body into what seems to be an empty office. There is a fire burning in the grate and untidy desks littered with cups and paper facing towards the hearth. The barred windows are filthy. The ceiling is yellow in places and the paint is peeling. Slezak throws me savagely to the creaking floor in front of the fire. It takes all of my strength to ensure I don't fall head first into the seething flames: perhaps that is what he intends. He demands that I look at him, but I keep my eyes focused on the fire: perhaps abandoning myself to the blaze is better than what I must now face in his brutal hands.

He pinches my chin hard between his thumb and finger, forcing my face upwards. I close my eyes because I know that I will urinate from sheer terror if I am forced to look into his scalding eyes.

"Look at your superior, Jewish scum."

His face is so close to mine that the stench of his breath reeking with stale cigarette smoke and whiskey makes me heave involuntarily with revulsion. This instinctive reaction seems to further ignite his rage, for he grasps great clumps of my hair in his other hand and yanks my head backwards. He removes his fingers from my chin and reaches down towards his shin. Before I recognise what is happening a shining, silver knife is thrust beneath my nose, its acute blade glinting menacingly in the firelight. He turns it slowly, allowing the cold edge to linger on my lips. At this, my bladder gives way and Slezak laughs.

He drags me from the fire to a desk and thrusts me backwards on its leather top as the contents slide across the room. He presses his body against mine and pulls viciously at my thighs. Belatedly I realise that a beating beneath Slezak's vindictive hands might not be the worst fate to befall me this bleak winter's night. I scream and once I have started screaming I cannot stop. I fight. I kick and punch; I claw at Slezak's body like a wild animal, drawing blood on his neck. The presence of the knife does not somehow focus in my mind at this point, for I am determined to escape this heathen with all my will.

The knife slicing my cheek from my ear to my mouth, muzzles the scream in my throat. Metallic blood trickles onto my tongue and I abruptly lose my strength. Just as I try to take a breath, Slezak forces his lips over my mouth and his voluminous tongue between my lips. He laughs inside his throat.

"Slezak, what is the crime of this Jewish scum?"

Slezak forces me flat upon the desk and stands upright to face the source of interruption. I watch him bluster beneath the gaze of the enormous SS officer standing in the doorway. He quickly lifts his arm in the obligatory Nazi greeting and straightens his uniform.

"She stole potatoes from the SS kitchen garden, Sir. She is a dirty thief."

"I see."

The SS officer eyes me with a detached loathing.

"I think, Slezak that you have so far failed to administer the appropriate punishment for such a crime."

Bizarrely, the officer reaches into his pocket and hands me a pristine white handkerchief. He gestures towards his blunt face, indicating that I should use it to staunch the blood that is streaming down my neck into the collar of my shirt. He eyes Slezak distastefully before lighting a cigarette, then reaching towards the wall above the fire. My body seems to implode when I see him grasp the leather whip that is looped across the wall like the endless body of a python. He hands the whip to Slezak and tells me to turn around and lean over the desk.

The fear is suffocating; I struggle simultaneously to control the movement of my bowels and the panic bulging in my chest. As I bend over the desk I stare dumbfounded at the sole document remaining there. The SS officer's voice rings clearly in my ears. My coat is roughly pulled from my body.

"Ten, Slezak."

Before the whip slices across my back, I hear a clock chime the hour and the officer vigorously exhale the smoke from his lungs. I smell the enticing aroma of coffee that Slezak has spilled over the desk during his assault. I am detached and strangely prepared for the gut-wrenching pain that courses through my body when Slezak brings the whip ferociously down upon my back.

I stare at the document. I try to disassociate myself by translating the German letter into French. I try to lose myself.

Crack, crack, crack. The whips falls. The last thing I remember is knocking my blood-curdled chin on the edge of the desk as I lose consciousness from the inexorable pain and collapse upon the floor.

When I wake next I am staring at the ground and it is moving. The whole world is upside down. I close my eyes and know nothing until I am gently lowered to the ground by a man with eyes the colour of storm clouds with a tweed cap on his head. He holds one rough hand against my face with a scrunched up piece of newspaper in his fist. I try to look around, but the pain in my back is overwhelming. I think I am in the infirmary. I think the capped man is a fellow Jew. I take a deep breath, as I comprehend that I have inconceivably escaped the clutches of Slezak and been given another chance to live, before I slither against the cold floor and close my eyes.

Anna's voice laboured as she completed her sentence. Theo stared at her. He was both appalled at what she had told him and concerned for her well-being. She began to cough. It was a deep hack that seemed to come from her guts. It disturbed Theo.

"I think," he murmured when the coughing subsided, "...that I need to go home."

"Sit with me... just for a while."

Theo reached out and took Anna's hand. It was cold. Her eyes were closed. For the first time he realised how old she must be; how tired. He thought about the vicious guard who had beaten her. Rage trembled over his skin. He pulled a tartan blanket from the wicker basket beside the sofa, gently laying it over Anna's still body. He held her hand until he was certain she was asleep.

Impulsively he leant down and kissed her grey head. Whispering his goodbyes, Theo let Blackie out into the garden for a few minutes before he left, ensuring the doors were safely locked behind him.

That night, he and Seb were treated to a trip to the cinema with Jon, leaving a petulant Nana Dora keeping watch over Sophia. Jon bought an enormous box of popcorn and more chocolate than they could eat. The film was an action movie about a karate expert being framed for a murder he didn't commit, but Theo found it difficult to concentrate. He thought about the nature of true violence; the devastation left in its wake.

In the car on the way home, Seb teased Jon about football whilst Jon ribbed him in return about his preference for motor sport. They bantered about players and drivers until Jon slid the key in the front door. For those few hours, everything felt the way it used to. Theo found it comforting. He ignored Nana Dora's waspish expression as Jon bundled her into her lilac jacket and out into the night. He ignored her sly commentary as she edged into her car and Jon slammed the door behind her.

Afterwards Theo laid in bed thinking about his fascinating day with Anna. Sleep eluded him, but for once it was not because of the panic over Eden. Anna floated through his mind. He thought of her bravery and her terrible suffering. She was the only person apart from Jon who had ever inspired him to be a better person.

CHAPTER TWELVE

THURSDAY, 18 FEBRUARY 2010

THAT night Theo dreamt about the last time he was happy. The day he had been to the kart track with Seb; the day after Eden was born.

The entrance to Carter's Karts was through an area of woodland. He and Seb had ridden their bikes over a carpet of old leaves mashed into undulating muddy banks. The air was icy. As they snaked between the tall trees glistening with frost, Theo thought they were ghostly in their unusual stillness. Splatters of mud spurted up from Seb's back wheel, smearing Theo's face below his cycle helmet. The squelch of their tyres echoed through the silence.

The new kart was already on the track when the boys arrived. Mac and his father were adjusting the tyre pressures. Theo and Seb leant their bikes against the old, metal cabin and headed for the race track.

"Didn't expect to see you two for a while!" George Carter looked up from the pressure gauge as Theo and Seb approached. He wiped an oily hand across his face. The grease emphasised his wrinkles.

"How's your mum?" Mac asked. He was a slim, blond boy of eighteen with dimples in his cheeks and a rugged complexion from being outdoors all of the time. He was Seb's best friend and although they were opposite in many ways, they shared a love of motor sport.

Seb shrugged. "She's still in hospital with the baby. There's nothing much we can do for her. Anyway it's Saturday, time to come down here and look at this beauty!"

Seb bent over to admire George's new kart. "How does she run?"

"She's amazing to be honest." George was grinning. "First time out today!"

"My turn!" Mac pulled his sparkly helmet over his head and fastened his neck brace. "I'll show you how it's done Dad."

"He probably will too," George agreed, smiling at Seb and Theo. "Bloody clever clogs! He beat Jason Ferdinand at the weekend, did you hear?" George looked exactly like his only son, but his thick hair was grey at the temples.

"Yeah," Seb said. "He phoned me this morning. Must have been awesome!"

"Jason didn't think so!" George unzipped his karting overalls. "So ends his winning streak. My boy did well."

"Very well," agreed Seb.

The three of them turned their attention to the track. The familiar odour of petrol filled the air. Mac was taking the kart slowly through its paces to get some heat into the tyres. As he expertly manoeuvred it around the tricky bends and corners, he began to pick up the pace. He carefully manipulated the boisterous machine, braking hard into the corners and accelerating just at the right point around the apex. Mac's arms wrestled with the steering wheel as he expertly managed the over steer and under steer. Strangely it was rather like watching a ballerina manipulate her body around a stage, for in spite of the roar of the engine and the vague screech of the slick tyres as they slid slightly on tarmac that was still damp in places, the precision and style of the driving had a certain elegance. He completed a rigorous twenty laps, during which time nobody spoke, before screeching to a halt in front of them.

Mac climbed out of the kart and removed his helmet. Theo bent down and switched the engine off.

"Awesome!" A wide smile spread across Mac's face. He was buzzing with adrenaline. "She's amazing; a real animal Dad! I love her. Thank you!" He drew his father into a mighty hug.

Seb was leaning over the lap timer on the kart. George pulled his grubby laptop out of an even grubbier bag so they could view Mac's lap times.

"Reckon you've got some good times," Theo grinned at Mac. "You looked fantastic out there."

George and Mac exchanged a knowing look.

"Take her out!" offered Mac. "See the power for yourself!"

Theo was utterly incredulous. Pink spots appeared on his cheeks. "You're kidding..."

"No, he's not," George grinned. The excitement ignited Theo's face. "Go and get your stuff."

Theo didn't wait around for them to change their minds. He could hardly believe his luck. He charged over to the cabin to change into his karting overalls. Armed with his helmet and rib protector he arrived back at the track breathing hard.

"Mac thanks so much. I..." Theo babbled.

Mac interrupted him, "Yeah, yeah, just get in and don't kill yourself. I don't want that on my conscience."

Theo fiddled with his chin strap.

"Get on with it," urged Seb hurriedly. "Throttle's on the right, remember?"

Theo grinned. "Ha ha!"

He eased the kart forward, a grin spreading over his face as he slowly rounded the first corner. Taking it easy at first, to warm up the tyres as Mac had done, Theo settled into the rhythm of the kart. Each kart was particular to itself, needing different handling on the track. The one Theo usually drove tended to bog down into the corners as it was not properly geared for this particular track and had limited power; this machine had no such problems. The moment he pressed the throttle the kart seemed to literally fly forward and Theo streamed down the straight at a speed he had only envisioned in his dreams. For the first time since the fateful day of his mother's scan, Theo's mind was empty.

As the kart demanded every shred of his concentration, Theo lived only in the moment; the danger and exhilaration coursed through his veins vanquishing other emotions. When he finally brought the kart to a standstill in front of Seb, Mac and George he had no idea how long he had been out there for. Lap after lap he had poured himself into the fabric of the machinery, becoming an integral part of it.

"Theo Drew I am immensely impressed," marvelled George as Theo lifted the visor on his helmet and turned off the engine.

Theo luxuriated in his words. He had seldom heard them from anyone.

"I think we need to move you on a bit," added George, thoughtfully. "I see some signs of genius in your driving."

Theo looked at him hard to ascertain whether or not he was just teasing him, but George's face remained completely serious.

"Dad's right!" declared Mac. "I was watching you. You've progressed a lot. I thought she'd be too much for you, but you handled her well. I'm impressed."

The unfamiliar feeling of happiness swelled up inside Theo. He found that he could not take the grin off his face. Seb was smiling too. He thumped Theo on the back and ruffled his dark curls.

"My turn," he said. "Let's see if I can beat your lap times little brother!"

"No chance!" Theo shoved him good-naturedly.

George was looking at the screen on his laptop, nodding to himself. "Actually Seb, I think you might struggle! Theo's done well."

Seb sped off. He took the first bend too quickly and the kart launched into a magnificent spin, narrowly missing the tyre wall at the edge of the track.

"Bloody good job he didn't hit those tyres," snorted Mac, holding his blond head in his oily hands. "He'd have been dead meat!"

"Think he found the damp patch!" mused Theo wisely. "It nearly caught me out on the first few laps!"

"He was going too fast!" added George, as Seb continued driving. "Not enough heat in the tyres to grip the track. Silly boy, he should know better!"

They all laughed. Theo was secretly rather pleased that Seb hadn't handled the kart as well as he had. Finally he may have found something he was better at.

The lap timer told the true story when Seb had finished his laps. After George had looked at the data he announced that Mac had achieved the quickest lap, but only by a fraction of a second. Theo's times were so close to Mac's that it surprised everyone, most especially Theo. He was much quicker than Seb and significantly quicker than George. If there had been a great deal of difference in their weight then they may have attributed Theo's remarkable speed to that, but all four of them weighed almost the same amount. Theo could hardly contain his pleasure. He had never been better than Seb at anything.

A gull woke Theo, calling mournfully through the fading darkness. The panic had returned, twisting with the knowledge of his perfidy; churning with his irredeemable guilt. The dream forgotten, an incandescent fury absorbed him. He punched at the pillow and kicked at random items scattered beneath the bed. He was consumed with self-hatred. On the small desk beneath the windowsill where he sat to do his homework sometimes, lay a pair of kitchen scissors he had used for a school project. The scissors were open, the blades taunting him. In a mindless state of adrenaline, he grabbed at the handle, placing the deadly blades over his good wrist. With an intense longing to eradicate his guilt, he closed the scissors over the delicate skin. The intense pain drained him of his anger. He grabbed a pillow from his bed, cramming it over his mouth, to muffle the sound of his screaming: the pain was frightful but also, in some perverse way, satisfying. He stared in wide-eyed horror at the blood trickling from his mutilated wrist onto the duvet.

His mind emerged from the deep fog spurring him into action. He threw open his wardrobe with his bandaged arm, pulling a dark jumper from a hanger and wrapping it around his wrist.

Hobbling silently into the bathroom, he rifled through the medicine cabinet until he came across a bandage that looked like it had been bought before he was born. He sat on the toilet, his heart thudding in his head, whilst he botched the bandage, one-handed around his tender, damaged wrist. The pain seemed to lessen, but the searing throb still numbed his despair. When he eventually returned to his room, easing the door closed behind him, he slid down behind it onto his bottom. He was breathing fast, holding his wrist in his other hand. He sat there until his breathing became calmer before dry-retching into his waste-paper basket. Before the silver dawn had even broken, heralding the promise of snow, Theo grabbed his warmest clothes and retreated to the solace of the sea until it was time to see Anna.

Anna, 1943

I do not know how long I am in the infirmary. The sleep that I sleep is unlike the usual slumber for I am, for once, aware of nothing that happens around me. My eyelids are heavy and I cannot rouse myself to even speak to those who care for me. I lay on one side, a swathe of dressings across my back and more across the side of my face. The pain is gone with the fear. I am left with a strange numbness and a floating sensation that leaves me feeling faintly nauseous.

At one point I am aware of a presence beside me; someone grasps my hand and another is crying. I force my eyelids apart and a vision of my friends swirls before my eyes. Berta, Sara and Rachel, with watery smiles on their pale faces, peer down at me. Struggling to raise my head from the pillow, I try to move my lips to ask a question, but the swabs prevent my attempt at speech. Berta squeezes my hand but Sara, who usually knows what I am thinking, sees the anguish in my eyes and reassures me that Isabella is thriving and that she is visiting her every day in my absence. I am perspiring with the effort of movement so I abandon my head once more to the worn out pillow.

Rachel explains that my wounds are infected and that I am being given drugs to combat the infection. I see hope in her eyes as she speaks and I am glad that I cannot explain to her the appalling lack of drugs and medical equipment available to the doctors here. I cannot tell her that the SS do not care if we perish in these beds, for they will happily burn our remains in their special crematorium.

Berta is oddly silent. I have seldom seen her thus, but when her eyes meet mine and tears flood down her pretty cheeks, she begins to rant about the insane brutality of the vindictive Slezak. I do not want to hear that she wants to wring his neck with her bare hands or slice off his appendages. It does not make me feel better. I do not yearn for justice over Slezak: I just never want to see him or speak of him again. I long for him to be wiped from my mind like a nightmare that cannot be remembered upon waking. Listening to Berta is allowing the memories to flood through my mind and I cannot abide listening. I try to use my hands to make her stop, but my breath is tangled in my chest. Everything hurts, everything is tight. Someone bustles in and bustles everyone else away from my bedside. She thrusts something in my arm and

I know no more.

It is many days before I am conscious of anything at all; before I can sit up without collapsing, before the impregnable dressings are removed from my face, before I can tolerate the pain in my back when I move. As the infirmary shifts around me and I become more aware of my surroundings, I yearn to see Isabella. Many times I try to rise from the bed only to fall in a heap of limbs that will not behave in the manner I am asking them to. Frustrated and despondent, I long for my body to recover. Absurdly, I dream of returning to my paltry existence in the ghetto because at least it will mean that my body has found a functioning rhythm.

On the morning I am finally well enough to leave, Sara dashes into the infirmary with eyes that are wide with fear. When I ask her to tell me what is wrong she shakes her head and takes my arm to lead me back to the barracks. The bitter cold bites into my face as we leave; the laceration in my cheek aches in time with the pulse beating near the whip marks across my back. I falter against Sara as I walk and she carries the burden of my weakened body.

She is constantly checking over her shoulder as we stagger along. I am worried and intrigued as to why she is not at work. A nagging feeling tells me that something is terribly wrong and instinct tells me that it relates to Isabella. When we are the solitary figures in a derelict street, Sara surprises me by shoving me violently into a hidden doorway. She leans her body into mine so that her face is level with my good cheek and her lips brush in the hair that covers my ear. She is extremely agitated and her body quivers.

"I must tell you something. Do not move and when I

have finished speaking promise me, you will do exactly as I tell you. Nod if you understand, Anna."

I nod. Fear bites at my subconscious; I blink hard trying to concentrate my mind on the here and now.

"I have never explained to you my job here Anna."

Sara's voice is almost hoarse with urgency.

"I have kept the details from you all for a very good reason. I am not merely an office worker for the SS... Indeed... I think Christians would call me the devil himself..."

A strangled cry catches in Sara's throat and I wait for her to gain her composure. She closes her eyes very tightly and her lips twitch as though she is praying.

"I place the names of Jews from all over Europe on lists for shipment to the east... men, women and thousands of children... they do not go to better camps..."

I back away from her in confusion, but the impregnable concrete wall behind me chafes my heels.

"Many times my own name... your name has appeared on the Transport list. Berta's has been on it on four different occasions. Each time I ensure the names are removed by my co-workers, but when we do this, another person has to be chosen to make up the complete Transport."

I shake my head.

"Please understand, Anna. This is my job here. I have had no choice. Just like you making coffins for the dead German soldiers. None of us has a choice in any of it. We are pawns in this monstrous game the Nazis are playing."

I try to understand; to digest the ramifications of what she is telling me, but the pain is muddling my mind. I am too weak to question her so I stand and stare. What is there to say? How we behave in the ghetto, the challenges that are foisted upon us, do not have any bearing upon our characters. It is a question of self, a matter of survival in which our moral guidelines are sometimes forced eschew. It is hard to hold anyone accountable other than those who emasculate us through this inhumane incarceration. Sara hurries on.

"I do not have time to explain this further, you must just trust me. Two transports of two-thousand-five-hundred people will be leaving. Today, Isabella's name appeared on the list."

I stiffen, falling backwards against the wall, as all the blood seems to drain from my body. I try to focus on Sara's voice.

"But right now there is a man at the gate. He has asked the Commandant for workers to labour in his arms factory near here because the men have gone to fight the war. He will take you and Isabella. At the end of this street, Rachel is waiting for you with Isabella and your bags. I will take you to her then take you to this man. I do not know if this is another elaborate Nazi circus to send you to your death, but I am certain that if Isabella is to leave on the transport tonight she will surely die. Anna, this is your only hope."

Adrenaline and the carnal instinct to protect Isabella, overcomes the shock and pain. I lunge at Sara, who is sobbing. As I clutch at her in one great hug that communicates all my love to her, I realise that I have never seen her cry before. She presses her face into my hair before pulling me out of the doorway and dragging me down the street.

At the far end, Rachel's anxious face peers around

a corner. I know we are close to the gate now and I can see a large vehicle parked outside. I run towards her, clutching Sara's hand. A bag is at her feet and mercifully, peeping out from between her legs, is Isabella. Quivering, I lean over and gather her in my arms, inhaling her glorious familiarity. She covers my face in kisses, stroking the dressings that cover my defiled cheek. I embrace Rachel, unable to convey my gratitude in words, but Sara is dragging us to the gate. She shoves us gently into the small delegation standing there. I am shaking with fear and anticipation. When the immense gates actually open, I cannot believe it is reality. Holding my bag in one hand and Isabella in the other, I take one last look behind me. At first it seems Sara and Rachel have vanished, but as my eyes pan around I eventually see their tiny faces watching us from behind a wall. For a fraction of a second, time stands still. I stand, hugging Isabella, smiling at them. I know they feel from that smile, love and gratitude warming the air between us. I know I have left them with something that words could never capture.

"You escaped the ghetto?" Theo marvelled.

Anna nodded, fondling Blackie's floppy ears as he lay across their feet. His legs were sprawled over the floor in front of the sofa.

"Because your friends helped you?"

"Yes, because Sara and Rachel helped me."

Theo frowned.

"What is it Theo?"

"I don't understand," Theo began, ruffling his curls in agitation. "There is something I don't understand. Why…?"

"Why?"

"Yes," Theo took a breath and exhaled, deciding to ask the pertinent question. "Why did your friends not save themselves instead?"

Anna blanched. She stared at Theo for several uncomfortable moments before opening her wrinkled mouth and laughing.

"Oh... the youth of today... think only of themselves."

Theo watched her in dismay. Did she really count him among the selfish? He didn't mean that Rachel and Sara should have saved themselves. He just needed to know all the facts. He could not imagine the gangs of boys at school saving each other. Would Seb save Mac before himself? Would Jon save Sophia if he was forced to choose between her life and his own? Had morality changed so much over the years?

Then, as Anna shook her head, marvelling at the differences in the generations that passed, Theo realised the truth for himself.

"I know," pronounced Theo, jumping to his feet. "Stop laughing Anna. I know."

"Tell me..."

"Because of Isabella. They loved her and they knew you were chosen to be her mother after Viera's death."

"Yes."

"Despite the fact they wanted to escape the ghetto more than anything, they let you take Isabella because she loved you and they loved her as though she was their own child!"

Theo took a deep breath; he was gabbling.

"It is possible to love a child who does not belong to

159

you with all your heart isn't it?"

"Of course, Theo. Of course."

Anna, 1943

We are bundled into the truck. I clasp Isabella tightly on my lap; she squirms and I relinquish my hold a little so that she may cuddle into my body. She tucks herself into my warmth bringing one hand up to stroke absently at the unharmed side of my face. I feel woozy as the truck pulls away. For the first time since Sara broke her news to me I am aware of the searing pain coursing through my cheek and across my back. Every jolt in the road makes me shudder slightly. Sometimes I think that my eyes close and I begin to lose consciousness, but I know that I cannot surrender to the hurt until I know that this strange archangel is not the devil in disguise.

He is sitting in the front of the vehicle next to a young, blond man who is driving. I have not seen the blond man's face, but the other man constantly glances over his shoulder at us. I realise that most of the time his eyes finally rest on me. I believe I can see concern and compassion in their blue depths. I hope that I am not delusional and marvel that I can still find faith in strangers after all that has happened to me. I try to focus upon his face to prevent my eyes from closing: he is a distinguished looking fellow with short balding hair that is swept back from his prominent forehead. High, expressive brows arch above intelligent eyes that are wide set and thoughtful. Below a long nose a well-groomed moustache settles upon a mouth that seems to hide a smile.

Unexpectedly he turns to the driver. We have driven deep into woodland with a dense canopy of trees. Speaking eloquent German he asks the man to stop the vehicle. In a gentle voice he tells everyone to get out of the truck. I eye him with wide-eyed confusion and Isabella buries her tiny face in my breasts. My faith, once again, I realise was utterly unfounded. This man is part of the Nazi circus that torments and kills Jews. We are to be lined up against the trees and shot down like fowl. Why? For the amusement of two men who persecute Jews for reasons that never really seem to become apparent in all the years since Nazi tyranny ruled over most of Europe?

I can hardly lift Isabella now because the pain is so severe. Just as I drag myself from the seat, the blond man's face appears before me and thrusts me gently back upon it.

"Not you. You are not well enough to go."

I gawp at him in disbelief. I do not have to be well to be shot! Garbled words flood from my tongue before I have even formulated an escape plan in my mind.

"I'm begging you... please. Take me... Shoot me for your sadistic amusement, but please take the child somewhere safe. She is the daughter of a prominent U-boat commander... She's called Isabella... Her mother was Jewish... But she does not deserve to die here... Please. I beg you, Sir."

As I speak I watch the man's brow wrinkle in confusion and his vivid blue eyes widen in horror. He reaches out to stroke Isabella's soft hair, shaking his head slowly.

"Please..."

He indicates that I should look at our duplicitous rescuer standing in the woods with the other Jews. There is no longer fear on their faces, but weary expressions of resignation. I watch as he speaks to them all, then marvel as implausibly smiles cross their pallid features.

161

Furthermore as I strain my neck to stare at them, I see them begin to vanish through the trees. I am beyond shocked. My lips tremble as I stammer to the blond man.

"You've set them free... you've... you've let them go..."

He nods, placing a strong hand over my own that tremble beneath his reassuring grasp. The archangel calls to him and he winks at me before telling me to lie down and sleep. He beckons Isabella to him and takes her gently in his arms to lift her into the front of the truck to sit between him and the archangel. I stare at the backs of their heads in pure disbelief. My vision is blurry. Gradually the three heads become a flurry of many, oozing into one another. Snow begins to fall over the inside of my eyelids and the truck spins over the bumpy road. I try to steady myself with my arms, but my head falls to the tatty seat before I can wrestle with the darkness.

A roaring fire crackles in the grate. The room is dim and the leaping flames flicker in front of my aching eyes. It is difficult to keep them open, to focus. Recent events flood my mind and I panic when I remember Isabella, but I can scarcely lift my head from the pillow. I sense movement at the table in the corner of the room. A man shuffles over to me and he bends down so that his face is visible. I know his face. I know not to be scared, but for a few moments I cannot quite place him.

"Isabella is quite safe." He speaks softly in German; his boyish features expressive. "She is sleeping. You have been very sick."

He peers down at a pocket watch with eyes the colour of Lake Geneva basking in the sunshine. Taking my arm delicately in his hand he feels for my pulse.

"Better. Your infection was very bad; at one point I did not think that you would make it Anna."

"How do you know my name?" I croak.

The man straightens up. I can see he is slight but muscular with messy blond hair that curls over his ears. He smiles and suddenly I remember him.

"You talk in your sleep. Many languages... everything you said, I could understand perfectly." He chuckles; a laugh that reminds me of the boys playing on the ramparts in the ghetto. His boyish humour puts me at ease, but I am still wary, despite the fact that he and the other man have set us free; despite the obvious pains he has taken in nursing me.

I try to sit up, but the room begins to spin with such ferocity that I have no choice but to lie down again.

"Do not try to get up. You need to rest. Your body needs time to recover from your ordeal. I can see you have had a terrible time Anna."

I watch his eyes darting over my cheek as he implores me with a kindness that I have not known since I last saw Father. Tears threaten to overwhelm me for the first time since the SS captured us in Lidice. Their unfamiliarity unnerves me and I swallow deeply. I regard this man with disbelief as the pain of my unshed tears catches in my throat. There are so many questions that I want to ask him; so much I need to know.

He slips out of the room. I close my eyes trying to remember the faces of my friends whom I left behind, but I cannot visualise them. The uneven fragments of their features muddle in my mind then scatter, leaving the eyes of the German penetrating the blackness. I think he must be a medic of some kind; a doctor perhaps.

"Here..."

I recoil at the voice so close to my face. He is standing before me, holding a spoon in one hand and a bowl of soup in the other. I am disconcerted by this man. For the first time I realise how young he actually is; he seems far too young to be a doctor. Although in the toil of this war it would not be surprising for it makes all of us older than we are: it makes all of us weary despite the bloom of youth. I know that, though I am still only seventeen, I am already an adult for I have been thrust into adulthood with a brutal, malignant hand.

He places the soup and spoon on a dresser where there are two mugs of diluted wine.

"If you permit it, I will help you sit."

I nod. Part of me wishes to resist him, but I am undone by his philanthropy. Any need for self-preservation is besieged by the basic human desire for reciprocal kindness. This time when I try to sit, the room does not gyrate. He holds me in his proficient hands until I find a position that is comfortable then kneels back on the floor. He waits for me to regain my composure before he hands me a weak mug of wine to sip. I take great gulps before asking for the soup. The smell wafting beneath my nostrils is mouth-watering. I do not know how long it has been since food passed my lips, but I am ravenous. My hand shakes as I spoon the creamy broth into my mouth. The taste is utterly ambrosial. I close my eyes to savour the perfect mouthful before allowing it to flow down my throat to my neglected stomach. I feel the warmth passing between my protruding ribcage, allowing delicate fingers of heat to pulsate through my empty body. After savouring the first few ladles, extreme hunger takes over. As I gulp spoon after spoon of the delectable soup, I see my benefactor smiling at me.

"What is your name?"

"Kass," he answers simply. "It means blackbird. I do not think my mother realised that I would turn out to be a curly blond boy! She says my hair was black when I was born but that it all fell out!"

I giggle, splattering soup onto the covers. Dismayed, I try furiously to wipe them clean. Kass leans forward and takes my hand.

"Don't. It doesn't matter. It doesn't matter at all. Would you like some bread?"

I swallow and nod, handing him the empty bowl and spoon. He smiles again, stroking my hair affectionately before leaving in search of bread. When he returns, he does not only have bread but also a pastry that seems to have a crust of sugar and a vibrant, beautiful, rosy apple. I know I am goggling at the food. I know it is bad-manners to devour it so with my eyes, but it has been so long since I have even seen food like this.

"Take it," urges Kass. "It is a relief to see you eating. I have been so worried about you. Please Anna. Shovel it in; do not think of decorum. Eat! I know that any food in the ghetto must be scarce with those monsters in charge!"

My eyes flit towards the door that is ajar. Surely it is not safe to talk in such a way. Surely it would be seen as treason. Seeing my concern, Kass smiles and nudges the plate into my hand. He lifts the apple, brandishing a small knife from his pocket and cutting it into small pieces. I try not to blanch at the sight of the knife, but Kass sees my face.

"Pieces," he shrugs. "Easier to chew."

I stare at him, taking a tentative bite of the apple segment handed to me. The divine juice trickles down my chin and I catch it on my finger to preserve every inch of the exquisite liquid.

"We can speak freely in this house, Anna. You do not need to worry. I have one housekeeper who is caring for Isabella. She is Jewish like you, but she has forged papers that I acquired for her. There is much you do not know Anna, but I must reassure you that you and Isabella are safe here. Yes... I am German, but I am not a Nazi. I am your friend and I will do everything in my power to ensure you never return to the ghetto. The man who was with me when we came for you at the camp – I cannot tell you his name – so we will refer to him as G, has acquired false papers for you and the child. As far as the Nazis are concerned you are a nurse who is assisting me here and Isabella is your child. Your husband died fighting the Allies at sea."

I try to absorb the information he is giving me. It is quite beyond belief. Why is this man helping me? Why did the man they call G liberate us from the ghetto? Surely they were taking tremendous risks. Surely if the Nazis discovered their subterfuge, their treachery, they would be shot point blank; exterminated. Why would they take that risk?

"Why?" I implore him, through a small mouthful of pastry; flakes flutter from my lips onto the white sheet that is tangled around my legs. My face throbs with every movement of my jaw, but I am too hungry to stop eating.

"Why?" he repeats frowning.

"Why did you do it? Why did you help us?"

Kass moves away from me and stands in front of the fire, staring into the soaring flames. His white shirt stretches over muscular shoulders as though it is too small for him. His body reminds me of Stefa.

"Because... what they are doing to the Jews is wrong." His voice is low, but trembles with suppressed rage. "Because I despise the Nazis and everything they stand for. They said they would make Germany great, but they have only given her reason to be ashamed. I love my country, but I hate this war and I cannot stand by and do nothing whilst Hitler murders innocent people. If lose my life to the cause then so be it. It will be worth the sacrifice to have saved lives; to have made a difference, however slight."

His speech overwhelms me. I cannot say anything because there is nothing to say. His bravery ignites a spark of hope within me. It feels alien to feel hopeful.

"You have helped others, you and this man G?"

"Yes," Kass nods solemnly. "We have helped many – but please do not ask me anymore Anna. Information makes all of us vulnerable. G is closely related to a prominent member of Hitler's regime. It enables him to call in favours when he needs to, but it also makes it especially dangerous for him."

Kass sighs, turning to face me with eyes that are glazed with tears. "It is imperative you remember at all times the danger we are all in Anna... Until this war is over we are never safe... Until the Nazis are defeated, like we must pray they will be."

I swallow and nod. The pastry has turned to dust in my mouth. I wanted to tell him that I understood, but somehow I didn't have the words to reassure this extraordinary man; this German. He crosses the room and takes the plate from me. Handing me the wine from the dresser, he urges me to drink it all, though the taste makes me shudder. I readily do his bidding then allow his gentle hands to lower me into a comfortable sleeping position. It is an effort to keep my eyes from closing as he draws the blankets up to my chin. The gesture reminds me acutely of my mother and I see her face clearly on the inside of my eyes.

"Sleep now, Anna. You need to be well again."

I nod, filled with an acute longing for Isabella that embraces my entire body: maybe tomorrow I will see her.

"In the morning you will see Isabella," Kass murmurs as though he has read my mind. "She will be so very happy to see you."

I smile and he pads quietly out of the dark room as shadows from the fire leap across the walls. Luxuriating in the glory of its unfamiliar warmth, I wonder if he will look back over his shoulder at me. He does not and I am curiously disappointed."

CHAPTER THIRTEEN

Anna, 1943

I am wide awake and sitting up in bed when a matronly lady with a round, smiling face bustles through the door with Isabella in her arms. At first she is captivated by the embers burning in the grate until her eyes pan around the room and come to rest on me. I have never seen her smile so sweetly nor strain towards me with such vigour. Still devoid of speech, she makes animated noises, stretching out her arms to me so that the woman has little choice but to plonk her onto the bed. Throwing her arms around my neck, she nuzzles into the unblemished side of my face. She smells of soapy flowers and fresh bread and as I hold her tiny form close to me, I am overjoyed not to feel her bones protruding so severely through her clothes. Suffused with love and gratitude, I realise she has been well looked after by these extraordinary people.

"How are you feeling?" The smiling woman speaks to me in Czech, fussing over my pillows and placing them delicately behind my sore back. The dressings are gone and I recognise that she was the one who probably removed them and ensured my wounds did not become further infected.

"Much better thank you. I really appreciate all the trouble you have taken looking after Isabella and me."

"It is the least I could have done in the circumstances. You have been through a terrible ordeal, one which I have avoided thanks to the good doctor."

I nod. Isabella shuffles her bottom into the crook of my legs, stuffing her thumb in her mouth and stroking my cheek with her other hand.

"Breakfast is on its way – my friend Frau Eberhardt's chickens have been producing more eggs than usual so I have been fortunate to acquire one for you."

Her goodness overwhelms me. I nod again, swallowing the emotion rising from within me. She bustles around the room, placing logs from a broken basket onto the embers of the fire. They hiss and smoke rises up into the cavernous chimney. She wipes her hands on the front of her apron, stopping to smile at Isabella cradled happily in my arms.

"She missed you. I kept her away because I knew that she couldn't possibly understand why you were always sleeping. She was very brave; my little shadow, helping me in my work."

"She is lucky to have had you."

"I think, actually, I am luckier for having her. I don't have children of my own. I couldn't."

Her eyes are suddenly sorrowful, but her wide mouth is still smiling.

"My name is Lara – anything you need Anna – you must ask me." She dabs her glittering eyes with a clean corner of her apron.

I struggle to find something to say that will encapsulate my gratitude, but I fail and settle with thank you once again as she hurries from the room, promising a breakfast fit for a queen.

Moments later she returns with the glorious smell of strong, fresh coffee preceding her. Eyeing what seems to be a plate of fresh meat and rolls with an egg settled beside it, I wonder how Lara manages to find such morsels in a place despoiled by war.

Lara places the coffee and plate upon a scrubbed wooden table top, then asks me if I would like to eat at the table. Gathering Isabella in her arms, she waits for me to shuffle my bottom to the edge of the bed and place my feet tentatively on the cold floor. I am shaking, but I want to move from the bed, not least because I am desperate to use the toilet. My head begins to spin as I lean against Lara, willing my legs to stop wobbling.

When I can stand without falling, Lara assists me in using the lavatory, but the small motion exhausts me in ways that I have hitherto not experienced. My frailty frustrates me and I describe my feelings to Lara.

"You need to give yourself time child," she insists warmly. "Did the good doctor explain how sick you have been?"

Exhaling, I fall heavily into the chair jarring the raw wounds on my back. Lara sees the agony cross my face and grimaces with concern. I wave my hand, trying to reassure her that I am quite well. I wait for the pain to subside before tucking into the heavenly breakfast Lara has prepared. Isabella sits next to me, looking miniature in the great wooden chair that sheaths her within its long arms.

The egg yolk crumbles on my tongue. The taste reminds me of Father and picnics in the Czech hills beneath a hazy sun. I savour every mouthful of my meal, scraping every morsel from the plate. Lara stands with her back to the fire, watching me delight in her food. Just as I swallow the final crumbs, Kass' smiling face peers around the door. Astonished I watch Isabella spin around on to her tummy and slide off the chair, running into his legs, squeaking with joy. He bends over and scoops her into his arms, planting an affectionate kiss on the end of her nose. She giggles, rubbing her nose before returning his affection with a loving kiss on his smooth cheek. The scene is endearing and I find the German doctor surprising me once again. He seems unaware of Lara and me watching him and quite sincere in his affection for my tiny charge. After the ghetto I realise that this place must seem like paradise to her, as it does to me.

"I am pleased to see you out of bed, Anna," Kass says, greeting me with a beguiling smile.

"She knocked her back when she sat," Lara cautions. "It is still causing her terrible pain."

"Time will heal," Kass reassures her and I know he is talking about more than my physical wounds. "I think we can remove the dressing from your face today Anna, if you permit."

I avoid his gaze. I have been dreading this point for I know that I am now deformed and ugly. I know that every time I look in the mirror I will be reminded of Slezak and the ghetto; a stark souvenir. There is a mirror hanging on the wall above my bed. I pointedly avoid looking at it as I agree to my dressings being removed.

If Kass senses my apprehension he does not show it, for his demeanour is breezy and positive. He asks Lara to fetch him a dish and bowl of warm water and tells me to stay seated at the table. Isabella wriggles out of his arms and climbs onto my lap. Looking into her beautiful eyes that are so similar to Viera's, gives me strength to endure what I must. As if she senses my unease, Isabella strokes the dressing on my face. Her face is solemn. Impulsively I kiss her soft cheek, allowing my lips to linger against her skin.

Kass works quickly, peeling the dressing from my raw cheek. Without the confinement of the covering, my face feels exposed and vulnerable. I am conscious that Kass and Lara will stare at me, or that Isabella will recoil from such ugliness, but these things do not happen. Isabella, distracted by a wooden train that Lara pulls from a cupboard in the dresser, plays on a mat in front of the fire and Kass talks about appointments he has that day. Lara tells me that she will fill a bath for me if I am feeling strong enough, and also that she has borrowed some clothes from somebody's daughter a few streets away. Nobody pays any attention to my bare face whatsoever and I feel rather foolish for feeling so self-conscious.

Leaving for his engagements, Kass grabs a greatcoat from the stand and a black bag from the top of the dresser. When he bends to pull on a pair of shiny, leather boots, I see his face wince in pain. I wonder, as he seems to hobble very slightly, what the good doctor's story is and why he is not away fighting this war.

The bath Lara prepares for me is blissful despite the small amount of water. I scrub myself with the soap, lathering it over my body as I have not done in so very long. To wash in such a way and feel clean is a luxury that I had not forgotten in my time of cold, dribbling showers in the ghetto. The lacerations on my back sting and I avoid soaping the hurt side of my face. Isabella pours water from a metal jug over my head, giggling as the water cascades down over my eyes and I make a comical face at her. Lara watches us affectionately from afar.

We are in a sizeable kitchen with a large pantry at one end and a vast range at the other where a kettle is boiling. Lara stands at an enormous wooden table, peeling vegetables into a white tin bowl. There is a window above a wide, oblong sink, but it reveals nothing except a block of steps rising upwards.

I long to ask Lara about the location of the house; I am clueless as to our whereabouts. She chatters about everyday things: the bread she hopes will rise, the illicit goods that should be arriving at the basement door from her source later; whether she has enough blue stamps to purchase meat for the good doctor's dinner. I murmur in the right places, enchanted and secure in the familiarity of the mundane yet essential throb of the house. It is unbelievable to me that Isabella and I are here, and I cannot quite rid myself of the chilling feeling that someone will arrive at the door and cart us back to the ghetto or somewhere even worse. My trust has been tested to extremes and, though I cannot help but depend upon the benevolent Lara and the man she constantly refers to only as the 'good doctor', I feel that there are questions that cannot remain unanswered. I need to engage fully in my new existence, despite the colossal extent of my gratitude.

Isabella and I spend many therapeutic, domesticated days with Lara. Both of us follow her around like two dependable spaniels. My bed has been moved to one of the rooms at the top of the house where I am treated to an urban view of streets and buildings. At first glance the location seems untouched by war, but if I crane my neck from the window I can see this is not the case.

Distinguished buildings stand between those I discern to be destroyed by bombs, ruins that are now no more than heaps of rubble and jagged blackened beams. Looking at them makes me shiver with fear for I cannot tolerate the thought of escaping the ghetto only to die in a bombing raid. It also signifies to me that I must be in an area heavily controlled by the Nazis to come under such vigorous Allied bombing raids. Being in a city again makes me feel uneasy; excepting Prague I have never really enjoyed their faceless anonymity.

Lara tells us that if the air raid siren calls then we must go directly to the basement, but she is careful not to mention our locality. I believe she pointedly avoids talking to me about anything that is not ordinary, for we have not spoken about her previous life or mine in the ghetto or anything related to the doctor. She is highly attentive to my well-being, constantly worrying that I am in pain or distress, and she commands that I rest for a good period of time each day. I know that she is helping me regain my strength and lessen some of the harm inflicted by living in the ghetto.

The doctor, who I am finding hard to call by his real name, is conspicuous by his absence. He leaves the house before I wake in the morning and does not return until nightfall, when he eats a supper concocted from the rations that Lara scrapes together at the table in front of the range. Sometimes I hear him out in the yard cutting logs for Lara to burn on the fires. Once I watched him from the window, with his shirt sleeves rolled up despite the freezing temperatures and a murderous look on his face as he brought the axe down to split the logs. Throwing them into a great basket like an Englishman tossing a cricket ball, he split one after another until the fury inside him was spent.

Though I long to know what angered him so, I know I should not ask. Despite telling me I can speak freely in the house, none of us has really spoken of anything pertinent at all.

As my physical well-being improves and I regain my strength, this frustrates me more and more. I also long to go outside, but I have not yet conjured up the courage to ask Lara if it would be possible, not because I fear her answer, but because I am highly conscious of the unsightliness of my face. Lara, Isabella and the doctor treat me as though I look normal, but I know that cannot be the case. I am not courageous enough to look in the mirror to see for myself. I avoid the mirrors in the house which is not difficult because as far as I can see there are only two. One in the room downstairs where I was convalescing, which I have surreptitiously covered with a cloth that no one has yet removed, and one on the landing at the end of a corridor which leads to the doctor's quarters.

The healing wound itches and throbs in equal measure, especially at night or when I am chewing my food; consequently I am fiendishly aware of it. Although the people around me do not stare at me in horror, I am afraid that I will walk down the street and passers-by will shrink away from my mutation and cross over. Absurdly, although I know I have confronted far worse things in the ghetto, I somehow still cannot abide the thought of this: my vanity will not allow it. I am miserable, but not because I am worried about my friends in Theresienstadt, or being recaptured, or Father's fate, but because I am a loathsome human being who is mourning her own beauty rather than the things that really matter. While I detest myself for the truth of this, I still cannot jolt myself free of self-pity.

One morning, I wake to discover that Isabella is not there. Searching the house, I fervently call her name, struggling not to panic. When I finally reach the basement kitchen, the doctor looks up from reading a newspaper.

"I've lost Isabella."

He folds the paper carefully, smiling at me. I glimpse a headline that is written in German. Flurries of snow fall past the window.

"She is not lost," he laughs. "Lara has wrapped her up and taken her out into the snow to play with some other children. She woke early and is very excited."

"Oh!"

"Take a seat. Here drink this."

He pushes a cup towards me filled with strong coffee. The aroma is mouth-watering. I slide out a chair and sit opposite him at the table.

"I was thinking," he says casually, delving into his black leather bag that rests beside him. "That today you could assist me."

"Assist you?"

"Yes," he insists as though he is merely asking me to do the laundry or clean the silver. "Your papers claim you are a nurse, so today, I thought perhaps you should be one."

"But I am not qualified..." I begin, but he stuns me into silence with a laugh.

"Are any of us? I have barely anytime at medical school before I find myself in the Wehrmacht, thrust upon the Eastern Front performing amputations on dying soldiers. Are any of us ready for that?" he exclaims with uncharacteristic bitterness.

I bite my lower lip, disappointed in myself for angering him. I have no idea of his history. How could I?

"My father was a doctor," I tell him, my voice trembling slightly. I have not spoken of him in such a long time and I really do not know why I mention him now.

The doctor pulls an arm band out of his bag. It is emblazoned with a red cross. He hands it to me across the table.

"I used to help him on his rounds sometimes, although I was quite young. His patients knew that I wanted also to become a doctor one day."

I smile at my memories, remembering an old lady who was suffering with recurrent nose bleeds, who would allow me to listen to her chest through Father's stethoscope. She believed that more women should become doctors, as she herself had once been a leading scientist, and encouraged my youthful ambition.

The doctor grins and raises his expressive, blond brows as though he is already in possession of this information and I feel wrong-footed. A small part of me wants to impress him and assure him I am entirely up to the task but I feel oddly deflated. He crosses the room to a pile of clothes that lie beside an old mangle.

"Wear these." He thrusts an armful of dark clothing into my arms and places the arm band on top. "We leave in fifteen minutes."

I do not know what to say so I stand in the middle of

178

the kitchen, holding the clothing, as he gathers his things together.

"And Anna," he says breezily, a chuckle hovering on his lips as he peers around the door from the hallway. "Make sure you eat something!"

Something snaps inside of me.

"Excuse me please. Could you just wait a moment?" The mounting fury bubbles on my lips.

The doctor, looking confused, re-enters the room and leans against the tall dresser with his arms folded, surveying me with unconcealed amusement. This incites me further.

"It may seem perfectly reasonable to you," I continue to bluster. "To request my presence on your medical rounds this morning after everything you have done for Isabella and I, for which, you must understand, I will remain forever in your debt, but what is not clear to me, what does not seem reasonable to me, is that I know absolutely nothing!"

"Anna," he says, his blue eyes twinkling mischievously, like a school boy playing in the mud. "You are beautiful when you are angry. Has anyone ever told you that?"

He does not look at me, but I feel a blush creeping across my scar. I feel oddly tearful. I want him to understand. I need to know where I am. I need to know the places where evil may linger.

I sniff, a sob escapes my throat. Kass looks up at me. The smile dies on his face.

"Anna," he whispers. "Oh Anna, I did not mean to upset you."

He sweeps across the room, gathering my hands

into his own. We both stare down at our hands locked together. Eventually, he speaks.

"I'm sorry you feel I have purposely kept things from you, Anna. Lara and I were of the opinion that you needed time to recover fully before we bewildered you with details. We imagined that the realities of this war have been real enough to you already." He glances fleetingly at my disfigured face. "We thought you had enough to deal with."

I blush, shame creeping up my neck as I fail to meet the eyes of this man who is scarcely more than a child himself, who has obviously experienced first-hand the savagery of this war, who has been protecting me from the fierce reality of the outside world, which has hitherto given me such a raw deal.

"I'm sorry," I breathe.

"Ask away, Anna. Ask me anything you like."

I stutter. "It... It... it doesn't matter." I withdraw from him. "I'm sorry doctor."

I feel him reach towards me, then drop his hands to his sides. I feel naked, eclipsed by a torrent of feelings.

"Anna," he gently tugs at my hand. "Anna, of course it matters."

I cannot look at him. He pushes me gently into a chair near the warm stove then sits down next to me. The snow outside seems to be falling even faster now; enormous snowflakes crystallise on the window ledge. "And please, stop calling me doctor; I am not even fully qualified yet: another casualty of this war. You are as bad as Lara. Please just call me Kass."

We are quiet for a moment, the silence heavy with unspoken words.

"Ask me, Anna. Ask me anything, I will try to be honest."

I take a deep breath. "Where are we?"

Kass takes a deep breath also. "We are in Prenzlauer Berg."

My eyes widen. "Berlin?"

He nods. "It is one of the only parts that has not been heavily bombed."

"But it cannot be safe," I blurt, fear overcrowding my thoughts.

He shrugs. "As safe as anywhere else controlled by the Nazis. The war is going badly for the Axis. The Allies have landed in Italy. They have more to worry about than us, I can promise you. Word is... they are planning a counter attack!"

I narrow my eyes at him. "You seem to know an awful lot..."

He sighs, rubbing his eyes, "Yes... I think sometimes too much..."

He looks exhausted.

"Anna," he continues, slightly exasperated and impatient. "Would it be too much to ask you to come with me today in a nursing capacity and just trust that everything will be ok?" He glances at his watch. "There are patients I must attend who will not wait, do you understand?"

"Then why take me with you... just go if you must." I cross my arms.

"Because whilst you stay here and do not nurse, people will be more inclined to ask questions."

"How can you be sure I will not embarrass you? How

181

do you know that I can dress a wound?"

I sound petulant. I do not like it; nor do I know why I am angry.

"I don't," he agrees quietly, looking at me like a small boy who has been reprimanded by his teacher when things at home are difficult. "But I know you are an intelligent young woman and you have mentioned a couple of times your personal desire to become a medic..."

"Mm," I huff. "I didn't think you were even listening."

"I was."

"Evidently..." I feel something shift inside me. I jump to my feet. My disfigurement all but forgotten, I grab a bread roll from the board beside the stove. "I'll be ready in five minutes."

Kass' face brightens. "I'll unearth an old coat of my mother's."

"Your mother?" I enquire absently, gulping coffee. "Why would her coat be here?"

"This is her house." His expression is suddenly grave. "My father lived here too until he was killed. Get changed."

Chapter Fourteen

Anna, 1944

IT is glorious to be outside, even in Berlin. The city is eerily silent beneath the veil of snow that falls steadily from the heavy sky. I am grateful for the leather boots and woollen coat that Kass found in a trunk of his mother's on the landing. He has even discovered a little hat that he has pinned to my head because, although he didn't say so, he knew that I would have been unable to look in the mirror and do it myself. He says I now look the part and that everyone will believe I am a nurse. He tells me that it is my presence beside him that matters more than the tasks I undertake today; that he will not ask me to do more than pass things to him when I assist him with the patients. I explain that I am more than happy to clean and dress wounds and that I will be an avid learner. I cannot keep the nerves and excitement from my voice.

Footprints snake over the carpet of snow, but they begin to disappear as snowflake flurries continue to settle on the ground. Every step is hard going, but I do not care. I imagine Isabella playing in its glittering depths, throwing flakes joyfully into the air. Motorcars and bicycles are abandoned in the street, plant pots seem to be scattered at random, upended. I stick my tongue out, trying to catch their truth as they fall. I linger behind Kass as he marches purposefully through the whirling flakes.

The landscape alters as we trundle onwards. What had once been majestic, old buildings rising towards the hovering sky housing important families have become burnt out ruins, devastated by bombing raids. Snow begins to fall on vestiges of homes that once resonated with voices. Everywhere I look there are the scorched remains of everyday objects, which alone are insignificant but amass to become a home. Kass walks onwards, burying his head in the collar of his warm coat as I traipse behind him. A deathly silence prevails, one which should not envelope a city such as this. Abruptly, Kass takes a right turn, along an avenue that seems mercifully untouched by the bombing raids. We seem to trudge for ages through the snow before he turns left and climbs the steps towards a grandiose front door. He knocks and I am wholly unprepared for the person who opens it.

Kass raises his arm, "Heil Hitler!"

I shudder behind him. There is a plump maid holding the door open with trembling fingers, staring in a petrified state at the two men exiting the building. They are dressed in imposing Nazi refinery, decorated in medals with boots that almost reveal their deleterious reflections. One has narrow eyes, reminiscent of an amphibian and a grim set mouth which is wider than it should be, almost reaching out to his large ears that could flap like the wings of a bird beneath his imposing cap. He surveys us coldly; my breath is suffocating, seemingly turning to water in my lungs. His corrosive eyes, travelling the length of my body, while the maid's full lips widen in dismay, finally rest on the band encircling my upper arm that is emblazoned with a red cross. I focus, with pure terror, on a tiny stain defacing the maid's clean apron, trying to bury my mutilated face in the cashmere scarf belonging to Kass' mother, swathing my neck. The static silence is broken by the second man, whose wide, jowly appearance is entirely pugilist, urging his comrade forward with undisguised impatience, down the steps onto the snow-entrenched path. He does not even glance at us.

"He's waiting for you," stutters the maid through wobbly lips. "He's in the library."

Kass nods, his eyes devoid of their usual vivacity, but he does not smile. He pointedly avoids looking at me and I am relieved. Why has he brought me here? He says I must trust him, but it is hideously unclear to me, why he would place me in such conspicuous danger by bringing me to the obvious home of an eminent Nazi. I know I am completely at his mercy so I steel myself to play a role in this charade. As we meander slowly through the hallway, our booted feet echoing on the marble floor, I stop holding my breath.

The library is dark; shelves, filled with every imaginable book, line the walls, reaching from floor to ceiling. A magnificent mahogany desk presides over the remaining space in the room, placed upon a luxurious rug that spreads elaborately over the shiny wooden floor. A smouldering fire burns in the grate of a wide-breasted chimney above which hangs the portrait of a youthful, blond man clad in military uniform. He looks impatient and agitated. His jaw is hard and his features are severe. The expression in his eyes perturbs me. I shudder as I realise with revulsion that he reminds me of Slezak.

At first it seems as though nobody is present, but presently a gruff German voice resonates from a covert corner of the library. To my surprise, the greeting is warm and Kass turns on his heel towards it.

A distinguished man with a lined face that belies his youthful eyes lounges in the corner of a vast leather sofa propped up by a wealth of velvet pillows. He is dressed immaculately in a starched white shirt with smart braces that reach over the shoulder. In one hand rests a glass of cognac despite the early hour and on his lap, a copy of Johann Wolfgang von Goethe's Die Leiden des Jungen Werthers. Prematurely greying hair rises from a high forehead that seems to crease in pleasure with Kass' arrival. Striking eyes, the colour of coal, glow faintly above a long nose and groomed moustache, but the man's face appears grey and pinched with pain. Expecting another Nazi greeting to take place, I do not know whether to feel anxious or relieved when it does not. It is only on closer inspection that I realise that the right arm of our host's shirt dangles languidly from his shoulder.

"How are you feeling, Oberst Von Fleischmann?" Kass asks him, falling to his knees on the smooth floor and opening his bag.

"My fingers tingle." Oberst Von Fleischmann smiles ruefully, picking up the cuff of his right sleeve and waving it like a puppet on a string. Strong, musky cologne drifts on the air, mingling with the scent of warm skin. It is oddly pleasant. "All night they tingle away... time seems to make no difference."

"It will get better."

"And this terrible pain?"

"That too – eventually."

"Are you telling me that one day you will not have to visit me three times a week? It is the highlight of my day Gefreiter Hartenstein. I went to great lengths to ensure you continue to be my medic."

Kass nods, a genuine smile lighting his face as he assists the man in the removal of his shirt. Slightly embarrassed and self-conscious, I hang back, awkwardly averting my eyes from the scene, scanning the bindings of leather books lining the imposing shelves.

"You like to read Fräulein?"

I jump. He is grimacing, but his black eyes retain the hint of a smile while Kass removes his dressing.

"Ja, Ich liebe es zu lessen."

"You are from the south of Germany. Stuttgart perhaps?"

I think quickly, my heart pounding, although the words on the papers Kass acquired are imprinted on my soul.

"Heppenheim Oberst."

"I have never been, but I hear it is very beautiful."

"Indeed, Oberst. The town hall is a most magnificent building."

"Maybe one day I shall visit."

"I can recommend it. The lake and the surrounding countryside are also striking."

"I see." Oberst Von Fleischmann nods at Kass with approval. "You seem to have found yourself a most handsome and learned assistant."

"I'm glad you approve Oberst," Kass murmurs, his eyes avidly focused on his task.

"Nurse, could you please pass me clean dressings from my bag."

I delve into his bag.

"Has he told you about my son?"

Belatedly, I realise that he is still speaking to me and I am unsure how to respond; I try to move my lips but no words are forthcoming. Kass intervenes, snatching the provisions from my hand and graciously soliciting Oberst Von Fleischmann to preserve his modesty, for he believes I have no desire to hear of battlefield heroics after the loss of my husband.

"You are young to be married Fräulein."

I stare out of the window at the breath-taking beauty of the snow falling from the sky, trying to eradicate the lie from my face.

"He was a friend of my father's."

Oberst Von Fleischmann flinches at Kass' delicate administration, saving me from further questioning.

I look up from his bag and cannot help but stare in fascination at the raw flesh that emerges where the Colonel's arm should be. A transhumeral amputation has taken place and all that remains of his right arm is a stump that reaches just below his arm pit. The wound is quite new, I believe, for it is open beneath the dressing. A flap amputation has not been administered because there is no skin across the laceration, which leads me to believe that Oberst Von Fleischmann had a wound that became infected resulting in the need to remove the limb. He has suffered a guillotine amputation, one which would have been performed quickly with the circuitous stroke of a knife preceding the slash of a saw. The sliced humerous is exposed to the air.

"It was a bomb," Oberst Von Fleischmann says simply as he watches me staring at his open wound. "My arm was practically sliced off by shard of glass. It became infected, so the butchers took it away!"

"Oh, I'm sorry... I didn't mean to stare."

"Stare away my dear; it's all that it is good for now."

While Kass works quickly on the Colonel's wound, I cannot help but feel pity for him despite the fact he is a Nazi and my sworn enemy. It is strange to think that if we were not adversaries in a Europe festooned in hatred, he could easily be a friend of my father's with whom I could willingly converse over afternoon tea. He seems so helpless, continual pain etched across his features; I cannot imagine this man condemning thousands of Jews to their death: a sheep in wolf's clothing?

High spots of colour have appeared upon Kass' cheeks. Concentration is etched across his face as he works adeptly; I sense he is anxious to leave. The Colonel's curious nature vexes him; I do not think he was expecting it for if he had then he surely would not have brought me here.

"Will you come again?"

The enquiry is undeniably aimed at me and in my desire to prove to Kass that I can execute the complex role he has assigned to me, I meet Oberst Von Fleischmann's penetrating gaze.

"I shall."

"Would you stay and read to me next time? It tires me greatly to read myself and with the loss of my daughter I am bereft of intelligent company."

As panic threatens to overpower my capacity for speech, I nod and swallow.

"I am sorry for your loss Oberst."

To my chagrin, tears fill the eyes of this diminished veteran of war. He tugs fiercely at a handkerchief lodged in his trouser pocket with his only thumb and forefinger.

Absently I place my hand over my open mouth, watching him in consternation as he shakes it then dabs at his sombre eyes.

"She died in the bombing raid in which I lost my arm. It was her husband's mother's house; a bright woman, a true National Socialist."

I swallow and nod, averting my eyes once again to the winter wonderland beyond the glass. Kass instantaneously rises to his feet and closes the clasp on his bag. He holds a hand out to the Colonel and waits for him to take it. He clasps it with indisputable warmth, thanking Kass for his time and dedication and also for giving him the opportunity to meet me. He tells me that he looks forward to our next meeting and that he hopes I will not change my mind about reading to him. Despite my anxiety I assure him, with a confidence that I do not feel, that I will not.

"You will not!" commands Kass as I slither and trip in the ice in my efforts to catch up with him as he marches purposely through the deepening drifts of snow. I am breathing heavily, wisps of my breath preceding me in the icy air.

"What?" I demand panting.

"Read to him. You cannot go there again. I won't allow it!" His brow is creased like a child being seduced from a tantrum.

"Really?" I raise my eyebrows in amusement. "So instead we raise his suspicions do we?"

"I'll tell him you are otherwise engaged."

I widen my eyes in scepticism. "And he will not ask questions?"

"He is welcome to ask what he likes!"

"That's preposterous; he is a wily individual who knows exactly what he desires. I have to go. It is the only way to validate our truth. I know that and so, I think, do you."

"I don't like it Anna. I didn't think he would take such a shine to you..."

"Because of my face?" I ask him, without any thought for what I am saying.

He stops mid-step, turning to look at me aghast. "No!"

He shakes my shoulder. "You must never say that."

We stand in the falling snow, staring at each other resolutely, as it settles on our clothing, glittering beneath a frail sun. Kass reaches out his arm and removes his dark glove. In an unexpected gesture, he strokes my spoiled cheek tenderly with the back of his hand. I feel the blood rising up my neck and in an effort to hide my embarrassment I scuff the snow with my booted foot. I can feel Kass' blue eyes burning into my short, uneven curls before he sighs and continues his journey to our next appointment.

I want to ask Kass where we are heading, but he seems fractious so I remain silent, meekly following his footsteps in the snow. He ignores me as I trudge behind him for more than three quarters of an hour. My hands are numb with cold and I stuff them within the confines of my new scarf in an effort to suffuse warmth into them.

Berlin is shocking, for bombs have fallen heavily here, wreaking their hideous damage. What astonishes me most of all are the ruins that fall between decorous buildings, both armoured by a unanimous layer of snow.

I lament that this beautiful city has been destroyed by its own undoing, by an ideology that can never be accepted by the outside world, by a treaty that did not predict that the ashes of confinement would unleash a far more sinister beast. I admire its historic splendour yet mourn its present.

Abruptly, Kass turns down a street that seems to be more industrial than those along which we have previously journeyed; although whatever was once manufactured here can be no longer for the buildings seem deserted and the snow leading up to the great doors of the workshops is untouched. I wonder what business we could possibly have in such an abandoned location, when Kass pulls my arm and drags me hastily up a path towards a dilapidated door with broken windows either side of it.

Shards of broken glass litter the ground. The remaining glass is caked in grime and therefore impossible to see through, so I crane my neck to look through the places where the window has shattered. Inside there are the remains of an ironmongery store, but the storage has been looted. Broken drawers have been flung to the ground, their contents stolen or rolling beneath cupboards and workbenches. The floor is carpeted with discarded nails and pieces of metal pipe. On a soiled worktop, saturated with oil, a cash register sits on its side with the drawer open and a lone five Reichsmark coin, displaying the Nazi swastika, settled beside it.

Kass pushes the door. It is unlocked and swings easily open. A fragment of peeling blue paint falls onto the snow and peculiarly Kass leans over and picks it up. He takes my hand and leads me wordlessly to the back of the shop. I tiptoe over the debris, trying to avoid catching nails or sharp tacks in the soles of my feet. A metallic aroma mingles with oil and wood shavings. Despite feeling bewildered by our presence here, I do not question Kass. His blue eyes are the colour of the sky before a rainstorm.

Behind the front of the store there is a staircase leading upwards. Tentatively, I follow Kass and our footsteps resonate on each wooden step. When we reach the landing he goes to a large window and opens it. I peer out noticing that the array of buildings surrounding us is at different levels. I notice that many of the outer buildings are much higher thus obscuring any view. Kass slides onto the windowsill, leaning backwards out of the window. Before I can cry in alarm, he hoists himself upwards by his arms so that he standing on the sill. I watch in apprehension as his foot slips on the ice encrusted ledge. A silent squeal escapes my lips but I hold my breath as he regains his footing. Only his legs are visible as he stretches upwards, ostensibly to grope around on the balustrade above us.

Moments later a rope is flung through the window, narrowly missing my face. It has knots tied all the way along it and the end is still attached to something that is beyond the casement. Like a monkey swinging through the trees, Kass soars through the window, his face glowing and his eyes wide with adrenaline.

"I'm climbing up. When I get there I'll throw the rope back down, when you see it hanging down, tie my bag on securely. I'll pull up the bag and send the rope back down for you."

I stare at him. "You want me to climb up there?"

"Yes. You have good boots. Just climb. I can pull you up a little, but you'll have to do some of the work."

I cross my arms, shaking my head. "No."

"Right," Kass mocks. "You'll sit and read to an afflicted Nazi, but you will not climb a rope. Do you realise how ridiculous that sounds." He climbs on to the sill again. "I'm going, see you up there..."

"Why?" I wail. "I hate heights."

"You'll see. Now stop prevaricating and get on with it."

With that, he vanishes out of sight, his long legs gradually disappearing until I can only see his boots suspended from above like the stockings of Christian children on Christmas Eve. If this had been a more frivolous occasion, I may have found the whole episode comical; however in Kass' current state of scornful derision, I dare not release the giggle bubbling inside me. Being prone to laughter when nervous, I hug Kass' bag to my chest, releasing a nervous chuckle. After what seems like seconds, the rope appears, swaying in the snowflakes cascading beyond the window. I grasp it firmly, resting the bag on the sill whilst I tie a secure knot. I give the rope a gentle tug to signal to Kass that it is safe to haul the bag. I watch in trepidation as it sways precariously, moving slowly upwards, before vanishing from sight.

Panic grips me. I wait for the rope to return, hoping that it will not; praying that Kass has changed his mind about our foolish sojourn across the roof of this neglected building on this snowy day in mid-winter in war-torn Berlin. How preposterous it all seems... I jump as the rope makes its next appearance. Moving cautiously towards the window, I clamp the rope between my shaking hands. Sick with nerves and talking aloud in a vain attempt to calm myself, I ease my bottom through the open window on to the sill.

My pulse quickens and I beg myself not to look down as I grip the rope between my thighs. With every ounce of available courage, I assail the offending, eternally shifting object. Keeping my eyes firmly focused on Kass' white face urging me on from above, I half climb, half scramble up the perilous line, gripping each knot between my feet and groping blindly upwards with tremulous hands. When eventually Kass' strong hands grip mine and haul me upwards onto an unstable roof, I feel the utter compulsion to slap him. Evidently seeing fury simmering in my eyes, he steps backwards, holding his hands up in a gesture of surrender.

"Hey, calm down... this is the only way... follow me and you'll understand."

Scowling at him, I remain quiet and resolute. Ignoring me, he picks up his bag, throws it over his shoulder and requests that I follow him over the icy rooftop. His demeanour is more comparable to a proficient soldier than a medic on a routine visit. My determination to stay angry with him is short-lived however because navigating the roof is hazardous and enormously challenging. Many times my heart seems to stop beating as I lose my footing and slip towards the distant ground. Sometimes I am able to regain my balance, but several times Kass' strong hands dart out and grip me to prevent me from falling.

The taller, derelict warehouses surround the hidden roof upon which we travel, but they are barely visible beneath the blanket of white; the snow is falling so rapidly now that I can only see a faint outline of Kass through the blizzard. Though we are both clothed in dark colours, our outer garments are now entirely white. I can no longer feel my fingers and the droplets on the end of my nose almost freeze above my top lip. The world is immersed in silence and the only sound I can hear is the rippling panic in my own rate of breath. My unease, combined with a smouldering rage that is resolutely directed at Kass, makes me uncharacteristically cantankerous and egocentric. I pull the now hard, freezing scarf over the wound on my cheek as it throbs painfully in time with the beating of my pulse.

Just as I think I am about to scream in sheer frustration, Kass stops abruptly and kneels down to scrabble around in the snow. I am balanced dangerously against an unused, crumbling chimney stack. Panic scorches my throat. I fumble, trying to maintain my balance, releasing a brick that plummets downwards, close to Kass' head bowed in the snow.

"Anna," he hisses, glowering at me. "Would you please sit down and stop trying to kill us both!"

"Me?" I hiss back at him. "Me? You're the one who has brought us up here in a blizzard. I'm pretty certain that I am not the reckless one here."

"Well," he mutters through gritted teeth, tugging at something in the snow. "Sometimes we all have to do things that we don't want to do for the sake of someone else. I'm afraid that for now you will just have to put up with it because the only way out of here is to follow me."

"Perfect," I exclaim, attempting to place my hands on my hips in a defiant stance, although I slip again and have to grab at the chimney stack that duly releases another brick which whistles past Kass' ear. Shaking his head in disbelief, he curses into the blizzard.

Somewhat contrite and realising that I might actually do some damage if I do not remain still, I crouch down, letting my bottom wiggle a protective hole in compacted snow. I remain silent; allowing Kass to do whatever it is he is doing. I imagine warming my hands on the wood-burning stove in his kitchen. Being this cold reminds me starkly of the ghetto and nights when the ice froze drips from our noses as we lay in misery huddled together to preserve warmth. I think of Sara and Rachel and the colossal sacrifice that they made for me. I wonder if they are still in Theresienstadt or whether they have been, at long last, placed on a transport. I shudder to think of them in that boarded-up place that once took Maksym away from me. I begin to shiver uncontrollably.

"Right!"

I try to rouse myself in the realisation that Kass is speaking to me. My mind feels distant.

"Anna."

I struggle to balance myself so that I may stand up on the slippery roof. Kass sidles carefully over to me. He leans down so that his face is so close to mine that I can feel the warmth of his breath defrosting my nose. His expressive eyes are blue again and snowflakes nestle, like tiny birds, in his wavy blond hair.

"I am sorry, Anna... really I am." He places a reassuring hand on my arm. His eyes, which are still those of a boy, are sorrowful and weary all of a sudden. They are sunken in slightly above his high cheeks.

Remorseful, I place my freezing hand upon his. We remain still for a while, shivering violently; each of us taking strength from the other.

"Come on; let's do whatever it is we have come here to do, shall we?"

My feet slide again as once more I try to get up. Kass and I hold onto each other, finding it impossible not to laugh at the absurdity of our predicament.

"I'm afraid we have to climb down."

"I was hoping you wouldn't say that, but somehow I knew that you would."

I grin at him, thinking that if I had managed to climb up without descending into blind panic then I could almost certainly manage to scramble down.

"It's actually a bit easier. You can go first this time."

"No, I would really rather not."

"Anna, do you want to get back down?"

"Yes," I stutter, regarding the second rope in his hand that is also knotted at intervals.

"Then take the rope and follow my directions – you are wearing gloves so your hands will be protected."

I nod, too terrified and pathetic to argue. He instructs me to hold the rope up high so that it is taut against the metal eyelet to which it is attached, whilst lowering my body over the side of the building. Quivering with fear I am certain I will vomit, until he tells me to look into his eyes the whole time he is speaking. I try to do as he asks, but flurries of snowflakes make it impossible to see more than a blurred outline of his head. I concentrate on that.

"Brace your legs against the wall and allow the rope to slip through your gloves. Even if you cannot stop the momentum, you will only slip as far as the next knot. You are such a slight, little thing that the rope can easily bear your weight. Look into my eyes the whole time, Anna."

Without knowing exactly how I have summoned the courage to do it, I feel myself slipping over the edge of the roof. Sticking my legs out, I feel the wall against my feet. Fleetingly I glance at it to ensure it is really there, but Kass insists that I look at him. When my hands slip too far over the icy rope, I am eclipsed by fear and a silent scream of terror rises in my throat. Feeling as though I am falling to my death, I am overcome when I actually stop slipping on reaching the next knot.

"Keep going Anna, that's excellent! Halfway down is a window. You go in there."

"How?" I stutter, but my words are lost in the snowstorm and regrettably he does not hear me.

I cannot even see the outline of his face anymore as he has disappeared into a white abyss; neither does there appear to be any sign of the window which only serves to increase my terror. Just as I think that it is impossible to hold onto the frozen rope any longer, because I cannot feel my hands and they refuse to do my bidding, something attaches itself to my booted feet. I scream as I am hauled through an open window, feet first and lifted off the rope by two dishevelled, furious looking men who pinch my upper arms hard in their strong hands.

CHAPTER FIFTEEN

Anna, 1944

ONE of them, with long dark hair and an unkempt beard, thrusts me forcibly into a wall and hisses in my face in a harsh German accent.

"Who are you? Who sent you here?"

His bloodless hands close around my throat while spittle from his mouth spurts in my astonished face. Trembling with fear and anger, I kick at his shins and flail my gloved hands in his face. I am propelled against a metal joist in a room that must be a disused office attached to an old warehouse.

"Curt!" The other man is shouting and my assailant's hands loosen on my throat just as I believe I will pass out.

"Put that poor girl down. Kass is here."

He drops me to the floor. I cough and splutter, taking great gulps of cold air. Kass is immediately by my side and an angry exchange in German takes place between the three men. I slide down the wall, pulling my knees into my chest. I close my eyes, struggling to eradicate the sound of their voices, and take the deep even breaths that I had taught myself to do in the ghetto when panic threatened to take hold of me.

"What is going on?" A woman's voice is very close to my

ear. I keep my eyes closed, my head bowed onto my knees. A gentle hand caresses my head.

"It's alright. Nobody is going to hurt you – Curt, Victor, what is going on here?"

I hear one of the men sigh, but I do not open my eyes. "I'm sorry – I didn't know she was with Kass."

"She is a nurse. She's here to help," Kass growls.

"She may have been a Nazi informant," insists the man. "I had to be sure."

"What?" snorts the woman standing beside me. "A slip of a girl like this, she is barely more than a child."

"And you don't think the Nazis use children as sneaks? How naive you are Ruth!"

"Perhaps, but it would have been better to have questioned her before trying to kill her, Curt!"

"I haven't killed her!"

"No, but you have nearly frightened her to death and potentially alienated one of our only sources of help. She may have been a friend of Ernest; he is no more than a child!"

"Ernest found this place for us," argued the man called Victor, gruffly. "He would never bring someone new here without first telling us!"

"Ernest brought Kass here to help..."

"Perhaps... but we needed him. The baby would have died without him."

"Stop," Kass commands. "It is my fault. I should have warned you. Please... let it go."

I feel him moving beside me then hear his voice whispering in my ear. "Are you alright, Anna?"

Finally I dare to open my eyes. Kass is kneeling beside me with a protective arm around my shoulders, and on my other side crouches a skeletal woman with hair that has fallen out in places and kind, brown eyes. She rubs my frozen hands between her bony ones. The two dishevelled men stare at us.

"Anna," she begins. "I am deeply sorry for your welcome. We have been hiding here for so long that some of us are prone to madness on occasion. Please accept our apologies."

Realisation filters slowly through my psyche. I stare at her sallow complexion and the droopy skin sagging from her patchy eyebrows. Kass stands up and begins taking supplies from his bag. He tells the men that the other one will come shortly with food and blankets. He explains that we had to scale the roof because our footprints in the snow would betray our presence here making it possible that someone could alert the authorities.

"I am a Jew also," I whisper to Ruth through chattering teeth. "The dd-doctor rescued me from Theresienstadt. How long have you been hiding here?"

"Longer than I care to tell – you survived that place? We've heard terrible rumours over the years."

I nod.

"Victor pounced on you because we are so paranoid that we may be discovered or betrayed. Only Kass, the youngster called Ernest – who risked his life to find this place for us – and another man know we are here. We must depend on them for everything, food, provisions, medical care... it is very hard." She appears utterly exhausted.

"Hard to trust..." I murmur.

"Yes," she confesses. "Sometimes..."

"I know."

She takes my other hand and continues the vigorous rubbing.

"Come," Ruth beckons, when we have sat in companionable silence for a while. "You must meet everyone else."

She stands to her full height, which is staggering, and stoops to offer me her hand. I take it, shuffling to my feet. Kass and the other men have disappeared from the dilapidated office to another part of the warehouse. My clothes are covered in dust from the floor. The walls, desks and shelves are strewn with a maze of cobwebs, over which spiders scuttle. Upon the shelves are cardboard files filled with stacks of yellowing paper from days gone by. Much of the paper is torn or partly eaten by something. I wonder if it is not only humans who suffer in this war.

Ruth leads me by the hand. I am unprepared for what I encounter on the other side of the door. My eyes fall upon machinery, covered in old, dusty sheets and pulleys and wheels attached to cables. Workbenches have been shifted in front of the equipment; they are lined up together to form makeshift beds which have no mattresses or pillows, only blankets. At first I am puzzled by this arrangement, but then I remember Berta saying that we were always freezing because the cold pervaded the floor. The room smells of treated wood and stale humans.

In an open space, between the wall and the benches, several children play. Two of them are fighting over an old wooden train that has lost one wheel and its funnel. Beyond the children, the adults gather in small groups. When I look at them I am immediately self-conscious because more than twenty pairs of eyes stare back at me, their expressions blank and unreadable. I feel ill at ease, as though they are accusing me of something of which I am innocent.

Ruth pulls me forward, a bright smile lighting her thin features. She introduces me and explains my presence in their sanctuary. Gradually, while she speaks about my incarceration in Theresienstadt, the eyes of the gathered crowd begin to thaw. Many of them murmur words of respect and conciliation. I am invited to sit with them and when they discover I am there in a nursing capacity they bombard me with questions about some minor ailments. Delighted to be accepted into their throng and even more delighted to be capable of answering their questions, I listen to their predicaments, making small suggestions and promising to ask Kass' advice. Most of what ails them could be fixed by fresh air, exercise and an abundant diet; this vexes me greatly.

One girl called Hannah, who is about my own age, confesses to me in a whisper that she has stopped menstruating. She is worried that the monthly bleeding may never start again, meaning that she will be unable to bear children when she is, god-willing, a prisoner no longer. I assure her that this was a common occurrence in the ghetto because the girls' bodies were starved of the nutritional requirements necessary to function properly. Relief floods her face. I ask her how they are managing to eat when food is rationed to everyone and she tells me that those who help them from the outside divide their rations somehow, although she has no idea how they possibly master it when the allowance is so meagre.

As we share stories, I am once again filled with a seething rage towards the Nazis and the fact that their determination to persecute innocent people has forced these blameless people into living like this: a half-life. This, like the ghetto, is a prison without bars; the reality of life for these people, their freedom blighted through no crime or immorality, just warped doctrines, elicited from the minds of those who, dallying with iniquity and insanity, misconstrue the unknown finding it threatening and intolerable.

Kass is in the corner, kneeling over a child who lies extremely still. The pallor of extreme sickness is upon his beatific face. I am overwhelmed with the longing to remove him from this place and care for him until he recovers. Kass talks to the adults who also crouch beside the boy in whispers. A tiny woman with very curly hair and wire-rimmed spectacles begins to sob quietly, gripping the child's inert hand in her own. I realise with horror that she has been told that the child will die and the pain pummelling her face is immeasurable. She leans forward until her cheek rest beside the child's. Her lips move sequentially and I know she is uttering prayers – "El maley rachamim shochen bam'romimhamtzey menuchah nechonah al kanfey haschechinah..." Although she murmurs the words almost inaudibly, I have heard them so many times now, more times than anyone should have to endure, that I know them by heart. Instinctively I feel myself muttering the words with her and slowly those around me join in. Ultimately the whole space is sonorous with vibrant prayer and the woman looks up from the face of her child to articulate, through eyes soaked with tears, her gratitude. All at once the boy's eyes flicker open. They search for those he knows best and when he finds them in her face so very close to his, they close once again for the last time. We are silent now; the sobs of the woman resonating through the open space.

Hannah tells me that the child is called Raphael; that his Spanish father perished in the Spanish Civil War and his mother returned to Germany with him to stay with her Jewish parents, once reputed jewellers, who were later rounded up and taken to the camps in the east. Raphael and his mother disappeared into hiding, soliciting the help of those who were privately against National Socialism and sympathised with the plight of the Jews. Hannah explains that poor Raphael suffered from Hodgkin's disease, a condition that she doesn't really understand, which meant he had swollen areas under his arms and around his neck, chest pain and difficulty breathing. His mother, she says, was not given a good prognosis and refused to administer the arsenic containing medicinal, suggested by a physician: a veritable poison that could slow the progress of the disease, but perhaps cause side effects that could also be deadly.

I watch Kass with a disquieting tenderness while he speaks to Raphael's mother, rubbing her back as she leans her head across the space between them to rest her forehead on his lower chest. I notice there are holes all the way up the arm of her scruffy jumper and the cuffs of her inadequate blouse are frayed. She wears trousers, like the ones I am wearing, hoisted around her tiny waist with a wide leather belt, that billow across her bottom and around her hips. These too are frayed and holey. Everyone in the warehouse is clad in insufficient clothing for state of the weather and once again I am reminded of the ghetto and how lucky I am to have escaped.

Our departure from the warehouse is via the method

of entry, only this time we are accompanied by the two men, Victor and Curt who first accosted me, carrying Raphael's body. When I finally make it onto the roof, shivering violently with cold and fear, darkness has descended. Our slippery, hazardous path is illuminated by the brightness of the snow, but I remain close to Kass at all times for his dark clothing is silhouetted against the night. Snowflakes are still falling relentlessly from the sky, although the wind that had hampered my earlier climbing escapade has died. The eerie stillness is strangely beautiful as every footprint I make is quickly covered with untouched snow. Low cloud prevents any glitter of starlight escaping its snowy sheath and the moon's silver beauty is conspicuous in its absence. I lament the dearth of light, but the men are quick to scold my naivety by reminding me that in darkness our business and our bodies remain inconspicuous. I feel foolish for my childish whims, but cannot help but wonder if the allies can still bomb Berlin through a snowstorm.

Raphael's body is wrapped in many layers of cloth. His mother had begged the men to leave him with her, but the women persuaded her that the warehouse could not accommodate his dead body without causing problems. As her deceased son departed through the window, she was led away to the other room by Ruth, stumbling to her knees in an outpouring of grief. I could not take my eyes away from her crouched form although simultaneously I could not bear to watch her pain; when it was my turn to ascend to the roof, I was almost grateful.

I am the last person to clamber into the open window of the ironmongery store. The landing is cloaked in darkness and I stumble on broken glass beneath my feet. The sound of it shattering echoes through the building and the three men stop in their tracks to stare at me in an accusatory fashion. Victor and Curt do not say goodbye to me after they dump poor Raphael's body at the front of the shop and disappear whence they came. The old shop creaks in the silence of the darkness and beyond the shattered windows an owl hoots mournfully through the snowy evening.

I think that Kass is crying when he orders me to stay in the old ironmongery and wait for him because his voice is rasping and he rubs his eyes too hard whilst he re-wraps the body in its cloths, preparing it for an unceremonious burial. I protest imploring him to let me go with him for the derelict shop seems to gently vibrate with the souls of the dead. I know it is a sin to consult the spirit world, but here I fear they may fasten themselves to me like a dybbuk; a detached spirit that can attach itself to the living, or worse, take possession of a body. I have never recovered from my good friend reading about them in the Torah and telling me all about it one day when we were snooping in Father's study. I do not know if it was the ovoths which frightened me most or the terrible scolding I received that night when she left.

Here the memory of Kristallnacht weighs heavily upon the recesses of my mind when, on the 9th and 10th November 1938, Jewish homes and businesses in Germany were ransacked by Nazi stormtroopers and buildings were destroyed with sledgehammers, leaving the streets covered in tiny fragments of shattered windows. In the Night of Broken Glass many Jews were killed and a quarter of all German Jewish men were transported to the camps in the east. After the introduction of the Nuremberg Laws in 1935, which restricted the civil liberties of the Jewish people, Kristallnacht was an act of violence which provided a small glimpse of what the Nazis were truly capable of, and a bitter insight, however slight, into the unspeakable atrocities that were to come.

Kass heaves the boy's dead body over his shoulder, dismissing my offers of help. His eyes are sunken and bleak and I have no words of comfort to offer, so I remain silent as he trudges out into the snow which is now so deep that it reaches above his knees. I watch him slowly depart, the darkness closing around him like a witch's cloak. The sounds of the night compound my sense of loneliness and unease. The scratching of mice amongst the scattered nails on the floor startles me and I spin around confronting nothing but stillness. My vision becomes more acute and I can begin to pick up more details in the gloom. Shadows sliding across the surface of the grimy walls are unnerving because I cannot find any source of light, except the brightness of the snow outside. Everything I know to be real and true in the light has a macabre notion in the darkness, for even though I find a solid wall to sit against, I still cannot dispel the sensation of spirits swimming around me; the ghosts of those, who, snatched from this world in an act of violence and resisting an untimely death, still mourn the lives they once had.

In an attempt to calm the ridiculous panic I feel in the presence of nothingness, I fix my eyes on a window catch and recite a prayer that I used to learn with my mother:

"Answer me quickly, O LORD, my spirit fails; Do not hide Your face from me, Or I will become like those who go down to the pit. Let me hear Your loving kindness in the morning; For I trust in You; Teach me the way in which I should walk; For to You I lift up my soul. Deliver me, O LORD, from my enemies; I take refuge in You."

I imagine her loving arms encircling me as I luxuriate in the lilt of her voice and the warmth of her soft skin oozing with the combined scent of her body and the perfume she wore. I feel the silk of her blouse beneath my cheek when I lean into her familiar body and inhale the moist, intoxicating air that fills the tiny gap between my nose and her soft neck when I gaze upwards to watch her lips moving as she reads.

By the time I have finished praying, reciting the prayer over and over, and conjuring a mind state of alchemy to transform my memory into reality, an extraordinary, unconscious thing has happened: for the first time, since all this began, I am crying.

Utterly powerless over this torrential grief, I howl like a small child, giving the deluge of sorrow, frustration, anger and heavy, debilitating, sadness that has been my capricious crutch for so long, freedom to leave my soul. I cry for Mother. I cry for Father, Matylda, Jurik and Michal. I cry for Viera, Agnes, Rachel, Sara and Berta. I cry for Maksym. I cry for Isabella and poor, cold Raphael. I cry for those devastated by the toil and iniquity of this war: for the Jews killed and persecuted; for the courageous men who die every day, in appalling circumstances, for their country; for the civilians inextricably bound by its complexity; and finally, ultimately, I cry for myself.

I do not know when Kass returns from burying Raphael. He pulls me to my feet, for I am incapable of standing alone, and together, arms tightly clasped around one another, we hobble away through the snow, his face also ravaged with tears.

CHAPTER SIXTEEN

Anna, 1944

I spend the next few weeks in my precarious nursing
role beside Kass whilst leaving Isabella in Lara's devoted
arms. The places we visit are often those hiding Jews in
miraculous places, but also houses where the families
of those sympathetic to the regime reside or those of
eminent Nazis themselves. Despite the fact that Kass
made it clear on our first morning together that he
would willingly answer my questions, the opportunity to
speak to him has not occurred; we are either too busy, too
tired or in a place where it is too dangerous to speak of
anything but the weather. The bombing raids on Berlin
are relentless. We spend more and more time sleeping in
the cellar, Isabella sleeping within the curves of my body,
like two perfectly shaped spoons in a cutlery drawer.
Lara snores softly on the floor next to us and more often
than not Kass is absent, though I know not where he
goes while Berlin burns beneath Allied fire. I know that
I should be frightened of the bombs and though I do not
wish any harm to be wrought upon Kass' family home,
the truth is that the bombs fill me with hope that Hitler
will be defeated and the Jews will be free.

Every morning we leave the house, trundling through
streets where the scorched fragments of buildings still
smoulder, smoke spiralling into the clear sky: a perfect

azure sky, ideal for bombing raids. People stand dismally before the shattered remains, hoping for news of survivors or grieving for their once treasured homes. Men hide their faces beneath trilby hats, tipped forward over their eyes. Sobbing is muffled by the jangle of ambulances and fire crews attempting to clear the wreckage from the pillaged roads where fallen, contorted lamp posts entwine with vehicles lying upside down amongst the rubble. The acrid smell of smoke carries on a vengeful wind whispering through the ravaged city.

Despite Kass' reservations I return to the home of Oberst Von Fleischmann. Sometimes I am escorted by Kass, but other times I go alone. I play a role which I quickly master. Mostly he requests that I read to him and our time together is predominantly pleasant and devoid of any probing conversation. Often he falls asleep to the sound of my voice, his head drooping forward, omitting a gentle snore. At this point I tiptoe from the library, making my excuses to the maid on the doorstep who is always anxious to usher me out of the door. On several occasions he has surprised me by requesting that I read English poetry to him in English. As I allow the beautiful words of Yeats, Tennyson and Byron to quietly drift over me, I wonder what the Oberst's superiors would make of this. When I chance upon one of my favourite poems and begin to read, the Oberst astounds me further by sighing and reciting the final two lines with me.

"I have spread my dreams under your feet; tread softly because you tread on my dreams... Dreams Anna," he continues wearily. The whites of his eyes are bloodshot, in deep contrast to the darkness of the irises. He looks ill and profoundly tired. "Do you believe they are worth it? My dreams are disappearing now so very quickly," he holds out his only hand to me "...like silver sand through my fingers."

I say nothing, for I know not what to say at a moment such as this.

"This war is no longer going well for Germany."

I blanch. He glances at my face, chuckling.

"Oh, yes, I know there are people who would hang me up for saying such a thing, but it is undoubtedly the truth." He rubs his right eye with his little finger. A gold signet ring gleams on the diminishing flesh below the knuckle. "The Scharnhorst is sunk; the upper hand has been taken in Africa and according to intelligence the Red Army is advancing further south-west from Leningrad and has taken back some important towns. Also we face heavy fighting in Italy."

I swallow, reminding myself of who I am when I am in this house.

"Perhaps it is only a glitch. Bad things have happened before."

"Not like this, Anna. Not like this. I had such high hopes for the Fatherland, now all I see are the shreds of greatness, the demise of a master race denied supremacy. It is... a tragedy."

I nod, unable to speak as the bulge of revulsion lodges itself in my throat, threatening to unmask my deception. I am saved by an uncommon interference from the hallway beyond the closed door. A kerfuffle of voices precedes, the bursting open of the library door, revealing a young, blond man clad in a Nazi uniform covered by a long, dark, double-breasted coat. He is instantly recognisable.

"Father!"

He crosses the room, smelling faintly of burning wood and sweat, enveloping his father in a demonstrative hug.

The Oberst, who seems to grow frailer by the day, tenses in his hard embrace, but the young man, whose harsh features are cruelly handsome, fails to notice his pain.

The Oberst's son straightens, regarding me with a roving, critical eye and a scornful smile.

"Father," he taunts, his pale blue eyes insipid above his taut, high cheekbones. "I see you have found yourself a most appealing companion. I might be tempted with her myself if she were not so horribly disfigured."

Mortified, I crush my hands around the English poetry book, thrust furtively between my thighs, to prevent my trembling hand flying to cover the unsightly scarring on my face. I stare down at the binding of the book, feeling my cheeks flush scarlet with humiliation. My dark curls cover my disgrace.

"Watch your tongue Friedrich."

The eyes of the Oberst Von Fleischmann ignite with an incandescent anger and it seems he may rise from the sofa, despite his appalling pain, to strike his only son. Disconcerted by this, I try to dismiss myself from my reading duties, but the Colonel's only hand lurches at my elbow as I begin to depart, leaving me with little choice but to stay seated beside him whilst his son turns his back, laughing derisively as he pours himself a drink from a decanter on the shiny, antique dresser below the window. Throwing himself into the seat, located at an angle to his painting above the hearth, the large whisky resting in his hand, he is clearly displeased that I have not been dismissed. The room hums with an uncomfortable silence. I focus my eyes on the ephemeral flames shooting up the chimney, wishing I could also disappear as swiftly as the smoke.

"Hartenstein rescued Friedrich."

Oberst Von Fleischmann's voice rings through the charged atmosphere, like Catholic Church bells in the silence of a Sunday morning.

"She is Hartenstein's strumpet?"

Again, I think the Colonel is going to strike his son.

"I will ask you, once again Friedrich, to watch your tongue." Oberst Von Fleischmann's thin form is shaking and I feel uncomfortable and flustered that my presence has ignited the disharmony between father and son. I want to disengage myself from this conflict but I know not how. I have no wish to antagonise the Oberst's son further.

"Anna is a nurse Friedrich and she has granted me the courtesy of reading to me during a time when I can barely lift a book."

The expression in Friedrich's eyes alters, but does not soften. His face loses its intensity, but his demeanour is more indifferent than sympathetic. I feel his eyes begin to ravage my body as Slezak's once did, then turn unexpectedly weary.

"I suppose you have told her everything." His tone is sardonic.

"I have told her nothing Friedrich."

"I wonder," Friedrich releases a contemptuous laugh, but his eyes remain closed. "How are Hartenstein's buttocks these days?"

I endeavour to keep the grains of confusion from sprinkling an honest portrayal of myself, but I have belatedly masked my deception for Oberst Von Fleischmann is eager to question me.

"Anna," he drawls a hint of amusement in his voice.

"Surely you have noticed how poor Hartenstein limps."

"Of course Oberst," I stutter, recovering my demeanour. "But I have worked with him only a short while. It would be inappropriate to ask such questions, most especially in a time of war."

"Liebe Anna, Hartenstein is fortunate to have acquired himself such a thoughtful assistant, but I believe you should know the truth about him. Hartenstein is a hero."

My mind is racing. Kass has a wound in the bottom that I have suspected but not dwelt upon, and now I am to learn more about it from a celebrated Nazi Colonel and his eminent son. I can feel a pulse beating in my disfigured cheek and hope that the Oberst cannot sense it. I stare at him in a manner of what I hope to be acquiescence. I meet the Oberst's eyes, but to my surprise it is Friedrich who speaks.

"You know what happened on the 5th December 1941?"

Now his eyes are open, glazed with the influence of the spirits; they bore into mine, threatening to overwhelm me.

I take a slow, deep breath.

"Yes, I do know... if you are referring to what happened at the Eastern Front?"

Friedrich has the good grace to look stunned. He narrows his eyes, sucking his lower left cheek between his teeth.

"If you are the expert... then you tell me."

I stare at him, thinking that if he were Italian or Hungarian he would gesticulate wildly with his hands. They lie flaccidly in his lap.

"We had M... Moscow within our sights," I stumble

over my words as my brain supersedes what I believe I can remember. "We had advanced many miles, to... to Mozhaisk through the autumn mud, then beyond despite Soviet resistance..."

Friedrich blanches as I speak and I take strength from his consternation, thanking God for the days spent at Theresienstadt preparing wood for coffins with Maksym. I thank God for his informants who were, by now, in all probability dead.

As I continue my voice rises and I am once more playing the role for which I am intended. "By December Panzer divisions were so close to Moscow that some of the Wehrmacht officers could make out many of Moscow's prominent buildings through binoculars. Moscow would soon be overcome!"

Friedrich laughs. The sound resonates through the library, over the fabric of the books and the vigour of the fire, though his voice when he speaks is flat.

"We were unprepared. We had no idea what obstacles the Russian winter would present. The cold... it penetrated your very soul. The clothing we had was inadequate despite the pleas we sent back home. Promises of winter supplies were far, far too late for what happened to us. Tell me, Liebe Anna. What happened to us?"

His voice is more pleading than disdainful now. He looks like a child, though I despise him nonetheless. I stare directly into his pale, roving eyes.

"The Soviets brought their troops from Siberia to stop you. They were fully equipped for winter warfare..."

"Yes," spat Friedrich, his former propensity for aggression burning in his eyes. "And we were halted where we stood. We were assailed by Russian fire power

219

at a time when we believed we were victorious... I was battling in the snow with my men... we had taken more Soviets than anyone else... we were doing well despite the hideous conditions and our pathetic attire. They assailed us from nowhere, clad all in white like war-mongering snowmen."

He pauses, lurching towards the dresser to pour another drink. He tips the tumbler into his open mouth, before pouring more of the amber liquor into his glass. Retreating to the chair, he leans forward, rubbing his blond eyebrows between his thumb and forefinger.

"We didn't stand a chance. One by one they came from nowhere. Our dark uniforms made us easy targets. We were surrounded in snowdrifts as one by one my men were hit. The snow was splattered with our blood. We could not hold our position. Before I could issue orders, I was attacked from behind. The brute stabbed me with his bayonet before leaving me for dead. The devil in angels' clothing..." Friedrich looks down at his front, gesticulating feebly with limp hands. "I remember my blood spurting into the soft snow before I collapsed."

Friedrich drains his glass then holds his head in his hand as though it pains him.

"The next thing I know Hartenstein is carrying me over his shoulder. I am numb. I see the Red Cross on his arm blurring with my blood. There is fire from behind us. Though there are principles against firing at an unarmed medic, Hartenstein was hit nonetheless. I remember him stumbling in the snow, dropping me, then once again hoisting me over his shoulder. I lost consciousness, waking in the field hospital. I knew Hartenstein had saved my life."

As I listen to Friedrich's story it is impossible not to

feel sympathy for him in spite of my intense dislike. I believe that the liquor has loosened his tongue; that the sober Friedrich would have painted a very different, less honest, picture of events.

"You see Anna... Hartenstein is a hero," declares Oberst Von Fleischmann proudly. "He is also a brilliant medic. When I knew I needed constant medical attention for my arm I requested that he be sent from his billet to tend to me. Now he lives in his mother's house in Berlin and tends to me. I believe his wounded buttocks would have prevented him returning to the Front in any case."

My mind is reeling. I am full of admiration for Kass Hartenstein, a man of great gallantry and honour; a man who continually sacrifices himself to save others. I calculate that Friedrich was not the only man to benefit from Kass' bravery on the battlefield. I believe he delivered many soldiers from certain death. Even now, when his front line war is over and he exists in less strenuous circumstances, he risks his life to rescue those who are persecuted by some of the very men whom he saved in battle. Kass Hartenstein is a very young man of great contradiction and, as I think of him, I feel the part of my heart reserved only for him, swell.

"Thank you for a most enjoyable afternoon, Oberst," I stutter, meeting his ebony eyes. He is fatigued. "But now, I think I should take my leave and allow you time with your son."

"As you wish liebe Anna... Please... come back soon."

He places his hand over mine, delving between my fingers to slide the poetry book surreptitiously beneath a cushion. Friedrich's eyes are closed. They fly open as my shoes click on the floor and he stumbles to his feet. The stench of whiskey on his breath makes me want to vomit and I cannot help but place a hand over my face as he wobbles close to me. He can barely stand.

"I will see young Anna to the door, Father then return to take a drink with you."

His words are slurred. I try to protest, but he staggers precariously after me, falling against the door frame. My pulse quickens as he lurches more rapidly behind me and bitter fear swells in my belly when he finally does what I know he has intended.

Friedrich's grip on my arms when he spins me around to face him is ferocious. He leers at me through glazed eyes, thrusting me upon the cold marble stairs. I fall violently and his body crushes mine. His rubbery lips slather over my scar.

A commanding voice hails from the door to the library.

"Friedrich! Leave Anna alone! Now!"

I struggle against his muscular bulk. His heavy form is sucking the air from my lungs. I try to heave him off me with my hands, but my arms are not strong enough to move him. I realise that his eyes are closed and his breathing is deep and nasal. He has passed out on top of me. I kick furiously with my legs, aiming my knee against him. He dribbles, groans then rolls off me onto a bed of jagged marble. Quivering I pull myself up and run to the door. I do not look back at Oberst Von Fleischmann as I leave his house for the last time.

I run all the way home. Kass is alone, seated by the fire, in the drawing room when I burst through the door.

"I know about Friedrich," I blurt, staring at him with blazing eyes.

"Anna!" He startles.

"I know you were a medic on the Eastern Front and you saved his life."

"The Oberst told you." He stares into the flames, avoiding my gaze.

"No," I shake my head vehemently. "Friedrich told me. You are a hero."

Kass stands. His face drains of colour. "Friedrich was there?" he asks incredulously.

I nod. "He's disgusting. He was drinking... he... he..."

Anger and fear cross Kass' face. "What Anna? What did he do to you?"

I am trembling. He holds my juddering shoulders in his wide hands, staring resolutely into my eyes. I stare back.

"I... I..."

It is impossible to tell him. Shame covers me like a shadow at dusk. I drop my gaze to stare at the buckle on his braces. Kass places his thumb tenderly below my chin.

"Did he hurt you?"

"I was trying to leave... he followed me... he assaulted me on the stairs, but the Colonel saw him and shouted... I couldn't breathe underneath him... he passed out drunk on top of me."

"Oh Anna..."

Kass pulls me into his arms, hugging me tightly. I succumb to his secure embrace, allowing the tears to fall.

When I pull away to wipe my nose, I see anxiety in Kass' eyes.

"What?"

He smiles at me sadly, pushing me gently backwards into the chair he has just vacated. The flames from the fire reflect in his eyes. He appears dishevelled and weary, his blond curls tousled like a child roused from sleeping. I feel a sense of foreboding.

"What?" I demand. "Please tell me."

Kass sighs, closing his eyes tightly. He throws his head back, grimacing before he speaks.

"I believe we have been betrayed..."

"Ww... what?" I stammer. "What does that mean?"

"I was sent word today of a betrayal that has filtered back to the Reich. I believe Friedrich was the recipient of this information and I believe that today he went to his Father's house to inform him."

"Bb... but he said nothing. I was there the whole time. He drank liquor, talked about Moscow then tried to molest me. Nothing untoward was said."

"Did he seem disappointed by your presence?"

"More intensely irritated. I wanted to leave as soon as he arrived, but I did not want to appear suspicious. Perhaps I betrayed myself."

"No Anna. If he had been drinking Friedrich would not have noticed your unease, and sober he would have revelled in it. He is an arrogant, vicious bully. Anyway by the time you were there it would already have been too late. Friedrich already knew there were individuals helping Jews close by, forging papers etc. There is nothing you could have done differently."

"Do you think he knows that it is you?"

Kass sighs, pinching the bridge of his nose.

"There is no way of knowing, but I believe I can bluff my way out of it. The trail is complicated and I do not think Friedrich will point the finger at me because of our shared history and his Father's favour."

"But you think they suspect me, don't you?" I whisper, my voice shaking.

Kass nods.

I stand up, exasperated. "But surely if the trail leads to me then it in turn, leads to you, to G, to Lara, to... to Isabella...?" My heart quickens with concern for my child.

"Isabella will be safe. I can ensure that."

"How?"

"I just can. Lara too, she has been my housekeeper for a long while now."

"But," I whimper. "You cannot protect me?"

Kass bows his head. "No," he whispers. "I am so sorry Anna."

I bite my lip, swallowing back the tears again like before, trapping the howling beast to give me strength to endure what I must.

"What will happen to me?" I sit back in the chair by the fire, wringing my hands; my face burns. "Must I leave?"

Kass doesn't answer immediately.

"A friend of G's will be driving to the coast tomorrow. He has friends in important places so border patrols will not pose a threat. He will carry enough fuel for the entire trip. From there you will board a boat to England where you will be met by my English cousin, Josephine. You will stay with her until the war is over. You will be safe."

"What about Isabella?" I whimper, searching his

desolate face for answers. "Will I ever see her again?"

"Yes," Kass nods vigorously, grasping my trembling hands tightly in his own. He gazes earnestly into my eyes as though he is begging me to believe him. I am struck once again by how very young he is; how very young we both are: children spat into adulthood by the savage jaws of war. I want to cry: why me? But I think of those still imprisoned in Theresienstadt and languishing in the certain hell of the camps in the East, and I know that to ask why is both futile and ungrateful. I am alive.

"When this wretched war is finally over, I will bring her to you." He leans his face close to mine. I can feel his warm, rapid breath on my lips.

He murmurs. "I will come back to you Anna." He pauses. "I... I want you to marry me."

Kass' voice cracks. He stares deeply into my eyes, kissing my lips. My mouth opens, embracing the exquisite tenderness of his tongue. My body burns with longing as I surrender to the man I love, kissing him with every agonising moment of my existence etched on my lips. A sound from beyond the door rouses us to the present. Kass cups my face in his hands, then lowers his face into my hands resting in my lap, kissing them also. I feel his tears trickling over my knuckles. My heart fragments with love for him. I bury my face in his hair. My lips are burning. He smells so distinctively like himself that I have to cleave my stomach in firmly and hold my breath to control my anguish. I breathe deeply, imploring my racing heart to be still.

CHAPTER SEVENTEEN

"SO that is how you came to be England!" Theo declared. "What a life."

Anna said nothing and for a while they sat in silence, depleted by the efforts of speaking and listening, allowing the sound of the wind and the gravity of the truth to wash over them.

Finally, with a voice full of awe, Theo said, "You must be special."

Anna stared at him with sad, steady eyes, shaking her silvery head.

"People like to congratulate themselves Theo, if life is kind to them: if they secure themselves a loving partner, children, a job they enjoy, money. But life, in the main, is a game of luck. Am I here because I was chosen from the masses who were massacred? Is pretty Mrs Read, who lives opposite me, happily married with two thriving boys and one adorable, healthy little girl because she is more special than anyone else? No. Nobody is chosen or special; they are simply lucky or hard-working. One shouldn't look down on others because they are different or less fortunate or inhibited by the grenades life has thrown at them; no, one should take a long hard look in the mirror and just be thankful."

Theo realised she was right.

"Did he come back for you?" Theo asked his voice cracking.

He saw Anna's eyes glaze with tears. They settled in the valley above her scrawny cheek before finally succumbing to gravity and coursing over her powdery face.

She shook her head.

"Why?" demanded Theo incredulously. "He said he wanted to marry you. He said he'd bring Isabella back to you!"

Anna nodded, unable to speak.

Theo jumped up, staring hard at her as though the answers would magically emerge, imprinted on her forehead.

"It doesn't make any sense."

Anna swallowed, then began to cough. She coughed so hard that Theo thought her insides would erupt from her mouth. He waited for the hacking to subside.

"At the time it made no sense to me either. I waited, living with his kindly cousin Josephine, for him to return. After the war was over and he didn't come for me, I fell deeper into despair. Eventually Josephine came to me one morning with a letter in her hand. She was shaking and could not speak as she handed it to me. Instantly I knew it was from him."

"What did it say?"

Anna shrugged, her eyes settling on Theo's bandaged wrist. He belatedly pulled his jumper down over the dressing, but she was already frowning hard at him.

"It said that he loved me," began Anna. "It said that he would always love me..." Her voice was gripped with emotion, tears rolled unfettered down her old face. She took great gulps of air as she tried to compose herself enough to continue.

"It said, it said..." She dabbed at her eyes with crooked fingers. "It said that our relationship would never be tolerated in any community in Europe. He said he couldn't come to England because he was German and had fought on the side of the Nazis. He said I shouldn't return to Europe because a marriage between a Jew and a seemingly patriotic German who had close connections to influential members of the Nazi regime, most of whom were now being rightfully tried as war criminals, would not be accepted. It said he would not condemn me to a half-life where we were taunted and shunned by those ignorant of the truth. It said he would always love me."

"But that's just tragic," declared Theo in disbelief. "Surely they would have understood if you explained that he had saved you. If you had stayed in Theresienstadt you would have almost certainly have been sent to Auschwitz or somewhere, then gassed. Kass rescued you. You are here now because of him."

"Yes Theo, of course you are right, but those were different times. People would not want to listen to the truth. Fear can lead to prejudice and prejudice to cruelty. I think everything he said was probably right. I think he was acting in my best interests."

"But it must have hurt," insisted Theo in a small voice.

"Oh yes," breathed Anna. "It hurt every day. But I did what I had always done."

"What?"

"I buried it."

"What about Isabella?"

"She stayed with Kass. She was happy with him and

Lara by then. She could probably barely remember me." Anna began to cry again. Theo watched with concern as the tears got trapped in the craggy furrows of her neck.

"They stayed in Berlin?"

"No," Anna sighed. "Josephine received a letter saying they were moving to a different part of Germany in the aftermath of the war so that Kass could continue his medical training. There was no forwarding address. It also said he had searched for Isabella's real father and discovered he had been blown up during the war."

"That was the last she heard of him?"

"Yes."

"What did you do?"

Anna leant her weary head backwards, closing her eyes against the weak sunlight spilling onto the floorboards.

"I let my grief drive me. I lived with dear Josephine and attended medical school."

"You actually fulfilled your childhood dream of being a doctor?" Theo's voice was full of awe.

"Yes, I worked very, very hard." Anna's face was grim.

"Did you ever get married?"

"No Theo, there was no man for me other than Kass. He was the love of my life; if I couldn't be with him then I would be alone. I certainly couldn't marry, although I was asked on several occasions."

"You were beautiful?"

"Perhaps," she shrugged. "But my cheek was a mess. Perhaps people used to stare at me because I was beautiful, now they look at me because I am not."

"Didn't you want children?"

"Oh yes. I had a daughter."

Theo was incredulous. "Did you?"

"Yes," Anna was matter of fact. "In those days it was a dreadful scandal: a child out of wedlock."

"Oh. I didn't realise."

"Well how could you? I haven't told you about her yet. I loved my daughter dearly, but I was a poor mother. Still consumed by a grief I could not acknowledge and by my work, I was only really half there; half a mother. In the end, Thea got fed up with it. She was confused and hurt. In her teens she started hating me and eventually went to live with Josephine. I tried tirelessly to make it up to her, to get her to speak to me but she refused. She married at a young age and simply vanished from my life."

"That's awful."

"Yes," agreed Anna. "It was. I missed her terribly and what was tragic is that I had no one to blame but myself. I still miss her. I was great at helping others, but I couldn't help my own daughter and I could not help myself. I was locked in the prison of a continuous cycle of grief that I could not break. I am still doing teshuvah."

"What is that?" Theo asked, thinking that it sounded like a Jewish thing.

"It means repent."

Theo nodded. "You are still repenting your sins?"

"Yes, I let Thea down despite loving her more than anything. None of it was her fault."

"Do you believe in fate Anna?" Theo asked in a solemn, sad voice.

Anna released air from her mouth like a balloon deflating slowly. "I do not know. Jews do not believe that it applies to them; we believe God has it all worked out for us."

"Do you think that is true? Someone told me that we are all exactly where we are meant to be; that the universe is unfolding as it should."

"Isn't that the same thing?"

"I don't know..." murmured Theo slowly. "I hadn't thought of it like that."

They were silent for a moment before Anna began to cough again. Theo refused to watch her as he waited for her to recover.

"Theo?"

"Yes."

He felt her unwavering eyes upon him; felt the imprint of her stare on his face.

"I believe we should be honest with each other."

"We are," Theo began, feeling blood thudding in his temple. "Aren't we?"

Anna shrugged.

"I've seen your arm... the other arm."

He didn't look at her. He pretended not to have heard what she had said. The blood in his veins seemed to stop and freeze. His mind searched for the right lie to tell her. She pressed on.

"I'm a doctor, but I didn't tell you what kind of doctor, did I?"

"No," Theo huffed, scuffling his feet on the floor. "But I think you are about to..."

"Don't be sarcastic Theo, it doesn't suit you. I'm a psychiatrist."

"Shit!" Theo groaned tapping his forehead repeatedly with a closed fist.

"No, actually I was quite good."

"What?"

"Nothing, never mind," Anna touched him very gently on the arm. Theo could feel the essence of her running through his skin. The unflinching, bound layers contorted within him began to uncurl with a flood of emotion that made him gulp suddenly.

"Look the point is," she continued. "The point is that I know you've been hurting yourself on purpose."

Theo stopped moving. He could not breathe. The layers twisted and writhed; every fibre of his body resonated with a shame that rendered him stagnant.

"There is a wound under those bandages that you inflicted upon yourself isn't there?"

Theo said nothing; not because he didn't want to but because he couldn't.

"You can tell me the truth Theo. You can trust me. There is isn't there?"

Eventually, Theo nodded. Did she know? Did she get it? Did she understand that the only escape from the suffocating noise and agony inside his head was to transfer the pain, however fleetingly, to the outside of his body? Did she know it was a blessed relief to concentrate on something else, on the blood and the horror of what he could do to himself?

"Because of the baby?" Anna asked gently.

Once again, Theo nodded. He closed his eyes; tears spurted through the thick lashes.

"Did you slash your arm in the woods that day because of the baby too?"

"I did it..." he wailed, rocking back and forth. Anna watched him with steady eyes.

"Did what Theo?" she asked softly, laying a compassionate hand upon his shoulder.

"I... I..." Theo's voice cracked. "I killed her."

For a while nobody moved whilst the gravity of what Theo had said rolled back and forth between them.

"How do you know?" asked Anna. There was no trace of judgement in her tone.

Theo was flustered. He glared at her angrily. "I just do. She was crying, alright? I hated her, but I hated the sound of her screaming more. I hated the thought of her being unhappy."

"What did you do?" Anna's voice was level.

Theo stared at her, looking for some kind of reproach or loathing in her face. He found none.

"I gave her a cuddle." The statement was weak and final.

"Just a cuddle?"

"Yes," Theo seethed. "I told you. I cuddled her, she fell asleep on me; I put her back in her cot and a few minutes later my mum was screaming. She was dead. I killed her."

CHAPTER EIGHTEEN

Theo, February 2010

IT was in the moment he heard his mother scream that Theo knew he had killed his baby sister.

Instantly he wanted to rewind time to the minutes before, when the only sound in the otherwise silent house was the irritating tick of the superhero clock that still hung on his elder brother Sebastian's bedroom wall. As Theo lay on his bed in the tiny box room, which was too small for more than a single wardrobe, reading his war books, his mother was sleeping downstairs on the sofa. He was glad of it because since the baby had been born she seemed agitated and exhausted.

"Mum's asleep," he had told Seb who was studying at the desk in his room. It was as though an explosion had taken place above it, depositing wrappers, empty cups and screwed up pieces of paper all over it. One of the cups had fallen over and was seeping black coffee over the pages of an open chemistry book. Seb was a genius, but he was also the most untidy person Theo had ever met. He had to clear away the debris just to get the bedroom door open.

"Where's Eden then?" murmured Seb, his eyes scanning the screen of his laptop as his fingers tapped furiously at the grubby keyboard.

"Asleep in her cot," Theo replied, cautiously kicking at a pair of crumpled boxer shorts that lay at his feet.

"Finally!" Seb marvelled. "Sometimes I wonder if that baby will ever sleep. She's gorgeous and all that, but her screaming gets on my nerves."

"She can't help it," muttered Theo, surprising even himself with the defensive tone of his voice. "She's only tiny. All babies cry don't they?"

"What? You've changed your tune. Thought you couldn't stand her," scoffed Seb glancing at him suspiciously. Theo looked down at his feet, focusing on the hole in his sock through which his big toe was escaping. "Anyway," Seb continued, screwing up pieces of scrap paper. "Last night it was so bad, I fell asleep with my earphones in. Get out of here, I need to learn this."

Theo sighed, yanking the door shut. Seb didn't know how lucky he was to be going away from this place. He had secured a place at Oxford University to study Biochemistry, a feat that the family could still hardly believe. He was all consumed by it. Theo yearned to talk to him about stuff, but it was like he had already left home in his head.

Theo was reading a book about the D-day landings when he heard Eden begin to moan. He tried to ignore it, struggling with feeling annoyed and concerned all at once. Eventually concern won him over and he trundled into her bedroom. The blind was closed. She was lying on a pink sheet, swathed in a pink blanket. Theo stared down at her; this creature whose arrival he had resented so bitterly. She whimpered piteously, meeting his stare with her wide, navy eyes. Theo sighed and picked her up. Perhaps she would settle if he gave her a quick cuddle. Perhaps he wouldn't need to wake his mother up. Eden snuggled into the warmth of his body, rubbing her nose on his shoulder. The feeling was alien to Theo, because he had barely touched her since she had been born, but not unwelcome. Strangely he felt she needed him, despite the uneasiness she ignited in the pit of his stomach. He knew nothing about babies, but it didn't seem right that she cried all the time.

Contorting his neck to a strange angle, Theo glanced down at her face. Her eyes were closed and her body moved with the rhythm of her breath. He felt oddly satisfied that she had found comfort in his arms and he gently leaned forward to place her sweet-smelling form on the soft sheet. He tiptoed out of the room to continue reading about amphibious landing craft.

Theo didn't hear his mother's footsteps on the stairs or the bedroom door brush across the carpet. What he heard was a cry that would, in time to come, wake him from his sleep at night. He and Seb collided in the doorway to Eden's bedroom, staring aghast as their mother tried to wake the sleeping baby. She was almost deranged as she desperately pulled the clothes from her daughter's chest.

"Ring an ambulance," she whispered. Her entire body was shaking. Theo and Seb were rooted to the spot.

"I SAID RING AN AMBULANCE."

This time their mother stared at them from a face they didn't recognise. Her eyes were wide with an emotion so raw it was terrifying to behold. Theo backed away onto the landing, towards the phone that sat on the windowsill in her bedroom. He dialled the emergency services and asked for an ambulance without hearing the voice on the other end at all. Instead he could hear Seb sobbing and pleading with his mother.

"Mum, Mum, I think she's gone."

"Mum, let me look at her... Mum..."

Theo returned to find his mother perched on the side of the bed, fiercely clutching Eden's inert body to her breast. Seb was kneeling at her feet, his face against the baby's side. Theo thought he was trying to detect a heartbeat.

"Ring Jon," Seb murmured, his terrified eyes darting over Theo's face, as if disgusted by his presence.

"The ambulance is coming."

Theo felt as though his voice was coming from somewhere else; as though he was watching himself from within the body of another.

"Theo." Seb was trembling, his eyes glazed with panic. "I said ring Jon."

Theo disappeared again. Once more clutching the phone in his clammy hand as he spoke to his stepfather in a voice that wasn't his, in words he could not remember.

The ambulance arrived and paramedics invaded the house. Theo tried to return to his mother, but the door was closed in his face, by a spectacled man who did not seem to see him. Muffled voices carried through the closed door, but he could not understand them. Panic rose in his throat like bile. Surely they would be out to get him soon. Somebody would work out that he had been the last one to see Eden alive, that he had been the last one to hold her; that he, Theo Drew, had accidentally killed her.

He ran to the bathroom and retched into the toilet, vomiting until nothing remained in his curdled stomach. Grabbing a towel to wipe his face, he belatedly realised he had used Eden's baby towel. It was still damp from her morning bath. He dropped it like a timed incendiary device.

Theo heard the front door open and charged down the stairs. Jon, his usually merry eyes clouded with dread, passed him on the second step. He touched Theo's head briefly as Theo sank down on the step.

"It's alright son."

Theo stared after his bulky form, knowing that they both knew he was wrong on two counts: it wasn't going to be alright and he wasn't his son.

It seemed a lifetime had passed before Eden's bedroom door opened and his mother and Jon followed the paramedics outside. Jon seemed to be carrying his mother who was still clasping the baby wrapped in a bundle of pink blankets. She didn't look like his mother anymore. Her face was ravaged and her glassy, staring eyes were bulbous and dead. He couldn't look at her.

Sebastian appeared at Theo's side, sliding down onto the stairs next to him. For a while neither of them spoke. Eventually Seb grabbed his arm. There was so much force behind the gesture that Theo had to bite his lip so that he didn't cry out in pain.

"She's dead," Seb stuttered. He choked on the words, coughing as the tears coursed down his face. "She's bloody dead Theo. Mum's precious daughter... Can you bloody believe it?"

Theo couldn't speak. He couldn't believe it. It was beyond belief. He looked at Seb. He had never seen his brother like this before. He watched as his body convulsed in grief, emanating a sound that was primal. It scared him; not because he didn't know what to do, which he didn't, but because he couldn't feel anything himself. There was nothing inside; just a gaping, cavernous hole where everything he once felt had been.

A memorial service was held for Eden. Her body had not yet been released by the coroner, as the cause of death could not be agreed by the pathologists. Jon had spoken to the boys explaining that he intended to hold a memorial service so that people could come and pay their respects to the family. He believed that the delay in the release of the body was having a detrimental effect on their mother; he hoped that the memorial service might bring her out of her silence.

Theo sat next to Seb and Jon in the first line of pews in the huge church that was filled to the brim with mourners. Theo hated church. God scared him. He didn't make sense to him. Why would he let all the wars happen? Why would he let Eden die? If God existed then Theo was very angry with him indeed. He thought everyone else should be too.

The vicar droned on about Eden. He had never met her, but he seemed to be an expert in spite of it. Theo couldn't bear to listen to him. Eden was just a baby who had tragically died because he had given her a cuddle, one cold February afternoon. What could this fat guy in a dress possibly know about that? How could he understand how it felt to live in a soundless house with a mother who didn't speak or cry or move from her bed? Did he know that Jon would sit behind the ancient coal shed in the garden, on the pile of old bricks, smoking illicit cigarettes and weeping softly into the sleeve of his jacket? Could he hear the silence of the night broken by Seb wailing in his sleep? Did he know that Theo hardly slept at all and that when he did fall into an exhausted stupor, dreams of Eden's dead form hung before his closed eyes? No. Nobody here in this ostentatious building could possibly know that. Nobody would ever understand anything about them ever again.

Seb was weeping quietly beside him. Theo saw the tears drop onto the dark fabric of his trousers and seep away. He wanted to touch Seb, but he didn't know how so he balled his hands into fists so that the nails hurt his palms. The pain was oddly soothing; at least he could feel it. On his other side, Jon held his mother. This gentle, dark-haired man may not be his biological father, but he was the closest he and Seb had to a dad. He was inordinately kind to both of them, patient and understanding, almost to a fault. Sometimes it made Theo want to scream, but he knew this was because he feared that Jon loved him far more than his mother did. He wished he was his real father and hated him because he wasn't.

Theo stole a glance at his mother. Her form was completely still. She did not crumple into Jon's arms, but remained rigid, like a statue. Theo wished that blood would flow from her eyes like it did from the statue in a film that Seb had once forced him to watch; at least then he would know there was some kind of hope. In the film it had signified a miracle of some sort. Theo thought that was exactly what they needed.

The vicar stopped talking and his grandmother tottered forward to the pulpit. She carefully climbed the steps in black, shiny heels and a skirt that clung to thick black tights above her knee. Makeup hung from folds of skin on her face. The feather on her hat pointed into the sombre air. She cleared her throat, daintily.

"My daughter," she chanted to the assembled crowd, "has done something that no mother should ever do – she has outlived her child. Not just any child, but her own daughter; a daughter that she has wished for, dreamed about, cherished. Today she must say goodbye to her dearest, dearest Eden when she has hardly had chance to even murmur hello." She paused to ensure the congregation were in rapture of her words, moving a tendril of dyed, straw-like hair away from her thin, fuchsia lips. "My Sophia was a perfect mother to her daughter Eden. She is also a perfect daughter.

"As mother and daughter we have never dealt in trickery and lies. We share an affinity in everything..."

Theo couldn't bear to listen anymore. His heart pounded in his ears, drowning out the monotonous whine of his grandmother's voice: how she aggravated him. Why was she bleating about trickery and lies? She was rattling on about her own life again; even in death she was selfish. It had nothing to do with Eden, nothing at all. He could see that Seb had covertly put his thumbs in his ears as he held his face in his hands. He found her insufferable too.

Although she almost ignored Theo, Seb did not easily escape her attention. Basking in Seb's superior intellect, she lavished excessive, wholly unwanted, affection on him. She would regale him with tales about how she was also gifted and special, but that her mother had held her back from greatness with her pernicious lies and jealousy. Seb suffered her attentions, but spent hours lounging on Theo's bed moaning about her. They had never met Nana Dora's mother and Seb longed to find out more about her. His innate inquisitiveness seemed to go hand in hand with his advanced intellect. Theo didn't care. He listened to Seb's theories about their weird family, their capricious mother, their absent father, with irritation. It mounted in him a loathing, a fury that scared him, rather than a detached curiosity. Theo couldn't let things go;

243

they festered inside him like spores of mould.

Nana Dora finally finished her speech with an inappropriate poem.

"I only know that summer sang in me, a little while, that in me sings no more."

Seb hissed in Theo's ear, "Stupid woman, this one isn't about death or Eden, it's about her! She could've at least have had the decency to do 'And you as well must die, beloved dust'. How is this ever going to help Mum? As usual she's just making more problems."

Theo raised his eyebrows in agreement, although he knew nothing about poetry. He opened his hymnbook upside down so that he could pretend to sing 'Blest are the pure in heart'. Nana Dora tried to hug her daughter as she passed, but for once Sophia was unyielding to her affection. She stared relentlessly, unblinking at the altar where a solitary candle burned upon a gold-encrusted, ivory table cloth. An immense stained glass window, depicting Christ's expulsion into the desert, presided over it; a clear signal to all that it was essential to do God's bidding.

When the service was over, everyone filed out of church behind the family. Theo's black shoes creaked as he walked slowly behind Nana Dora over the icy flagstones. He looked at the ancient headstones that sat at awkward angles in a disorderly fashion throughout the graveyard. Shuddering involuntarily, he hoped that his mother and Jon would not choose to bury Eden. Theo could not bear to think of the worms and insects crawling over her little body. The appalling thought caused an explosion of raw emotion to course through his veins like adrenaline. Theo was momentarily eclipsed by it. Seb pushed him forward into the car.

"Are you alright, mate?"

"Yeah." Theo rubbed his eyes.

They bundled into the back seat, sliding over the leather.

"Are you sure? You look like you've seen a ghost!"

"I'm fine," Theo insisted abruptly, resting his head backwards and closing his eyes. The tears hadn't come. Would they ever come?

The house was teeming with people when they arrived back. Nana Dora had arranged for outside caterers to prepare a buffet. Seb grumbled that if she had really wanted to help then she should have done the wake at her house so that they wouldn't have to clear up. Soggy sausage rolls and cucumber sandwiches rubbed alongside slabs of dry fruit cake. The sight of it made Theo's stomach turn over. He edged through the throng of people, most of whom he had never met before and unlocked the back door which led into the garden. Taking gulps of icy air, he settled down on Jon's pile of smoking bricks. It was hidden away from the back of the house. He wished everyone would just leave them in peace. The whole memorial thing didn't seem to be helping his mother at all: she had charged through the front door, straight upstairs to her bedroom, slamming the door behind her, leaving a bewildered Jon on the doorstep.

Theo heard the back door squeak as it opened again. There were footsteps on the path followed by the sound of heaving sobs. It was Jon. Theo was embarrassed. Part of him wanted to hug him, but he didn't know how. Instead he remained rooted to the spot as the door opened again. This time he heard Nana Dora's voice,

"Oh, Jonny, you poor, poor darling," she crooned.

Jon sniffed and gulped air. "I don't know what to do Dora," he sobbed. "She won't talk to me. She won't talk to anyone. Even you! It's like she died too. I can't bear it. I lost my daughter, my beautiful, baby daughter, I can't lose my wife too; I can't!"

Theo felt the blood freeze in his veins. This was entirely his fault. He should surely tell the truth, but how could he when they would hate him for it? Misery hung over him like a damp fog. How could he disappoint his mother even more than he did already? There would be no hope for him with her then. She would be lost to him forever. Once again he felt the heavy burden of guilt immobilise him.

"It's only been days Jonny," insisted Nana Dora. Even the sound of her voice grated on Theo's nerves. "She'll come back to us."

"But she doesn't even cry; she just sits there in that bloody room."

"The loss is too much for her."

"It's my loss too."

"Yes, but for her it's different."

"Why is it different? I loved Eden too."

"I know that and she knows that. But it is different for Sophia because this was her daughter. She had longed for her for so many years; trying not to be disappointed by having one boy and then another. Then finally she met you and Eden was born. She was satisfied at last."

"The boys are great." Jon's tone was defensive. "She loves them."

"I know she does darling..." soothed Nana Dora. "Especially Seb; but it's not the same you know! Every woman needs a daughter. I've been telling her that for years."

The fury bubbled in Theo like molten lava. He made two balls with his fists, squeezing them tightly so that the nails cut into his palms. He had listened to her telling his mother this over and over again for as long as he could remember. They would sit together at the kitchen table as Nana Dora offered Sophia warped advice about her life. Oblivious to Seb and Theo listening from where they were perched at the breakfast bar, Nana Dora would drone on in a theatrical whisper.

"You need a daughter darling. I won't live forever you know."

"Mummy, how can I possibly have a daughter when I don't have a husband," insisted Sophia, staring into the depths of her coffee cup.

"We need to find you one!"

"They don't grow on trees. I can't just pick one!"

"If you went to that dance class I told you about, I'm sure you'd meet someone."

"I don't want just 'someone', Mummy. I did that last time and look where that got me – divorced with two boys. Hardly ideal is it?"

"There's time!"

"So you keep telling me," Sophia would answer in a tired voice.

"You'll get there. Your looks will ensure it."

Sophia would cast a glance at herself in the mirror, rubbing her hand over the smooth skin on her face and into the mass of dark curls that fell below her shoulders. She was indeed beautiful.

Sophia sighed. "I'm sorry I've been such a disappointment to you Mummy; I have tried."

Seb scribbled a note on Theo's English book. It read, "So have we!!!!!!"

Theo charged past his stepfather and grandmother, knocking a load of bricks from the pile. They tumbled to the concrete floor with a violent crash. He couldn't do it anymore. He felt like a ticking bomb. The timer was clicking round and round, monitoring the minutes left before his guilt was finally uncovered. These were his moments of freedom before he was chained in cuffs by some policeman, but he didn't feel free. He felt shackled by guilt, held captive by the icy hand of fear that seemed to grapple at his throat, constricting his airway. He was already imprisoned.

"Theo!" Jon called as he streaked past him.

"Leave him," declared Nana Dora. "You can't

do anything. You're not his father. He's not your responsibility."

"Of course he is," insisted Jon irritably. "Those boys need me. You're interfering in things again, Dora. You promised you wouldn't do that. I've told you before how I feel about those boys..."

Theo didn't hear anymore. He had made his decision. He was going upstairs to tell his mother the truth. The burden of guilt was crushing him and he had to get rid of it even if she never spoke to him again or sent him to rot in jail. His mouth was parched as he slowly climbed the stairs. He had to force himself to put one foot in front of the other. He was breathing hard as he found himself confronted with his mother's bedroom door. His heart hammered in his chest, pounding a beat that was deafening to his ears. Nausea clung to his stomach. He lifted his trembling hand to knock at the door, but instead of completing the movement he froze with his hand in mid-air. Swallowing twice, he tried again, but his brain would not send the signal to his arm. He stood on the landing quivering from head to foot, just staring at the door.

He couldn't do it. He was a coward. He couldn't tell his mother the truth. He couldn't confess to killing Eden. A surge of savage anger began to veil his fear. He threw his body forward, brutally head-butting the doorframe. Pain coursed through his head; he felt dizzy and disorientated. Swaying dangerously from side to side he stumbled into his bedroom and collapsed in a crumpled heap on the bed.

CHAPTER NINETEEN

Theo, February 2010

ON the morning after the memorial service, Theo crawled out of bed early after another sleepless night. He was relieved that it was half term and he didn't have to go to school. School was torturous at the best of times; today it would be unbearable. His head ached from where he had head-butted the door frame and a quick glance in the bathroom mirror revealed an enormous, ugly bruise on his forehead. He felt stupid. The green and purple lump covered the width of his brow.

The house was still silent. He hurried down the stairs, grabbing his tattered trainers and winter coat from the murky cupboard under the stairs, and headed out into the gloomy February dawn. The icy air was a welcome friend. Theo took several deep breaths before breaking into a run towards the seafront. He knew he wouldn't be missed at home. They were all too absorbed in their own problems to worry about him. Seb wouldn't even come out of his room until midday when he would take a break from studying to grab a sandwich, and Jon was due back at work today. He had wanted to take more time off with Sophia, but owning a shop and being self-employed, it just wasn't possible. Theo knew that the chances of his mother surfacing from her bed at any point were acutely slim, even with her meddling mother inevitably hovering around the house.

Theo yearned to be where he always wanted to be when he needed to time to think; at the beach. More than anything Theo loved the sea. It was his constant companion in good times and bad, soothing him with its formidable power. Stormy days were his favourite, when the wind stole the breath from his lips and the salt clung to his stinging cheeks. Today was laced with a bitter cold that permeated the eerie calm that seemed to settle over the assorted rooftops. As he climbed up the grassy bank onto the grey shingle, the steely sky upon the horizon cast a faint line over a sea of polished silver. It shimmered in the stillness of the morning. Gulls arched over the beach calling to each other as they swooped down to feed from the surface of the water. Dark, wet sand fell away from the shingle as the falling tide left gifts of translucent rock pools and revealed a jungle of jagged pebbles that stretched along the sand as far as the eye could see.

Theo crunched over the shingle, heading for the bench where he always sat. The panic and anger within his gut jostled for dominance, leaving him jittery and nauseous. The sea could not calm him as it usually did. Instead he was left with a feeling of mindless desolation.

What was his life worth now that he had killed Eden? What did he have to look forward to apart from an existence in some sordid prison being beaten and worse by the dregs of society? The dregs, among whom he now counted. Icy fear clutched at his heart as he imagined filthy, bulging men leering at him as prison officers led him to his cell. His fate seemed unavoidable after his heinous crime. What options were left to him now, apart from running away? He could leave today, but where would he go? He didn't know anyone, even vaguely, that he could run to. Theo thought about his biological father, but he knew it was a wasted thought because he was useless and had never even cared enough to send a birthday card. He could hitch a lift to London or another city like kids he had watched in movies, but he knew he wouldn't last long sleeping rough on the streets. Martial arts had never been his thing so his only defence would be to slash at someone with the penknife that nestled in his coat pocket.

Burrowing his hand amongst old receipts and crisp packets, Theo grasped hold of the knife. The casing was smooth like ivory. He rubbed it with his thumb enjoying the way it felt across the pad of fleshy skin. Theo had found it at the bottom of one of Seb's drawers several months ago when his mother was floundering beneath the weight of her pregnancy and Theo was helping her out by putting the clean clothes away. He didn't usually snoop through Seb's stuff because he would hate it if Seb did the same to him, but he had seen the marbled effect of the knife casing sticking out through pairs of Seb's odd socks. The shiny item winked at him, taunting Theo to satisfy his curiosity. Plunging his hand beneath the socks, he merely glimpsed at the knife and slid it into his pocket before Seb came out of the bathroom. The lock on the door unlatched just as Theo, his body coursing with guilt and adrenaline, was throwing the knife into the back of his wardrobe for later inspection.

The knife seemed to pulsate in his hand as though it was alive. The beat of the blood in his palm throbbed with his desire to submit to the temptation of the blade offering itself to his culpable skin. Theo flicked the knife open. He rubbed his index finger lightly across the blade. It was sharp he knew, for he had used the knife sharpener in the kitchen to whet the blade. He remembered the satisfaction of hearing the metal writhing against the rock as he rolled the knife back and forth across the worktop. When he had finished he had removed a tomato from the fridge and practised cutting it. The blade had sliced effortlessly through the skin, easing through the flesh of the fruit to its fluid core. Theo had smiled with satisfaction as a perfect slice hit the plate.

Theo began to shake as he eyed the knife with awe and trepidation. He licked his lips, but the saliva seemed to be absent from his tongue. Prison and leaving, he knew, weren't the only answers to his crime. The knife offered answers of its own. The magnificence of the blade could not only obliterate the utter desolation with a pain so violent it was overwhelming, but it could also deliver the promise of oblivion. Theo knew this in his gut for he had imagined the moment a hundred times before.

He dropped the knife into his lap, pressing the sweaty palms of his hands over his eyes. The pressure formed a vacuum of nothingness. Theo tried to empty his mind and focus on the void of darkness. Would death be like this, without thought or feelings? Would he have a soul that would depart from his body to live forever in purgatory, as some religious people suggested, constantly replaying his crimes of murder and suicide, until he begged the devil to deliver him to hell? No. There would be nothing, he decided, exhaling a deep breath that he did not know he had been holding. There would be nothing but an escape from this world that could offer him no more than he could offer it. He wasn't good enough for the happy things, and he could no longer see the beautiful things. A butterfly was just an insect; the prey of a bird after a hasty snack.

His family, he knew, would be better off without him. At least if he had the courage to kill himself then his mother would know that he was more than the average criminal. She would be saved the agony of hating him and the years of his incarceration. She would know that in killing himself he had done the right thing by relieving the world of his shameful presence. At least through death, he was paying in the same way Eden had. The difference being that she had been blameless. He could no longer censure her for taking away his mother's love because he knew with an absolute certainty that he had never deserved it in the first place. Maybe Sophia had known that.

Theo hauled the sleeve of his coat up to his elbow, staring at the perfect white skin that seemed almost translucent in the silvery light. The bulky material of his coat limited the movement of his left arm as he ran the blade of the knife over the sensitive crease of his wrist as though it was the long nail of his mother's index finger. He saw his hand trembling and the dirt present beneath one of his finger nails. He saw his knuckle tighten in anger around the casing of the knife.

What a coward he was even now, with death breathing down his neck. Theo knocked his knuckles painfully upon his forehead before shoving the open penknife into his coat pocket. In his clenched fist, he held the blade as he turned his back on the ocean and headed to the line of trees that stood behind him. Sprinting over the stones, his feet spat pebbles that filled his shabby shoes and made it painful for him to run. Increasing his speed Theo wondered at the question they were often asked at school: were people born evil or made that way? Now, in his final moments, he believed he knew the answer. He was born evil. He knew with devastating clarity that it was not his mother's fault that she could not love him, that it was not his father's fault for abandoning him. He knew now that it wasn't even Nana Dora's fault for finding fault in everything, for she had been born with her own brand of wickedness. No. He, Theo Drew, was born into this world as a worthless, malicious being and now he was going to finally have to find the courage to do something about it.

Breathless, Theo skidded to a standstill in front of a great willow tree that was somewhat hidden from the muddy path that ambled through the trees. He looked up into its glorious boughs hoping that the calm emanating from its branches would silence his quivering body, despite the absence of leaves. Sliding his back down the trunk, Theo felt the rough bark chafe his protruding spine. He imagined the red marks it would leave behind.

Despite the onset of winter, there was still an assortment of autumn leaves composting beneath his shivering form. They were almost comforting in their willingness to supply a malleable covering that may save his festering body from potential predators.

Once again Theo removed the knife from his pocket. This time he did not look at it, but lifted his chin towards the sky with his eyes squeezed tightly together. He placed the point of the knife at his wrist and allowed his right hand to draw it up his left arm. He stopped at the point that he believed was his elbow crease but when he opened his eyes he realised that touch had been deceiving him. Furious, he stared at the knife, jabbing his left palm upon the point so that it drew blood. Theo smiled. He could do this. He could finally do the right thing. He could rid himself of his own sorry existence.

With a tremulous breath he closed his eyes and held the knife aloft in his aching hand, then with a ferocity he didn't recognise, Theo sliced at the inside of his forearm with jagged, purposeful slashes. The agonising pain was almost overpowering. Muffling his cries, he thrust his upper arm between his thrashing teeth and opened his eyes. Blood seeped from the wounds, dripping upon his jeans and soaking into the leaves beneath him. Theo could feel the intense pain, but the roaring in his ears obscured all thoughts and feelings. His head was twisting and swimming in time with the blood that coursed from his open veins. Theo could no longer feel who or what he was as the sensations of his body took over. He struggled to slash at his arm. He stared at the blood and propelled the knife savagely forward towards the open wound. He had to do it. He had to get the job done.

Theo's whole body shook as his confession unleashed the desperate clawing of grief. Anna let him cry. She rubbed his back with her arthritic hands. When, after a long time, his sobbing subsided enough for him to absorb her words, she spoke, "That's when I found you."

"Yes," Theo's voice was muffled by his hands.

"Theo?"

"What?"

"Theo," Anna was persistent. "Theo, I think you might have got it wrong."

"W... what?" Theo lifted his ravaged face from his palms.

"I don't think you killed her..." insisted Anna.

"How c... could you know, y... you weren't there. I... I cuddled her then she died," surmised Theo bitterly. "It's as simple as that."

"No Theo." Anna was insistent. "I really don't think it is. You cannot kill a baby by cuddling her unless she was smothered or strangled or poisoned. Did you do those things Theo?"

"God no," cried Theo in horror. "Of course I didn't."

"Then I believe," continued Anna wisely. "That there was another cause of death. Something medical; you just happened to be the last person to see her alive."

Theo jumped up, staring at his friend in pure and utter disbelief. He tapped his feet on the rug, his jaw clamped so tightly shut that a pulse ticked in his cheek.

"But," he whispered as tears rolled into the collar of his jacket, "I cuddled her and that made her die... that's what happened."

Anna shook her head.

"No Theo, I really don't think that is what happened. You cuddled her out of concern and love. I imagine that your mother was sleeping because she was exhausted and you, not wanting your sister to wake her, got up and comforted the baby yourself. Am I right?"

Theo nodded, unable to meet Anna's kind, wise eyes. He wanted to believe her more than he had ever wanted anything. He wanted to believe in his innocence so that the immense burden of guilt would shrink away to nothing, leaving the sadness behind.

"You comforted the baby despite your jealousy and unease; despite your loathing."

"Yes," he whispered, falling to his knees.

"Sometimes love and hate really is intertwined. It is possible to hate someone and love them all in the same breath. Human emotion is a complex web of trickery; sometimes the mind doesn't know what to think."

"I want to believe you so very badly, but the coroner hasn't decided the cause of death yet. He may say it was me!"

"I think," continued Anna, "the chances of that are extremely slim. What you must do Theo is go home; you must tell Jon, and your mother eventually, the truth. I am absolutely sure that they will do what I have done and allay your fears. They will agree with me that your caring embrace with your baby sister could not have killed her."

Theo shook his head and started to cry again. "I can't."

"Yes, you can. You must."

"But…"

"Do you trust me Theo?"

"Yes," he sobbed. "I do trust you."

"Then go home," Anna was kind but insistent. She spoke with her hands and arms. "All really will be well, I promise."

"Do you really think I am brave enough to tell them the truth? How can I tell them that I hated that little baby? It makes me seem like a monster! In fact, I am a monster for feeling that about her so they'd be right to think it wouldn't they?" He ranted through his tears, his bruised face almost demented with anxiety.

"No, they will not think that about you because you must start by telling them how you and Sebastian feel about your grandmother; about your mother's need for a daughter. When you explain this to them, your feelings towards your sister will seem justified and they will not be mortified because you loved and hated her all at once or because you were jealous, they will be mortified because they caused it; because their child is hurting so badly that he has cut himself to feel something other than the pain inside… that he felt life was no longer worth living. They will be mortified that they have let you down."

"H… how do you know?" murmured Theo. It was such a relief to finally talk about it that suddenly confessing his feelings to his mother didn't seem so very daunting any longer. Theo felt so tired.

"Because I know. It was my job to know things like this remember?"

Theo nodded. "Sometimes the noise inside my head makes me want to scream. It's like all the awful feelings have voices... I just need to escape myself. When I hate myself the noise makes the hating worse..."

"Yes."

"When... when I cut the noise goes," Theo whispered. "When I cut there is white in my head; an empty white that kills the hate."

"Yes," Anna said. "But now you must silence the noise yourself by talking to your mother."

Theo nodded. He felt exhausted. His mind was silent.

"And don't take this the wrong way, but I don't want to see you for a couple of days."

"Why?" Theo frowned.

"Because if you don't come, I'll know everything is ok. You need this time with your mother now."

Theo nodded.

"Before you go..." Anna cleared her throat and looked faintly embarrassed. "When your mother gets better, I would like you to give her something." Leaning over the arm of the sofa, she retrieved a covered wicker basket and handed it to Theo.

"I think what is in there may help her feel better in time. Please allow her to open it herself."

Theo stared at her for a long time before taking the basket. He saw the snowy wisps of hair, the lines of her life criss-crossing her face in the many directions she had travelled both willingly and unwillingly. He saw the white skin beneath the dreadful scar that burned purple in the cold air. He looked into her indefinable eyes that sparkled with a youth that seemed trapped in time. Anna. Survivor, doctor, mother, friend: but so many other things as well, so much that even words, with their myriad of voices, were futile in the face of the silent beauty eclipsing the space between those words.

Theo placed the basket on the front step. He leant towards Anna as she smiled at him, trying not to cough. Taking her face tenderly between his palms, he surprised both of them by placing a gentle kiss upon her scarred cheek.

"Thank you."

CHAPTER TWENTY

THEO sensed a change in the atmosphere of the house before he even pulled open the back door. He could hear the chink of glasses and a rumble of laughter. His senses remembered this in a time before Eden was even thought of. Unsure of what the kitchen would reveal, he took a deep breath before stepping across the threshold. The warmth embraced his cold skin as though he was stepping into a hot bath.

Seb, who was standing by the sink rinsing a glass, looked relieved to see him.

"There you are! We've been waiting for you for ages. Where have you been?" He frowned but became instantly distracted. "What's with the basket?"

"Nothing. It's nothing."

Theo avoided his probing eyes, pushing past him to deposit his shoes and coat in the cupboard under the stairs and hide the basket in the mess he knew would help him. He scrambled about in its depths for several moments before Seb peered at him through the darkness.

"What are you doing in there? Ok, no! Don't tell me! Maybe I don't want to know." He shook his head in bewilderment as Theo reappeared with glowing red cheeks.

"Listen," Seb hissed as they shoved past each other. "Mum's up. The coroner has declared cause of death..."

"W... what?" Theo stood instantly still. His heart throbbed in his ears as all the blood from his head flooded to his feet. He tried to ask Seb about the coroner's verdict, but his voice had vanished too.

Seb gave him an odd look. He grimaced. "Don't you want to know what he said?"

Dumbly, Theo nodded.

"Theo!" Jon thundered down the stairs interrupting the boys' premature conversation. He looked less pained than he had in the last few days; the deathly, pinched pallor had disappeared from his face. He enveloped Theo in a massive hug. Theo could feel his affection pouring from his skin.

"Mum's up," he whispered. "She's in here. Come on."

They went into the lounge. Sophia was curled up in the corner of the leather sofa, staring into the flames that were starting to lick the dry logs in the fireplace. She looked drawn and thin. Theo felt a shiver of fear as he looked at her. Was she going to leap forward and fling a log from the fire in his face?

"Sophia!"

Jon bustled past his stepsons, easing himself into the sofa beside his wife, taking her hand gently in his own and rubbing it.

"Theo's back!"

When he spoke, Sophia seemed roused as if from a coma. The realisation crossed her face like the words were printed on her lips.

"Theo," she murmured when she finally laid eyes on

him. She flew from the sofa into his arms, knocking him into the door frame. Embracing him in a ferocious hug that nearly drew breath from him, she whispered the word sorry over and over again in his ear. Theo wanted to cry so badly that the lump in his throat stuck like unwanted food.

Pulling back from him, Sophia stared horror-struck at the bruises she had inadvertently inflicted upon his face. Bringing a shaky, tender hand up to his chin, she touched him gently all over his face before finally cupping his cheeks in both of her hands and kissing him.

"Please forgive me. I didn't know what I was doing. Jon told me everything: how I threw stuff at him; at you. I don't remember..." she whispered, her voice trailing away. She looked so exceptionally lost that Theo knew that she was telling the truth.

"Mum, are you ok now?" he asked her in a small voice.

He trembled as she gathered him in her arms like she used to when he was very small. Her skin felt wonderful beneath his cheek, like the spring sunshine after a cruel winter. He took a deep juddering breath, inhaling her glorious familiarity. She clung to him so desperately that he felt he might actually have the strength to tell her what he must.

"Mum," Theo began urgently, disentangling himself from Sophia. "I need to tell you something..."

His mother placed a warm finger across his lips interrupting him.

"Me first."

Theo nodded. He felt relieved that he did not need to tell her yet, but also deflated as the adrenaline deserted him.

"We… we know why Eden died."

She began to wring her hands together, breathing deeply before she continued.

"There was…" Her voice cracked. She swallowed. "There was something wrong with her heart. It didn't work properly. It didn't… well no one knew that when she was born. It was a rare condition." She shook her head as though reassuring herself. "We couldn't have known. Nobody could have known. The doctors… they couldn't have prevented it."

Tears flooded her dark eyes as she bit her bottom lip and clasped Theo's quivering hands tightly in her own.

A small primal sound erupted in his throat. The deafening holler of blood pounding in his ears making him light-headed meant that he could not be entirely sure that he heard her correctly.

"W… what?"

"Eden had a rare heart condition Theo."

"Oh," he wailed, tears coursing down his face. He tried to speak but the words came out in strangled sobs.

"What?" Sophia's eyes widened in dismay as her son crumpled before her. "What is it Theo?"

"Theo please… please, tell me."

Theo closed his eyes, breathing deeply until he felt calm enough to speak coherently. He thought of Anna. He thought of her strength.

"I cuddled her."

"What?" Sophia looked confused. She was instantly still. "What do you mean?" Theo met her eyes with a courage he did not know he possessed, speaking his truth to his mother's core.

"The day she died... you were asleep... she cried... I didn't want her to wake you so I picked her up. I gave her a cuddle Mum and she fell asleep on my shoulder."

"Oh," murmured Sophia, her brows knitted. "That was... kind... of you."

"No," Theo protested fiercely. He began to cry hysterically as Sophia held him. She begged him to be calm, to explain.

"I thought I killed her."

"Oh darling," Sophia looked aghast. "You couldn't have done. A cuddle couldn't have killed her; her heart did that. You were giving her love Theo..."

"But I wasn't," he screamed. "I hated her..."

He watched his mother's face flinch in pain. He thought about the times he had fantasised about saying that aloud to her, but now that he had done it he felt ridiculous and cruel. Nevertheless, he continued babbling. Now that he had begun his confession, it was impossible to stop.

"I was jealous of her. I didn't want her around. Seb and I knew you wanted a daughter more than you wanted us. We've heard you and bloody Nana Dora talking about it enough," he spat into his mother's horrified face.

"I know I've never been good enough for you because I wasn't a girl..."

"Theo no," she protested, but her words fell on ears that could no longer listen.

"I know you had Seb first and he was a boy and that was alright, but then you had me when you really wanted a girl and that wasn't ok was it?" His eyes rolled like a terrified animal confronting a predator.

"I remember Nana Dora saying, 'Oh darling, if only

he'd been a girl!' And you never stopped her; you never defended me. I was just this useless second son you didn't want. Nothing I do has ever been good enough. Nothing I do can ever be good enough because I wasn't the girl that you wanted to begin with." He was shouting, but he stopped suddenly and said in a whisper of deflated acceptance, "I know you didn't love me Mum; not the way you were supposed to. Not the way you love Seb and Eden."

Sophia opened her mouth to protest, but shut it promptly again and Theo, taking this as a sign he was right, glared at her with disgust. He waited for her to respond, to say something, but Sophia seemed stunned into a bewildered silence. He stared at her, challenging her to regain her equilibrium.

"Theo." Her voice was a whisper that sounded like a prayer. She closed her eyes, tilting her face upwards. Her hands were outstretched and her feet tapped furiously at the carpeted floor.

"Theo – I am so, so sorry how for how this seems to you..."

Theo wouldn't look at her. The guilt and self-loathing no longer constricted his conscious mind and without it, his brain felt unusually quiet. He didn't know what to do with the space. Instead of the waves of relief he expected to feel upon making his confession there was only emptiness tinged with foolishness and an antipathy towards his mother: how could sorry ever make a difference?

"I... I..." Sophia stammered. "I don't know how to explain it to you."

Theo's eyes focused on the empty coffee cup resting on the leather coaster in the centre of the old, oak table. His mother's ruby lipstick made a stark imprint against the perfect white porcelain.

"The truth is Theo that I've allowed my mother to bully me... all my life." Sophia closed her eyes tightly then peered upwards, biting her lip and sighing before she spoke into the silent space between them.

"Your grandmother is an unhappy woman. I believe also she was an unhappy child. Her relationship with her own mother was strained to say the least. I think she poured herself into me to make up for it. In many ways, she has been a good mother: supporting me, caring for me, being both mother and father after your grandfather died when I was only a little girl. Sometimes I think if she had remarried and I had had brothers or sisters, the pressure on me may have been less; if we had shared each other. But she expressed no desire to remarry. All she had ever wanted was a daughter to cherish and I had given her that. She always believed that the most sacred of all relationships was the one between mother and daughter."

"What about mother and son?" muttered Theo, swallowing hard.

Sophia smiled faintly. "I quite agree. The relationship between parent and child is sacred. There are so many kinds of love Theo; all of them sacred in their own way."

"But you agreed with her..."

"What do you mean?"

"You agreed that you needed a daughter; that it was sacred."

Sophia sighed, pinching the bridge of her nose. "I didn't. Not really. I wanted to please her. She was always going on about me having a girl and I wanted a girl so that she would just stop going on about it!"

Theo regarded her doubtfully. Sophia sighed again.

"I liked the thought of having a daughter. I think those

people who are blessed with both are very lucky. But if you and Seb had been girls then I would have liked the thought of having a boy. None of it meant I loved the two of you any less. Before I met Jon, I didn't even think I'd have more children and truly you boys were enough for me. I loved you fiercely... with all my heart... I still do..."

"Then why didn't you tell your mother that? Why didn't you tell her to shut up?"

"Because she wouldn't listen," explained Sophia sadly. "She doesn't actually listen to anything I say. She thinks she's right all of the time. She thinks she is beyond reproach. My mother doesn't do guilt. She twists everything so that everyone else is wrong and she is the victim."

"Maybe you should have tried harder," insisted Theo frowning. "Nobody can live a blameless life. We all do things wrong sometimes and then we have to say sorry."

"I couldn't Theo... you can't win with people like that. It's like ploughing headfirst into a brick wall every time you open your mouth; and it hurts just as much!"

"Surely you could have done something... maybe you didn't try hard enough," Theo wailed. He stood up and began pacing the room fretfully.

His mother looked apologetic. "Maybe not... but I remember my father trying; I remember the rows..." Sophia murmured. Her voice was distant yet grave. "I learnt that the only way to live around my mother without constant conflict was to let her believe she was right..."

"But your father didn't... he stood up for himself." Theo stared out of the window. The sky was thick with snow clouds.

"My father killed himself Theo."

Sophia's words hung in the silence of the room. Theo

felt his attention withdraw from the outside world; he whirled round to stare at her.

"What?"

"He couldn't take it," Sophia whispered. "One day he walked into the sea and didn't stop."

"What?" repeated Theo. "How do you know?"

"His body washed up on the shore a few miles away. The whole thing was declared an accident, but I didn't believe it. I mean, who swims in the English Channel in February? I knew an old lady who did it, but she was slightly batty. In my heart, I knew there was something dubious about it all and when I was twelve I found the note."

"What note?" asked Theo slowly.

"The suicide note."

"Christ... what did it say?"

"Pretty much what I told you... that it is impossible to live with someone who negates you the whole time. He wrote that he could not go on crashing into the wall that was her conceit. He wrote that he could never live up to the impossibly high expectations she placed upon him when the expectations she had of herself were so low. He said she had broken him. He said that not all prisons have bars."

"Christ!" said Theo again. The picture of his life seemed to be shifting. Nothing was where he had painted it any longer and even the brush strokes had changed. He shook his head, marvelling at his mother's confession and her ability to deal with such a momentous childhood tragedy. He saw her differently, admiring her for the way she had coped with a lifetime of living with a difficult, unyielding woman. In his head, the pieces of his life began to fall together. The missing fragments, which had been such an enigma to he and Seb, slotted between the truths of their lives.

"Does she know that you know? Nana Dora, I mean..."

Theo sat down and looked into his mother's face. Her cheeks were flushed, but her eyes brimmed with absolute affection. He turned around to see if there was someone behind him. There was nobody there. Sophia was looking at him. He yearned to reach out and cup her soft cheeks in his trembling hands.

"No," breathed Sophia. "I could never tell her. It wouldn't change anything. She would just twist the truth written on the page; twist the truth of my father's feelings that I know to be true because they are my feelings too. I couldn't allow her to do that to his memory. My feelings about her are validated by the words he wrote in that letter. Without that validation I think I may have gone mad." Sophia paused. "I couldn't allow her to take my sanity."

"So," declared Theo, almost to himself. "You tried to please her by having a daughter because that was what she wanted for you; that was what she said you should do..."

"Yes." Sophia began to wring her hands again. The ruby in her engagement ring glimmered in the lamp light. "I made a bad match in your father who believed he wanted children, but could not cope with the reality of them. I was blessed with Seb and then you. When each of you was born I was thrilled until my mother peered into the plastic hospital crib with a disapproving, disappointed look on her face. I instantly knew that in her eyes, I had failed again and her displeasure rubbed constantly at my joy. In the years after your Dad left, she went on and on at me to find a new man so that I could have a daughter."

"I remember," sighed Theo ruefully. He reached out to place a tentative hand over his mother's. She grabbed at it, clasping it so tightly that Theo felt the blood begin to drain from his fingers.

"Then," she continued, relinquishing her hold on his hand a little. "I was lucky enough to meet Jon. He is my one true love Theo. You know? Like the books say…"

Theo felt a blush creep over his throat as Sophia spoke.

"He loved me, and he loved you and Seb like you were his own. He was content not to have a child of his own, but happy enough when I suggested we try for a baby together. When Eden was born he was, as you know, overjoyed." Sophia choked. She sucked in her cheeks. Her breathing became quick and shallow as she tried to continue speaking.

"When… she… died…" she gasped. "I was… devastated… I am devastated… It is the most awful thing, the most dreadful of all things, to lose a child: not because she was my daughter but because she was my child. I loved her so much, Theo." Sophia stared up at him and Theo felt his heart crack open in his chest. "Why did they have to take her?"

Sophia's voice broke and she crumpled into her own lap. Theo threw himself at her, wrapping his arms around her so that he could exhume her pain as she cried. He felt part of her, for the first time in his memory.

"I love you," she choked. "I've always loved you and I'm so desperately sorry for all the hurt I've caused."

Theo said nothing, feeling the impasses within his body begin to dissolve.

CHAPTER TWENTY ONE

FRIDAY, 19 FEBRUARY 2010 ONWARDS

IT took several days for Theo to digest the information his mother had divulged about her life. In the quiet of his room, he unfolded the layers one by one, inspecting every detail, unravelling every nuance until he found himself able to understand her with empathy. Sophia became a completely new person to him. Instead of someone who was unreachable and ungrateful, he found her a victim of her mother's suffocating love and impenetrable arrogance. Dora, Theo realised was the antithesis of himself. Her arrogance was as damaging as Theo's lack of self-worth. She was beyond criticism, beyond the opinion of others. She cared about nothing except her own good opinion. She had no moral code or ability to form lasting relationships. She had no desire to foster an equal relationship with another human being based upon mutual respect and love. Dora wanted to dominate, to bully, to oppress. Dora wanted to inflict her power over others by making them weak. Sophia was not her child but her victim.

Dora was not present at the house that weekend. Theo could not remember a weekend that she had not at least popped in to see Sophia. Theo wondered if his mother had spoken to her, made it clear that she should stay away. Theo wondered if bringing him into her confidence and feeling his support had empowered her to stand up to her mother. Was it him or Eden's death that had been the catalyst? At some point he would ask her. He was stronger now. He was brave.

Without Dora's interference the family spent the weekend quietly together. Nobody said very much, and although the heavy sadness over Eden's death loomed in the house, it no longer loomed between them, separating them from one another, but swathed them together in difficult yet necessary bindings. Sophia did not take to her bed, but rose with Jon every morning and drank coffee with him in the kitchen whilst he prepared eggs like he usually did on weekend mornings. The radio played quietly in the background and Theo and Seb were content to do their own thing with their mother close by.

Theo went back to Anna's house on Saturday afternoon but she wasn't there. He wanted to tell her about Eden and how brave he had been to confront his mother. He knew Anna would listen and be proud of him. It was disappointing to find the house empty. He decided to try again the next day.

On Sunday he left the house with Jon calling after him that a special breakfast feast would be ready in an hour, so Theo took his bike to the beach instead of running. Once again the house was empty and Anna was nowhere to be seen. Worry began to gnaw inside him.

He spent the day watching movies with Seb and his mother. Jon lit the fire and the freezing logs sizzled as they were thrown into the flames. Sophia curled up between her sons on the sofa. Sometimes Theo sensed that she was crying softly beside him, but instead of feeling worried he felt comforted that her grief finally had an outlet. He watched Seb slide his hand gently into hers.

Later on Sophia decided to cook dinner. It was the first time she had mentioned food since Eden had gone and Seb grinned at Theo over her head. It was almost like old times as they all marvelled at the wonderful smell emanating from the big pot bubbling on the hob. Jon was half watching a documentary with Seb as they jovially emptied the dishwasher. Theo glanced at the screen, feeling his mother's body fold around him from behind. As the view on the screen changed, he felt Sophia stiffen.

"Turn it up!" she commanded, urging Jon to reach for the remote control.

They all stared at Sophia's blanched face and then at the television. There was a male television presenter standing in the darkness somewhere, dressed in a beige raincoat. He was talking about a man who had died.

"I need to sit down," declared Sophia.

Seb brought a stool up behind her. "Why?" he asked. "What on earth is the matter?"

Sophia gestured towards the screen with a limp wave. "That man. The one who died. It's Nana Dora's father. He's my grandfather."

Theo felt his mind begin to spin. He tried to listen to the reporter as Seb and Jon peered in bewilderment at the screen over Sophia's shoulder.

"There is a profound belief," the presenter was saying, "that this gentleman's name should be added to the Righteous Among the Nations, the honorific used by the State of Israel to describe non-Jews who risked their lives during the Holocaust to save Jews from Nazi slaughter. Up until recently the heroics of this man have been shrouded in secrecy but since his death, during a cross channel ferry crossing, his daughter has decided to honour his true memory. She has revealed that, despite fighting on the side of the Nazis as a very young man on the Eastern Front, throughout the Second World War he also saved the lives of countless Jews. Apparently this secretive German doctor was not all he seemed, for although he was highly regarded by many of Hitler's generals, he was surreptitiously undermining the regime by helping Jews to flee Europe and caring for numerous others who were in hiding. His daughter claims that the number of people he helped probably totalled nearly one thousand. One of the most heart-rendering aspects to this remarkable tale is that his daughter was actually a Jew who he rescued and took into his home. Apparently the good doctor acquired forged papers for the child, then later adopted her when it became clear her mother had perished in one of the Nazi death camps."

"I don't believe it!" Sophia marvelled, her eyes glued to the reporters face. "So it was the truth all along."

"What?" insisted Jon. "What was the truth?"

Sophia shook her head from side to side as though shaking her thoughts into place.

"You know I told you about my mother and her mother?"

"Yes," said Jon, looking vague. "You said they argued about Dora's father, but you didn't tell me much at all."

"Yes," continued Sophia thoughtfully. "I didn't really understand it all until now, but now it makes perfect sense."

"What do you mean?"

"My grandmother was a Jew. She came to England near the end of the Second World War. She was pregnant."

"Pregnant?" interrupted Seb. "With Nana Dora?"

Sophia nodded. "Yes. When my mother was old enough to understand, my Jewish grandmother told her that she was rescued by a German from a Jewish ghetto in the Czech Republic. She explained that he cared for her whilst she was sick and that she eventually fell in love with him. Thinking they had been betrayed to the authorities, the German sent her to England to live with his cousin so that she would be safe. He promised to find her after the war was over but he never materialised."

Theo thought he was living the days of the past week over again. He was flabbergasted as he listened to his mother. His mind was whirring and he couldn't keep his hands or feet still, but when he opened his mouth to speak nothing came out except a strangled cough. Seb frowned at him as though he smelled distasteful.

"My mother thought my grandmother was lying about being rescued by the German, because she was ashamed about betraying the Jews by having a relationship with a Nazi. They have, as you know, a strained relationship."

"Do they?" marvelled Seb. "I didn't know your grandmother was still alive!"

"I'm not sure she is," said Sophia. "My mother doesn't mention her. I've never even met her, but I know she didn't live far from here."

"Mum," exclaimed Seb excitedly. "Don't you think you should contact her? You know... after everything that has happened recently... Jon told me you've told Nana Dora to keep her distance, which I have to say, makes me happy! You don't have any reason not to contact your grandmother; maybe she'd like to meet us all!"

Sophia looked worried. "Maybe... she must be in her eighties by now..."

Theo opened his mouth to speak again, but closed it abruptly when the television screen panned to a lady standing below an arch above which was written, "Arbeit macht Frei." The presenter began to interview the woman. Theo felt his family stiffen around him as they listened to what she had to say.

"My mother died here shortly after I was born. I know her name was Viera, but I know nothing more. After she died my mother's best friend took care of me. I can remember sleeping in the crook of her body on a bed of straw, but I do not remember anything else about our time in the ghetto."

Theo knew at once that the woman standing in the archway was Isabella. He knew that she was standing outside Theresienstadt. He knew that she was talking about Anna; his Anna. He struggled to take hold of his thoughts, to stop them spinning beyond his control so that he could listen to what Isabella was saying.

"My father and another man known to us only as G, rescued my adoptive mother and I from the place you see behind us. They pretended they needed labour to work in their arms factory. When we left my adoptive mother was very sick. The medic, who was to become my father, took us to his family home in Berlin at great personal risk to himself and acquired false papers. I became Isabella Levine and my mother Anna Levine. We lived with him until he believed we had been betrayed to the authorities, then he sent Anna to England to ensure her safety. I remained in Berlin without her. After the war was over I begged him to go to England to find Anna, but he refused saying that no one could tolerate a love affair between a German who had fought with the Nazis and a Jewish woman. He said he loved her too much to make her live a lie, because nobody would believe the truth. She was the love of his life. There was never another."

The images on the screen changed again.

"Mum," asked Seb incredulously. "Are you really saying that this German man was your grandfather and this Jewish lady Anna is your grandmother and Nana Dora's mother?"

Sophia nodded. She was shivering all over.

"Mum!" interrupted Theo urgently.

"But," continued Seb, scratching his scalp. "Nana's name is Dora Drew?"

"Mum!" exclaimed Theo again. Sophia looked from one son to the other, seemingly unsure who to answer first. Theo thought she was looking at him the way she had when he was five and he had crammed an empty cereal box on his head and run full pelt at the garden wall.

She turned her attention to Seb. "Her married name is Dora Drew. Her maiden name, her birth name, is Theadora Levinsky. Theo was named after her."

Theo felt sick, then elated. This time he shrieked at Sophia. "Mum!"

"What Theo?" she asked with exasperation. "Just say it, whatever it is that you want to say!" She spoke with her hands as well as her voice.

"Your grandfather," urged Theo breathlessly. "Was his name Kass Hartenstein?"

"Yes," she murmured. This time it was Sophia's turn to look surprised. "How on earth do you know that?"

Before Theo could explain further, their attention was drawn back to the screen. A different presenter was speaking. Sophia continued to shake and unbeknown to her, Theo trembled beside her.

"The interview conducted with Isabella Hartenstein about the heroics of her father Kass Hartenstein was conducted several days ago, only a week after his death. Isabella was due to fly to London yesterday in search of her adoptive mother who was living under her given name of Anna Levinsky. Unfortunately news has broken pertaining to Anna Levinsky, who was living by the coast in the south east of England. In the early hours of Saturday morning police found the body of a dead woman on a bench on the beach, close to the village of Ferring. They have identified the body as Anna Levinsky. Her death is not being treated as suspicious. She was eighty three years old. Her dog, a Labrador will not leave the scene of her death, despite repeated attempts by the local dog's home to tempt him away."

"Oh no," wailed Sophia. "I'm too late." She grasped hold of Jon, leaning her head into his chest. "I can't believe it."

Theo stared in disbelief at the plastic features of the television reporter. Surely he was wrong? Surely Anna wasn't dead. He would have known wouldn't he, deep inside, if anything bad had happened to her? Anna: his great-grandmother. Tears stung his eyes and he rubbed them vigorously. Why hadn't she told him? And what would happen to Blackie now that she was gone? Had she known on some unfathomable, subconscious level that Kass had left this world? It must be a certainty that the cross-channel journey he was undertaking was due to a profound, inevasible desire to be with Anna once again. Had she known that before she died?

"I need to tell you something," Theo blurted, tugging his mother from Jon's arms.

Sophia raised a sardonic eyebrow at him, and Seb and Jon looked at him as though he was quite mad.

"Something else... yes... I know what you are thinking, but this time it's a good thing. First though, I need to show you something. Wait there... and also, we're going to have a dog if it's ok with you. I'll look after him."

"Good gracious," groaned Sophia. "I really don't think I can take much more of this. Do stop talking in riddles Theo! A dog?"

Dashing into the hall, Theo dived headfirst into the cupboard under the stairs to retrieve the basket Anna had given him. His initial shock and sadness over the news of her death had been replaced by the knowledge that he had something that could ease his mother's sadness. Finally Theo had the answers.

Just as he was easing the basket past the pairs of smelly boots and discarded school bags, Theo heard the doorbell ring. Believing that it might be Nana Dora, returning to berate Sophia, he bounded towards the front door before anyone else could emerge from the kitchen. As he opened the door, the freezing night air blasted against his face and a strange woman stood on the garden path. Flurries of snow fell from the night sky, settling on the silent world around her. Theo could not see her face, but the woman was gracefully dressed in a velvet hat and long navy coat.

"Excuse me..." she began in heavily accented English. "I am sorry to give you bother."

She sounded like she had been crying. When the door remained open, she stepped onto the front step. Now Theo could see her face clearly. She was older, but not yet old. Her soft face was elegant and distinctive.

"I have come all the way from Germany," she continued hesitantly. "My name is Isabella Hartenstein. I am the adopted daughter of Kass Hartenstein and Anna Levinsky. My father, Kass, recently passed away and I am coming to England to find my mother Anna. Unfortunately..." Isabella paused as though she was groping around for the right vocabulary, although Theo thought that she was actually trying not to cry. "Unfortunately the police tell me, when I come here, that Anna is dead. They say they found her body on the beach..."

Delving into the pocket of her coat Isabella withdrew a tissue. She dabbed at her eyes and wiped her nose as Theo waited politely for her to continue speaking. Plump flakes of snow settled on the hollow of her cheeks below her eyes, melting instantly like teardrops.

"I have come here because I believe that Kass and Anna's biological granddaughter lives here. I believe her name is Sophia Grace, born Sophia Drew. I have only recently known of her..." Isabella looked up into Theo's face. He nodded, unable to speak.

"Good," continued Isabella seeming visibly relieved. "Then you must be..." Once again her hand delved into the pocket of her coat. She pulled out a crinkled scrap of paper. Her brow furrowed as she narrowed her eyes to read the words written on it. "Sebastian?"

Theo shook his head.

"Theo?"

"Theo!" shouted his mother from the warmth of the kitchen. "What are you doing? Who is at the door?"

Theo stared at Isabella and began to smile. Isabella smiled warmly back at him.

"A friend," he called back finally.

"Well," said Sophia, bustling into the hallway and regarding her guest standing on the doorstep. "Don't leave her out there in the snow. Invite her in to the warm!"

Sophia smiled and Theo leaned forward to take Isabella's arm in his hand. He guided her over the threshold of his home, gently leading her in from the cold.

About the Author

RIA grew up in Worthing, West Sussex in a rowdy, loving family of six with parents who suffered her short stories with harassed smiles. They inspired her to do many of the things she still enjoys today including sailing, swimming, reading and riding horses. She is married with four sons and lives on a farm. As a qualified literacy teacher of Key Stage Two and Three age children she used to write and adapt school plays for the amusement of the children and, following the birth of her second son, wrote and self-published her first book for teenagers called 'Storm Savers'.

Ria went on to have twin sons who were born prematurely. During their early months, a time of intense worry about the babies, she secretly began writing 'Inflicted'. Ria says, 'I felt unable to reach out to those around me when my identical twin boys were premature and unwell. I couldn't surrender to vital sleep in the critical hours when the house finally fell quiet so I started to write'. Locked in a web of guilt and worry Ria poured her anxiety into her book which is based on the premise that we all have a need for reciprocal human kindness.

She believes her friends would describe her as someone who is fiercely in love with her four little boys, an avid reader, and a crazy lady who enjoys the thrills of wake-boarding, distance running and go-karting.